THE SCENT
OF
REDEMPTION

THE SCENT OF REDEMPTION
© 2016 Harl Goodman III
Cover illustrations by Asser Elnagar
All cover art © 2016
All rights reserved
ISBN: 9781519077509

Printed in the United States of America

First Printing, 2016

www.HarlGoodman.com

There are several people I would like to thank who were instrumental in the creation of this work.

I would like to thank my wife Liz Thomas who endured many hours alone while I secreted myself away to write in private. Without her encouragement and sacrifice, I would have given up a long time ago.

I am indebted to Peyton Adams and Flint Goodman, who helped with editing and gave me encouragement at every turn. I would like to thank Bonnie Hazlewood for helping me identify errors that even my professional editor couldn't.

And finally, my mother Pam Thompson. Though she left this world a long time ago, she left her heart and soul with me to give me the inspiration for this story.

CHAPTER ONE

Flint Westbrook drove his National Park Police truck east along the narrow lanes of Highway 4 which cut deep through the dark, brooding pine forests of northern Escambia County, Florida. In the distance, he spotted the dark gray underbelly of rain clouds which only worsened his apprehensive mood. There was nothing about this operation that gave him hope. In his experience, search and rescue missions ended in only one of three ways; someone lived, someone died, or someone was never heard from again. His gut told him this time there would be no survivor, only a ten-year-old victim.

He passed a weatherbeaten brown and yellow sign announcing his arrival at the Lost Pines RV Park, slowed his truck, and turned north onto the asphalt road leading to the campground. Bella, Flint's nine-year-old German Shepherd search dog, sensed they were getting close and started to whine, the way she always did when they arrived on an active scene. She was eager to get to work.

The tall trees hiding the park from the main road gave way to a large, open area full of RVs and old travel trailers. Some appeared to be old neglected FEMA trailers that hadn't seen movement in years. Broad washes of green algae slathered over their dirty white exteriors indicated they had been stewing for a long time in the sweltering northwest Florida heat and humidity.

Flint stopped the truck near a worn out mobile home with a sign near the road asking customers to stop and register before taking a site. It had to be the office. Seeing no one there, he scanned the campground and spotted several law enforcement vehicles through the trees on the opposite side of the RV loop. He figured they were his best chance to get information on the lost child he and Bella had been called in to locate.

As he rounded the loop, Bella's whine turned to excited barking. Knowing it would be impossible to get her to stop, Flint lowered the windows of his truck to lessen the assault to his ears and, as a result, Bella announced their arrival to everyone in the campground. The sight of police cars and cops in uniform always got her adrenaline racing. She wasn't a patient dog.

Flint parked the truck off the side of the road near a group of officers gathered around one of the squad cars. "Hang on, girl," he said, looking at Bella. She stopped barking, tilted her head, and looked at him sideways, causing him to smile despite his mood. The quiet lasted only a moment, though, as her barking resumed as soon as he exited the truck. She obviously didn't appreciate being left behind.

Flint removed his sunglasses which had fogged as he left the air conditioning of his truck. The southerly wind bringing moisture from the Gulf of Mexico made this early June afternoon particularly oppressive. Flint's tan and black police uniform and bulletproof vest made it even worse, but there was nothing he could do. It was Park Service regulation that he wear it anytime he was on duty. It didn't matter if he was on duty at Ft. Pickens National Park, the park he managed, or in this little backwater campground assisting local law enforcement. If he was in uniform, it had to include his full tactical gear.

"Hello, Flint!" said a familiar voice from the crowd of officers.

Flint recognized the man as Sergeant Frank Martinez, a deputy from the south end of the county. He was usually stationed in the downtown Pensacola office, but the higher-ups must have decided he was needed here today. Flint was glad to see him. He had worked with him several times before and knew him as a good officer.

"Hello, Frank," Flint replied. "Any luck finding the girl?"

"No, afraid not," Frank answered, shaking his head. "At this point, we still don't know if someone took her or if she wandered off into the woods. I was hoping you and Bella might help us with that."

2

"Sure, we'll figure it out. Tell me what you know."

"Well, see that fine, outstanding human being over there?" Frank said without bothering to hide the disgust in his voice. He was pointing to a tall, thin lady with long, stringy black hair talking with an officer near a dirty, worn-out camping trailer. "She and her equally fine husband decided their ten-year-old daughter was old enough to spend the night alone with her one-and-a-half-year-old brother in that piece-of-shit trailer while they went gambling in Biloxi." Frank looked back at Flint again, making no effort to hide his anger. "They came back this morning around ten and couldn't find the girl anywhere. Another camper found the boy wandering around the campground wearing nothing but a dirty diaper."

"Damn," Flint said under his breath. "So, if the boy was outside the trailer, the door was obviously open. I don't think he could reach the handle, could he?"

"I doubt it," Frank said, looking back in the woman's direction. "We're still trying to figure out if the girl left the door open when she went outside, or if someone went into the trailer and grabbed her. There are no signs of forced entry and no witnesses. We don't know yet what time it happened."

"Is there a description of the girl?" Flint asked.

Frank pulled out a small notepad from his shirt pocket. "What we know so far is her name is Abigail Day. Her parents call her Abby. She's ten years old, four feet two inches tall with brown eyes, medium length brown curly hair. She was wearing white shorts and a blue tee shirt with a dolphin on the front."

"What have you searched so far?" Flint said, writing the girl's description into his notepad.

"We've made contact and entry with almost all of the trailers in the park except for two because their owners weren't home. We know she's not in either of them," Frank said, pointing toward the north end of the campground. "We've searched a three-hundred-yard perimeter around the campground with no luck. We're hoping you can help us figure out what direction she went."

"Do you know how many people went into the woods looking for her?" Flint asked.

"Not exactly, but probably at least ten. Maybe a couple more. That includes volunteers and officers." Frank squinted as he looked at Flint.

"That's not a bad thing. It's just with that many people in the woods leaving their scent trails, it's going to make it a little harder for my dog to locate someone specific. We'll make it work."

"Guess I didn't realize that might cause a problem."

"It's no problem, Frank. You had to begin the search somewhere," Flint said, not wanting the deputy to feel he'd done something wrong. "Bella is primarily an air scenting dog. She doesn't usually track smells on the ground like a hound. I mean, she can do it, it's just that she's better at picking up scent in the air. We may end up having to circle upwind of the perimeter, but we'll try a ground track anyway. It might save us some time." Flint stopped writing on his pad and looked up at Frank. "Is there something the girl recently wore that can give us a good scent?"

"Yep. When I heard you were coming, I got the mother to give me a shirt the girl wore the day before. It's in my patrol car."

As Frank walked away to retrieve the child's t-shirt, Flint began surveying the campground and quickly decided on the obvious. There was no water to be seen, so it was unlikely the girl drowned. At least not in the campground. He spotted a sign not too far from his truck marking the beginning of a trail into the woods. He decided to start there knowing it would be a lot easier for a child to travel the path of least resistance rather than bushwhack through the low-lying shrubs and barbed wire marking the edge of the RV park.

Frank returned with the child's t-shirt haphazardly folded in a plastic bag and handed it over to Flint. "Good luck," he said as he reached out to shake Flint's hand. "If you find anything, call me. You've got my cellphone number, right?"

"I've got it. I will."

Flint returned to his truck, unloaded Bella and put the work harness on her. He followed up with her search and rescue vest and leash. He pulled a bottle of water from his rescue kit and poured it into the dog bowl that he kept in the back of the truck. Bella needed to stay hydrated. *The poor dog probably lost half-a-gallon of water panting so hard from excitement on the hour-and-a-half trip up from Ft. Pickens.* He drank half of one himself, capped it, and threw the plastic bottle into the back of the truck. "Okay, girl, let's go!"

Flint walked Bella to the trail head where he paused for a moment to gather his thoughts. Looking up through the clearing, he saw the sun begin to slip behind one of the thunderheads in the distance. It was a welcome relief to the heat. The view down the trail was dark and shadowy, the air heavy and dank. What little sunlight making it through the dense pine canopy was absorbed by the dark forest floor.

Flint knew this would be a difficult test for Bella. Separating the scent of a dozen or so humans from that of a ten-year-old girl who may or may not have walked this same trail wasn't in the training manual for an average air scenting dog. Bella, however, was a trained police dog, and though she preferred to find her targets by air scenting, her ability to also ground track is what made her special. She and Flint had tracked many a thief and drug dealer on the streets of Dallas when they worked together as a K-9 team on the Dallas Police force. They were good at it.

After checking to make sure his portable radio was turned on and his gun secure, Flint opened the clear plastic bag that held the girl's shirt. Bella knew what to do next. She stuck her nose into the bag and, after a few seconds, sat next to Flint, indicating she was ready. She had the scent locked into her brain.

Flint paused one more time, staring down the trail. The thought of a little girl lost and alone somewhere weighed on him. He thought about his daughter Samantha. She was close to this girl's age. He hoped the girl was only lost, and that something worse hadn't happened to her, but he just couldn't shake the bad feeling he had about this one. With a heavy sigh, he leaned over, patted Bella on the shoulder, and shouted, "Seek, girl! Seek."

Keeping Bella on the long line was necessary to keep her focused on the trail if she was going to be successful at ground tracking. She regularly worked hundreds of feet away from him when she was air scenting. Unleashed, she could cover a lot of ground in a hurry, but that wouldn't be necessary right now. She needed to concentrate on the trail.

Flint watched as Bella alternated her nose from the ground to the air trying to find the scent her brain had memorized from all the others that clouded the area. It wasn't long before they had their first promising find.

They were about a hundred and fifty yards from the campground when Bella stopped and investigated the trail with renewed interest. She turned and pulled Flint in the opposite direction for about twenty yards, then headed south, off the trail, dragging Flint with her through the brush. Flint's heartbeat quickened. He knew she was on scent. He stopped, removed her lead, and let her run. She shot off with her nose in the air.

Bella ran through the dense brush with ease, running twenty or thirty yards left, then changing direction and searching twenty or thirty yards to the right. It was a positive sign that she had a scent cone figured out. It was common for Bella to disappear, though she would always come back to make sure Flint was following. After one particularly long occasion of being gone for several minutes, Bella reappeared carrying a stick in her mouth which she promptly laid down at Flint's feet. It was the signal that Flint had been hoping for. She had found her target.

"Where is she, girl?" Flint said, trying to convey his excitement. "Take me to her!" Bella raced off as Flint tried to keep up. Feeling sluggish from the heat and humidity, he suddenly felt re-energized with the sudden turn of events. "Abby! Shout out if you can! Abby!"

Flint caught glimpses of the main highway through the pines, and his heart sank as the thought of a body dump crossed his mind. Ahead, Bella crawled under the barbed wire fence separating the roadway from the woods and sat near the road. There was no girl. Flint carefully made his way through the fence to Bella, who was still sitting, her tail wagging proudly. He could barely hide his disappointment when he saw what she had alerted on, a black wooden baton. It was the kind of baton that law enforcement sometimes carried with them. One of the deputies must have dropped it during the initial search. Bella was following the wrong scent and probably had been since they first started. Flint was afraid that might happen with so many people wandering around the area looking for the girl.

"Nice try, Bella." Flint could tell the lack of excitement in his voice confused her. Usually, she would be rewarded with playful petting and a game of tug-o-war with her favorite chew toy. Feeling bad for her, Flint leaned down and scratched her between the ears. He couldn't reward her for finding something other than what they were searching for.

"It's all right, girl. We'll start somewhere else."

Flint picked up the baton and placed it on his equipment belt. He would give it to Frank later who would return it to the rightful owner.

Flint and Bella took the easy route back to the campground by walking along the highway right-of-way. Flint reported their unsuccessful results to Lieutenant John Barnes who had taken over Incident Command from Frank so he could get some rest.

Flint grabbed another bottle of water from the truck, made sure Bella drank some from her bowl, and looked for another logical place to start. The searching continued for hours with no results. Flint grew frustrated with Bella. It seemed as if she wasn't up to her usual game and, with a little girl's life at stake, this was no time to falter.

A helicopter from the Escambia County Sheriff's Office flew in around dusk to search with their infrared camera, but had no luck. Frustration mounted as the hard decision was made to call off the search when darkness approached. It would resume in the morning.

Flint was exhausted. He and Bella had walked several miles through the surrounding woods with nothing to show for it. He didn't want to give up the search, but Bella wasn't performing as well as she usually did. He thought she might do better tomorrow with some rest. Flint loaded Bella into his truck, checked out with Lieutenant Barnes, and headed for home. He would need to be back by six in the morning.

Flint decided to pick up dinner for himself at the Blue Dolphin Diner about twenty minutes north of Pensacola. Samantha was spending the night with friends, so the only mouths to feed tonight were his and Bella's. He decided there would be no limiting himself to healthy options. Hamburgers would be just fine.

He pulled the truck into the diner's parking lot and shut off the engine, leaving the windows down for Bella. There was a good breeze now that he was out of the thick pine forest surrounding the campground. Having eaten here a few times before, he knew it wouldn't take long.

Inside, Flint grabbed a menu and took a seat in the waiting area near the hostess station. He decided on a chicken fried steak sandwich which he knew was the absolute worst thing for him, and for Bella, a cheeseburger would make her feel better. She loved burgers, and he was feeling awful about not being able to reward her for today's work, though he was concerned about her performance. He would need to put in some long training hours with her.

While waiting for his food, the waitress struck up a conversation. It was obvious she was flirting with him, which he didn't mind one bit. Since Rachael died, female companionship had been rare. Though he never thought so, he was a good looking man. He still possessed the muscular, athletic body type that carried him through Texas Tech University on a full-ride baseball scholarship. His dark brown hair had the occasional gray aberration, but it was his brown eyes that people loved most. They would often betray him to Rachael when he wasn't telling the truth about how he was feeling, their expression always communicating what was going on inside.

The waitress asked about the police uniform he was wearing. She was used to seeing the formal, all-black uniforms the county deputies wore when they came by for lunch, but his intrigued her. Flint told her about his job as the park superintendent at Fort Pickens National Park near Pensacola. The conversation turned to why he was in the north end of the county, to which he explained he was looking for a lost child with his search and rescue K-9, but that sadly, they were unsuccessful. She gave a polite condolence, then went to the back to check on his order.

Flint glanced at his cellphone and saw several text messages from Samantha. She was having fun with her friends. He sent a text to see if she needed anything. She replied she was fine, and asked if she could stay the night with her friend Beth. Flint sighed. He and his best friend Troy, along with Troy's wife Liz had planned to take Sam fishing on Troy's boat tomorrow. Sam loved to fish, and it was supposed to be a Saturday morning surprise for her. They would have to do it another time. 'Go ahead honey but only if it's all right with Beth's mother' he replied. It was probably best. He had to be up early to make it back to the RV park by sunrise.

The waitress brought his food from the back and motioned Flint to the front checkout.

"How much do I owe you?" he asked.

"Nothing," she said, smiling at him. She pointed to the dining area. "See those two men? They paid for your order, tip included. Said they like to support law enforcement when they can."

"Wow, you don't hear that very often these days," Flint said.

"Not often enough, I know," she replied. "Take care of yourself. Come back when you have more time." She winked at him and walked to the back.

Flint looked over at the men who were staring at him. Deciding it would be rude to duck out without saying thank you, he picked up his food and walked over to their table.

"Hello, fellas! I sure appreciate you paying for my dinner. That was a nice thing to do." Both men stood and reached out to shake Flint's hand.

"No problem, Officer. My name is Jake, and this is Travis," the bigger one said. "We just wanted to let you know how much we appreciate what you do."

"Well, that's kind of you. It's been a rough day and this just made it a lot better."

"Oh? Why so rough?" the smaller one, Travis, asked.

Flint wanted to blow off his statement by saying something polite and leaving, but he didn't want to appear to be ungracious. "My K-9 and I have been looking for a lost little girl. No luck yet. We're going to give it another shot in the morning."

Jake cleared his throat. "Yeah, we heard about her. That's awful. Good luck with that. We hope you find her."

"We'll find her," Flint said, trying to sound confident. "Take care, guys, and thanks again."

"Our pleasure, Officer. You be safe," Jake said, reaching out for Flint's hand once again. It wasn't unusual for someone to thank him for his police work, but it was damn unusual for someone to buy his meal. *I guess there are still some good people around*, he thought to himself as he made his way outside.

Flint put the food on the passenger seat of the truck, drove out to the highway, and settled in for the drive home. He checked his review mirror and saw Bella with her nose in the air, no doubt hoping there was something for her in the food bag. "We'll be home in a bit, girl," Flint said as he reached back to scratch her between the ears. She bumped his hand with her muzzle and sniffed at it intensely. She let out a loud bark and stared at him. "Oh, you smell your hamburger, don't you? A hamburger you can find, but a ten-year-old girl, not so much." He regretted saying it as soon as it came out of his mouth.

Feeling guilty, he tried petting her again, but she wouldn't let him reach above her head. Instead, she placed her nose against his palm and, after giving it several more whiffs, barked once more. *That's strange*, he thought. Bella, who could spend an hour barking at fish in the water, never barked for food. *She must be starving.*

Flint turned his concentration back to the road as Bella started to whimper. "We're not going back to work, girl," he told her, thinking she might be confused about where they were heading. "We're going home. We'll come back and try again tomorrow." Her whimpering got louder, punctuated now and then with more barks.

Flint was getting concerned. He thought about pulling over and giving her part of the hamburger now. It might help her quiet down. He pulled off the highway and stopped the truck as Bella put her paws over the front seat to see what was happening. Flint pulled the hamburger from its foam box and trying not to make too much of a mess, tore it in half. He put half back in the container, the other half he offered to Bella. She sniffed at the burger but surprisingly, seemed more interested in smelling Flint's hand. Flint was confused. He had never seen her refuse food before, especially a hamburger, which was a rare treat.

"What's bothering you, girl? It's a hamburger, for God's sake!" He put the food back into the box and looked at his dog. She stared back at him and barked. "Bella, what do you want?"

After a minute of trying to soothe her, he gave up. Whatever it was, he would have to figure it out at home. He pulled the truck back out onto the highway and headed south. Bella continued to whimper.

After a couple of minutes, the whimpering stopped, and he heard her scratching at the floorboard behind the front seat. Flint thought at first she might be looking for a mouse that had gotten into the truck at the campground. "Get it, girl!" he shouted, looking into the rear view mirror. Bella put her paws on the back of the front seat and dropped something next to Flint.

Expecting to find a dead rat, he was surprised instead to see the police baton he had picked up near the campground during the search. Deputy Martinez was gone when they returned to the campground, so Flint decided instead to put the baton in the back seat of the truck and give it to him the next day. It must have rolled onto the floorboard. "Sorry girl, no playing while I'm driving." Bella began to whimper again. He reached back to calm her but again, she blocked his hand with her nose and sniffed at his palm. This time, she barked and sat down in the back seat, instantly getting Flint's attention. It was the signal she used during search and rescue operations to indicate she had found something. He looked down at the baton, then looked at his hand and immediately pulled the truck over to the side of the highway.

Exiting the truck, he quickly walked to the passenger side. Opening the door, he reached into the back seat past Bella and grabbed his search and rescue bag. He unzipped it and pulled out the plastic bag with Abbie's shirt in it, careful not to touch the shirt when he opened the bag. He let Bella out of the truck.

"Here you go, girl." She stuck her nose into the bag. "Okay, seek, girl! Seek!" Out of habit, Bella ran for the bushes at the side of the road, but immediately returned, nuzzled Flint's right hand, and sat. She barked once.

Flint was stunned. He grabbed the baton out of the truck with his left hand and laid it on the ground in front of her. She smelled it for several moments before sitting, and barking once again.

"Bella, I'm sorry for being such an idiot!" He went down to one knee and hugged his dog. She had been right from the beginning. The baton didn't belong to a deputy, or maybe it did. One thing was sure though; it belonged to whoever kidnapped Abby, and it had her scent on it. Bella had tracked the little girl's scent after all. Whoever grabbed her took her down the trail and bushwhacked south to a waiting car. They must have used the baton on the girl, or maybe it fell out during a struggle to get her into their vehicle.

What it didn't explain though, was Bella's fascination with his hand. Some of the girl's scent could have transferred from the baton to his hand when he picked it up from the roadway but it had been hours since he'd touched it and besides, Bella wasn't interested in his hand until after they left the diner. He didn't recall touching much there. He touched the front door, the menu, and the food bag. He touched the table where he was sitting, and he shook hands with the guys who... That was it! He shook hands with the two strangers in the diner! If they'd manhandled the girl, her scent would be all over them, especially their hands! He needed to get back to the diner now!

"Okay, girl, load up!" Flint helped Bella back into the truck, picked up the baton, and tossed it into his bag. He tossed his bag into the back of the truck as he ran to the driver's side. After starting the truck, he turned the wheel hard and headed north back to the diner. He had to find out who these guys were before they left.

Once he got the truck up to speed, he pulled his police radio from its holster and keyed it up. "Forty-seven ninety-two Park Police to dispatch."

"Go ahead, forty-seven ninety-two," a female voice responded over the radio.

"I may have some information on the missing child from Lost Pines Campground. Could you send an officer to meet me at the Blue Dolphin Diner on Highway 29? I should be there in four to five minutes.

Have them meet me outside in the parking lot."

"Understood," the dispatcher replied. Flint mashed the accelerator to the floor.

Flint turned off his headlights as he entered the diner parking lot, making sure to park on the south side of the building so he couldn't be seen from someone inside. He didn't want to rush in and arrest anyone until he was certain his hunch was correct. Getting out, he reached into the back seat and put the short lead on Bella. He moved his seat forward and let her out. Her excitement told him that she was ready to prove herself once again. They walked to the other side of his truck so Flint could get into his search and rescue bag. He retrieved the plastic bag with Abby's shirt, opened it, and let Bella sink her nose into it once again.

There were three trucks and two cars in the lot. Flint started with the truck closest to him and walked Bella completely around it. She didn't alert. The vehicle next to it was an old Honda Element which didn't interest her either. The next vehicle was three parking spots closer to the front door, and there was no way Flint and Bella could get close enough without being seen through the diner's front windows. He didn't remember seeing it parked there earlier, so he decided to make it the last car to inspect. There were two trucks parked across the lot from the front door in an area that was relatively dark. If he were lucky, the lights inside the diner would make it difficult for anyone to see him nosing around outside.

Flint stayed well away from the yellow glow of the sodium lights illuminating the parking area from the front of the diner by taking a long semicircle walk through the shadows at the edge of the lot. From the far side of the lot, he could see the two men he had met earlier through the front window. They were still sitting at the same table, though their dirty dishes had been picked up. They might still be waiting on the check. Good!

Finally reaching the first truck on the back row, he could see Bella perk up, but she didn't alert as she circled the truck. It wasn't until she walked to the last truck two spots over that Flint thought they might have something.

Bella started at the front of the truck and walked around to the driver's side, where she stopped and took several deep sniffs. She continued to the back of the truck, then made her way back up to the passenger side door. After inspecting the crack around the bottom of the passenger door, she pawed at the truck and sat. That was the sign. She had found Abby's scent.

Flint was astounded. Bella was right all along, and he had made her feel like she'd done something wrong. He would have lots of time to make up for that.

Looking through the diner window, he saw the two men stand and start to walk toward the front door. Backup hadn't arrived yet, and it was beginning to look like he would have to handle this situation on his own.

Flint used his flashlight to look through the passenger window, but the dark tinting made it difficult to see if anyone was inside. He pointed his light through the front windshield. If Abby was in there at some point, it didn't appear she was in there now, and that could be bad for her.

He turned his attention back to the two men now coming out the door and heading for the truck. They stopped short when they saw Flint and Bella standing next to their vehicle.

"Hello, Officer," the big one said. Flint remembered his name as Jake.

Flint didn't say anything at first as he sized up the situation. *That guy is huge*, he thought. He had to be at least six feet tall and well over 300 pounds. His hair was short with some sort of buzz cut. The short one looked more manageable if things became physical. He was 5'8" or less and not as fat as the big guy.

"Hello, fellas. How was dinner?"

"Fine," the small one said. They started walking toward Flint again.

"Hold up right there, guys. Let me see your hands!" Flint shouted as he pulled and aimed his Glock pistol at the two men. Bella recognized his words and went on high alert. Flint reached for his radio. "Forty-seven ninety-two Park Police to dispatch," he said.

"Go ahead, forty-seven ninety-two," said the same female dispatcher from earlier.

"Have my backup step it up! I have two suspects at gunpoint in the parking lot at the Blue Dolphin Diner on Highway 29. I need immediate backup!"

"Understood," the dispatcher said.

"Suspects?" the big one shouted. "Suspects for what?" The little one started walking toward Flint.

"Stop right there. Do not come any closer!" Flint shouted, aiming his gun at the small guy. Travis stopped moving.

13

"Hey, dude! Just wait a damn minute! What is your problem?" he protested to Flint.

Bella barked with a ferocity that caused both men to freeze at the sound. Flint trained her to know the difference between a good guy and a bad guy, and he could tell she'd already made a decision on these two.

"Just stand right there! Don't move! You understand me?" Flint warned them. "Where is she?"

"Where is who?" the big one said.

"The girl. The ten-year-old girl you took from the campground!"

"I don't know who in the hell you're talking about, buddy! You're crazy," the big one shouted.

"You know who I'm talking about! You kidnapped her, and you put her in your truck. What did you do to her?" Flint was angry and losing his patience. Out of the corner of his left eye, he finally saw flashing blue lights far down the highway. He saw the two men look down the road at the same time. They knew Flint's backup was coming.

"Jimmy," the little one said to the big one. "We've got to go. We've got to go now!"

"Jimmy," Flint scoffed. "You told me your name was Jake. What the hell *is* your name?"

"Look, man, it was an accident," the big one said. "We didn't mean to hurt her. She walked out in front of my truck, and we hit her. We picked her up and tried to take her to the hospital, but she died before we could get there. It's as simple as that."

"Bullshit," Flint countered.

"I'm telling you, it was an accident. See for yourself. There's damage to the front of my truck, and besides that, she's still in there."

Flint was taken aback for a second. He hadn't seen a body when he looked into the truck nor did he notice any damage to the truck when he and Bella walked around it. He would have to look one more time.

"Don't move," Flint shouted. "If I see either of you move, I'll shoot. Do you understand?"

Both men nodded. Flint pulled back on Bella's lead and started walking backward to the front of the truck. He was heartbroken with what he saw. There was damage on the right front brush guard. Not much, but some.

He walked forward to the passenger side door, still holding Bella's lead. With the gun in his right hand trained on the men, he shined the flashlight with his left hand into the cab of the truck. The dark windows once again made it difficult to see the floorboard, so he leaned forward, taking his eyes away from the men for just a second. That was the mistake of his life.

Flint saw movement from the men but had no time to react. The first shot hit him in the left arm, causing him to drop Bella's lead as she bolted for the shooter. The second shot hit him square in the sternum, causing him to fall backward to the hard concrete. Through the fog of fear and adrenalin, he aimed his gun at the little guy who was moving up on him. Another shot hit him in the rib cage just as he squeezed the trigger.

Bella reached the little man as he dropped lifelessly to the ground. No longer a threat, she lunged after the big man who, after struggling with his enormous belly to remove a pistol from his front pocket, fired a shot at Flint. The bullet sparked as it bounced off the concrete parking lot and hit Flint in the right forearm, causing him to lose the grip on his pistol.

The last thing Flint heard before losing consciousness was another gunshot and a whimper from Bella.

Chaotic visions clouded Flint's intermittent moments of consciousness. There were sounds of sirens, lots of them. Bright lights were hurting his eyes, and people were shouting things at him he couldn't understand. In his mind, they were all annoyances keeping him from falling sleep. He was so tired. So damned tired.

Rachael gently awakened him by touching his shoulder. "Roll over baby," she asked him in the sweet way she always did when he snored too loudly.

"Am I snoring?" he asked.

"No, you're not snoring. You just need to breathe. You're not breathing," she said.

He tried to roll over, but couldn't. "I can't, sweetheart. I'm too tired."

"Let me help you," she said. He felt his body move and with it came searing pain. He was finally able to catch his breath, but it still required too much effort.

"Thanks, honey. That made me feel a little better," he said. "Are you home for the night?"

"No, I have to leave again in a bit. I just wanted to make sure you were doing all right. Good thing I did. It looks like you need some help."

"I'm okay," he said, finally getting his eyes open just enough so he could see her

silhouette through the bright light. "I've missed you so much. Sam misses you, too. When are you coming home?"

"It'll be a while, my love."

Flint began to feel the same God awful pain he felt the night he learned Rachael had been killed in the line of duty. Why they called it a heartache when it was so obviously a gut wrenching pain was beyond him, but he had been living with it for two years now.

"Maybe Sam and I will come stay with you?"

"I'm so sorry baby, but you can't do that right now. I don't know why, but I just know you can't. Believe me, I want you to, but that would just be selfish. Flint?"

"Yeah, babe?"

"I need you to breathe again, sweetheart. You have to remember to breathe," she said to him gently.

"No, I don't think I want to. I miss you. I need to be with you. So does Sam. And you know what? Bella misses you, too. I think we've waited long enough to be together, don't you?"

"Flint, Sam can't be with us right now. She still has a lot to do, and I need you to take care of her for a while, so please honey, breathe!"

"I don't think I want to. I just need to sleep." Flint was bone weary and tried to shut his eyes. This was all too confusing.

"Flint!" Rachael rarely raised her voice, so it caught him off guard. It always amazed him how she could be so quiet and unassuming at home, but could transform into such a hell on wheels while working a patrol shift. She was born to be a cop. Born a cop, died a cop.

"Flint!"

He parted his eyelids a bit. "Yes?"

"Breathe baby, please!" Rachael pleaded.

"Will it make you happy, Rachael? Truly happy?"

"Yes, Flint. It would make me very happy. You know who else it would make happy?"

"Who?"

"Bella. She's right here, and she wants you to breathe."

"That's weird. Usually, all she wants is a hamburger."

"Yep. She's here with us, and if you don't mind, I think I'll take her with me. She's tired, too, and needs a rest."

"Okay, but will she be gone long? You know, she just did the most incredible thing."

"I know, sweetheart. She's an amazing dog, and she's saved a lot of lives, but if you don't mind, I think I'd like to take care of her for a while. But you have to breathe, or she won't come with me."

Flint was confused, but somehow he knew it was the best thing to do.

"Take good care of her, okay? She's been a really good dog. And Rachael?"

"Yes, honey?"

"Please tell Bella I'm sorry. I'm sorry for thinking she failed when she had really done a good thing."

"She knows, Flint. She knows it with all of her heart and soul."

Flint felt a new sadness begin to creep up from his belly. It was bittersweet.

"If I breathe, she'll go with you?" he asked.

"Yes, and she'll be much happier knowing you're all right. She loves you very much."

"All right. I'll try," he said softly.

"That's great, baby. That's good news," Rachael said.

"Rachael?"

"Yes, my love?" Rachael replied from far away now.

"Can I sleep now?"

"Yes, Flint. You can sleep. I love you."

"I love you, too," Flint said, closing his eyes. He slept the deepest sleep he had ever known.

CHAPTER TWO

Flint's hearing was the first of his senses to return.

"Wake up, Flint! You need to wake up, honey." The voice didn't belong to Rachael, but the distinctive allure of its Southern drawl beckoned him forward from the haze anyway.

Slowly his eyes focused on the dim lights above and colorful flashing lights all around him. Not entirely unpleasant and certainly better than all those glaring lights from before.

"There he is," the voice said. "Our hero is back!"

With great effort, Flint tilted his head just enough to see who was speaking. A tall, middle-aged woman dressed in green medical scrubs with short black hair and tired, brown eyes lowered her clipboard and joined him at the side of his bed.

"My name is Susan, and I'm your nurse. Do you know where you are?"

Flint tried to speak, but unable to translate his thoughts into actual words, he moved his head just enough to indicate no. It nearly exhausted him.

"You're in the intensive care unit at the hospital. You've been hurt." There was a long pause. "Do you understand what I'm telling you?"

Flint couldn't move his head again to answer. He just laid there trying to understand what she was saying.

"You've just come from surgery and you're waking up from the anesthesia. It may take you a few minutes to get your bearings, but you're going to be okay."

Flint shut his eyes and tried to go back to sleep, but Nurse Susan was having none of that. "Wake up, Flint. We need to know how you're doing. Are you hurting anywhere?"

Flint managed to nod his head.

"Where are you hurting?" she asked again.

His throat was sore, and he could barely speak. "Arms," he said, scratching out the words.

The nurse reached across him and carefully touched his left arm. "Both of your arms are going to hurt for a while, baby. You've been shot in the upper left arm and your right forearm. The bullet that hit you in the left arm also went through your rib cage and punctured a lung." She gently placed her hands on his chest. "You were also shot twice in the chest. Once right here and again right here," she said as she softly touched him where the bullets impacted. You're lucky you were wearing your vest because it stopped both of those bullets. This spot near your sternum is badly bruised, sweetheart, and it's going to be sore for a while. This other spot isn't so bad, but we have you all fixed up now and you'll be chasing bad guys again in no time." She patted his shoulder and quickly checked his IV.

"Can I get you anything?" she asked.

Flint didn't answer.

"I'll be back in a couple of minutes. You've got some nice folks in the waiting room worried about you. I'm going to tell them you're awake now, and a few of them should be able to visit with you shortly." She disappeared behind a curtain.

As the fog from the anesthesia began to recede, the memories of what happened slowly creeped back into his consciousness. There were glimpses of the search for someone, he couldn't remember who just yet, the ride home, and stopping at the diner. He remembered the bright lights in his eyes and talking to Rachael. *Rachael! How was that possible? She's been dead for two years and where was she taking Bella?*

He struggled with his thoughts, trying to make sense of them. As his mind became more lucid and his memories clearer, the replay of the gunfight began to play over and over in his head. First in small snippets of action and finally as one long streaming vision. When he came to the end of the scene playing out in his memory, one thought struck him particularly hard. He remembered hearing the sound of a gunshot and a yelp from Bella. Tears welled in his eyes for the first time since Rachael died. The thought of losing Bella was unbearable, and the only way to lessen the sadness was to succumb to his desire for sleep.

"Pop! Can you hear me, Pop?"

"I hear you, Sam," Flint answered, smiling before he had even opened his eyes. When he turned his head, he saw her next to his best friend Troy, both standing beside the bed.

"Oh, Pop!" Her face crumpled as she began to cry.

"Hey now, none of that," he said softly. He tried to reach out to her with his left arm, but the pain wouldn't let him do it. "Come over to this other side and give me a hug." She walked around the foot of the bed and raced to his open arm. He squeezed her as tightly as he could until the pain in his forearm told him to ease up. "I'm fine, little one." He felt her nod her head as she buried her face in the sheets covering his chest.

"Hi, Troy," Flint said.

"Hello, Flint. How are you feeling?"

"Well, not so great at the moment. It looks like I got into a little bit of trouble."

"Yeah, you did," Troy said, turning his trademark grin into a full-on smile. "You got shot up pretty good, but the doctor told us you're going to be fine."

"That's what I heard," Flint replied. The two locked eyes for a moment. "Troy, tell me. Bella?"

The smile left Troy's face. "I'm sorry Flint."

Flint took a moment to absorb the news, then quickly redirected himself to Sam. He wanted to drop the conversation about Bella for fear of upsetting Sam even more.

"Are you going to be all right Samantha?" he asked her gently.

She looked up at him. "Yes, sir. Mr. Troy told me that Bella saved your life. She kept a man from shooting you."

Flint looked back at Troy. "Is that true?"

"Yep. It's true. Do you know Deputy Jim Dawson?" Troy asked.

"No, the name doesn't sound familiar."

"Well, Dawson arrived just as the gunfire started. He saw Bella break free and run toward one of the men who was shooting at you. He said you'd already shot one of them and Bella attacked the other guy just as he was getting a good aim at you. The dude had to fight with her just long enough to give Dawson time to draw his gun and shoot him. The bad guy shot Bella during the struggle Flint, but the few extra seconds she gave Dawson saved your life. Everyone is talking about it."

Flint couldn't speak for a few moments as he tried to fight off the overwhelming sadness.

"Let me tell you something that might make you feel better," Troy said. "You and Bella are both heroes. You know that girl you were looking for, Abby? The Sheriff's Department found her alive! One of those guys you fought with last night had a house nearby. They found her locked in an old storage shed behind his house. She's here at the hospital and she's going to be just fine!"

"That's great," Flint said. "I thought they'd killed her. They told me they hit her accidentally with their truck. I started to believe them when I saw some damage to the front of their truck, but I pulled a rookie mistake and looked away from them for just a second. That's what got me shot and Bella killed."

"Don't even go there. You saved a young girl's life, for God's sake." Troy paused for a moment. "I have to know something though. Everyone is wondering how you knew those guys kidnapped her?"

"I didn't."

Troy squinted. "What do you mean?" he asked.

"At the campground, Bella tracked the girl's scent down one of the trails leading into the woods. She left the trail and bushwhacked south all the way to the main highway. When we got to the side of the road, she alerted on a police baton that was just lying there."

Sam lifted her head and stared at her father's face.

"I thought Bella had gotten confused and followed the trail of one of the deputies who had been in the search party. I assumed one of the deputies dropped the baton accidentally." Flint stopped talking for a moment and swallowed hard. The anesthesia had worn off, but his throat was still sore from the breathing tube. "I didn't realize until later what Bella had been trying to tell me all along. It belonged to one of the men who took her. They either parked their truck on the highway and walked in or they found her lost on the side of the road. I don't know which, but the baton had her scent on it. Was she injured? Did they hit her with it?"

"I don't know," Troy answered. "I'm not sure anyone knows yet. They didn't bring her to the hospital until a couple of hours ago. I'll go and ask some questions in a minute, but first, I'd like to know how you tracked them to the diner?"

Flint closed his eyes to gather his thoughts. He still had to think through what happened before he could put it into words. "That was pure luck, at least on my part. I stopped at the diner to get something to take home. Two guys paid for my dinner, so when I went to thank them, they fed me a bunch of garbage about how much the appreciated cops and shook my hand. One or both of those guys must have had the girl's scent on their hands because Bella acted weird from the moment I got back into the truck. She kept smelling my hand and giving me the alert signal." Flint paused. The guilt of not understanding what Bella was trying to tell him was torturing him, and his voice was beginning to break from the emotion.

"So you figured out what she was trying to tell you?" Troy asked.

"No, but I should have. I thought she was smelling the hamburger I bought her, so I ignored her. She found the baton I'd thrown into the back of the truck and practically dropped it into my lap. When she did that, I knew she was trying to tell me something. If she hadn't done that, I would've never known something was wrong and that little girl would probably be dead by now. I'm not the hero, Troy. Bella is, and she died thinking she was a failure." Flint looked down at Sam, who had been standing stoically next to him. She smiled a sad smile.

Troy spoke softly, "Well, I disagree with you there. She died doing her job, and she knew it. She protected you from the bad guys. It just so happens that she also saved a young girl's life in the process."

"I guess so," Flint said, giving Sam another hug.

"Why would two guys who should be avoiding cops at all costs, especially after what they had just done, be so stupid as to call attention to themselves by buying your dinner? I mean, that's just ignorant."

"I was wondering that, too. I guess they were just arrogant idiots, trying to show how smart they were by buying a meal for a cop they knew was looking for them," Flint said. "Remember when we worked in Dallas, the bad guy would sometimes come back to the scene of the crime and hang out in the crowd?" Troy nodded. "Being intelligent isn't within the skill set of most bad guys."

"Stupid dumbasses." Troy looked at Sam. "Sorry kid. Didn't mean to use a bad word. Do you want to stay here while I check on the girl?" She nodded. "I'll be back in a bit," Troy said as he walked toward the door. "Damn," he said under his breath, which caused Flint to smile for the first time.

Flint eased himself into his favorite brown leather chair, which was no easy task considering his left arm was in a sling, and his right forearm was in a cast. He was tired and a little gloomy, but thankful that he was still alive and *able* to feel tired. Flint heard Troy's voice, "Goodbye, folks. Thanks for coming," followed by the sound of the front door closing. Troy headed to the kitchen to help Liz and Sam with the clean-up. Some of the folks attending the service had stopped by Flint's house afterward to pay their respects in person and the last of them just left. There was quite a turnout for Bella's memorial service that morning. To give Flint time to recover enough from his injuries so he could attend, the service was held two weeks to the day after Flint left the hospital. There were hundreds of people at the service Flint had never met, but nonetheless, felt the desire to be there.

The ceremony was honorable and uplifting. The Escambia County Sheriff's Department organized the entire thing, and at least seventy-five or eighty of their officers dressed in Class A uniforms where present to give their final respects to Flint's K9 partner. There were many officers present from other parts of the country, too. Flint met one who came from as far away as Vermont, and like Flint, he was a K-9 officer and understood the bond between a police officer and their dog. Several officers came from other national parks, though Flint didn't know most of them.

A surprise guest showed up at the memorial service as well, someone no one expected, Abigail Day. Flint's heart filled with emotion when he discovered she was there. He had seen pictures taken of her after she arrived at the hospital, but they were taken after she had been roughed up by the two monsters. He'd never seen her in person until now. She was a gorgeous little girl.

Her grandmother brought her to the ceremony who Flint was told afterward had custody of her now. Flint insisted they sit up front with him and Sam. She told Flint she was sorry he lost his puppy and thanked him for saving her life. Flint, overcome with emotion from hearing her say that, could only respond by nodding his head and hugging her. He tried to tell her she was welcome, but the words wouldn't come out of his mouth.

The chaplain for the Sheriff's Department gave the eulogy and was kind in choosing his words. He could have downplayed the ceremony somewhat considering that Bella was, after all, a dog. It wasn't the same as if a human officer had fallen in the line-of-duty, but the fact that 'the dog' had given its life protecting a human while at the same time saving another human from a horrible fate, well, that deserved honor and dignity, and his eulogy did just that. Flint was pleased.

Once word spread about what happened, condolences and offers to help honor Bella, the K-9 hero, came flooding in from as far away as Canada. There were gifts of money to help with the K-9 program even though there was no official K-9 program for the National Park Service. There were offers to help with Flint's medical expenses and rehabilitation, but because he had been injured in the line of duty, it was all covered through work. Flint would either have to return the checks or make sure they got donated to an agency like the Humane Society. He would be off from work another several weeks, so he had plenty of time to sort through all of it. Sam opened a lot of the mail for him already, but there was still a big stack on his desk in the spare bedroom and another stack that had come in just today on the table next to his chair.

Flint felt a hand on his shoulder. He looked up and saw Troy's wife Liz. "Flint, would you like a cup of coffee?" she asked.

"I'd love one, Liz, thank you." He reached out to her and grabbed her hand. "Liz, thank you for helping me around here with Sam and the house. I really appreciate it!"

"You're most welcome, sir," she said, letting go of his hand and patting his shoulder. "You know how much we love Samantha, and we think you're okay on occasion, too. I mean, now that you're a big freaking superhero of some kind, it's just a pleasure to bask in your light." They both laughed over that one.

Flint, alone again, took a moment to shut his eyes and rest. The day's memories fluttered through his mind. How proud he was of Samantha, trying to be brave, and take care of her daddy. He knew she loved Bella as much as he did.

Bella had come to the Westbrook home when Sam was just six. Flint was thirty-four at the time and had been an officer with the Dallas

Police Department for almost twelve years. He was growing bored with busting drunks and drug dealers so his wife Rachael, also a Dallas Police Officer, talked him into trying something new, joining the K-9 program. Flint wasn't too sure about it at first. He thought maybe he would do better as a detective or a member of the SWAT Team but Rachael knew his heart wouldn't be happy with those things. His was a soft heart that wanted to do good things.

In the end, Flint listened to Rachael and gave the K-9 program a try. The program gave him Bella and she turned out to be everything he needed. She gave him a renewed outlook at work, and he'd never been happier. He put everything he had into the program so that he and Bella could be the best there was.

Their training and hard work paid off. In a short amount of time, Flint and Bella developed quite a reputation for being able to hunt down the bad guys. Criminals would throw themselves face-first onto the street rather than risk being bitten by the large German Shepherd. As a team, the duo had been responsible for taking tons of drugs off the street and the guns that usually went with them. Together, they made a big difference on the streets of Dallas. They saved lives. Bella was ferocious when she needed to be, but sweet and gentle otherwise. Especially with Sam.

Coming home from work, Bella would turn into a different dog. She would sit patiently for hours while Sam would dress her up and have princess parties. They played together constantly and even slept in the same bed together. They were best friends. It was never as apparent as after Rachael died.

Flint heard footsteps plod across the wooden floor, and soon Troy appeared, handing Flint a cup of much-needed coffee. Troy sat on the couch across from Flint. "How are you doing?" he asked.

"I'm fine. I'm going to miss her," Flint said.

"She was a great dog. She did a lot of good things in her life," Troy said.

"Yep, she sure did. I was just thinking of how she had helped Sam deal with losing Rachael. Sam found more solace in that damn dog than she ever got from me. I didn't know how to help her, but Bella did."

"Dogs seem to know how to listen better than humans do. They don't try to fix things; they just listen to your problems," Troy said.

"That they do," Flint replied.

"Hey, I need to tell you about a phone call I got at the office this morning," Troy said as more of a question than a statement. Flint met his gaze.

"I know this is way too soon, but I got a call from a lady you may be interested in talking to. I wasn't going to tell you about it until later, but you might want to know."

"I'm listening," Flint said.

Troy pulled a yellow piece of paper from his shirt pocket and unfolded it. "Have you ever heard of Coffy Summerfield?" Troy asked.

"I don't recognize the name."

Troy studied the paper. "She owns an organization called Colorado Search and Rescue Association."

"I've heard of the organization," Flint said. "I think they raise and train search and rescue dogs. They're pretty good at it."

"Are they?" Troy asked. "She said they train them, but I wasn't sure if it was an amateur thing or if they were legit."

"No, they're legit. I know they give a lot of seminars and stuff around the country, and now that you mentioned the name of the organization, I do recall her name. She's written several books on handling search and rescue dogs. She's supposed to be really good at it." Flint leaned back in his chair and started to rub his aching arm.

"Well, like I said, she called. She didn't know how to get in touch with you directly, but she wanted me to pass along her phone number." Troy stood and handed Flint the piece of paper. "She wanted me to tell you that she heard about what you and Bella were able to accomplish with the rescue. She was sorry to hear about what happened to Bella, and wanted you to come up to Colorado and let her set you up with another search and rescue dog."

Flint looked up at Troy.

"She said only when and if you're ready, and that her organization will cover all the expense." Troy placed his hand on Flint's good shoulder and walked back to the kitchen.

Flint, took a few moments to think about what Troy had just said. Bella had been a police K-9 who had never been used for search and rescue until Flint and Bella retired from the police force and moved to Florida. Because Ft. Pickens National Park had never been a hotbed for crime, he had cross-trained her for search and rescue as a hobby. Bella was good at search and rescue but was still a police dog at heart. He wasn't sure if he wanted to try it again. As a handler, he felt he wasn't that good. He didn't understand what Bella was trying to tell him and, as a result, he was injured, and she was killed. Tracking criminals and finding drugs, that was easy. Finding people who needed help and might die if he failed, that was a whole other ballgame.

Flint woke the next morning after a terrible night's sleep. As had been the norm since he left the hospital, his dreams of what he'd done wrong kept him from resting peacefully. They always ended with the sound of a gunshot and a yelp from his best friend.

He got up, dressed, and wandered into the kitchen to make himself a cup of coffee, which was no easy task. The fingers in his right hand were still uncooperative. He had to relearn some of the basic things in life because of it. Even zipping his pants had become a challenge.

He walked out to the front porch and settled into his favorite rocking chair. Pensacola Bay was flat and calm, with no wind to disturb the mirror-like surface. He spotted several people already on the park's public fishing pier this morning, but it didn't look like they were having much luck. His mind wandered to the day he last saw Bella on the pier and what a good time she was having waiting on Sam to catch a fish. He smiled a sad smile and began rocking to sooth his mind.

After an hour or so, the increasing temperature and humidity sent him indoors to see what was on television, but as usual, trade-school commercials and lawyer ads encouraging lawsuits for everything from incontinence to truck accidents drove him out of his skull. He shut off the TV and tried to nap in his chair. If he didn't get back to work soon, boredom was going to kill him.

After his failed attempt at sleep, he opened his eyes and reached for his coffee cup. Stuck to the bottom of it was the yellow piece of paper Troy had handed him the day before. Flint peeled it off the bottom of the cup and stared at the phone number. *What the hell? It probably wouldn't hurt just to talk to the lady. If I sit around here doing nothing but park work, I might as well plan my own funeral arrangements.'*

Flint pulled his cellphone out of his shorts' pocket and dialed the number. The coffee had blotted out one of the numbers, so he took a chance on whether the last number was a one or a seven. He opted for a seven. He got the answering machine.

"Hello, you've reached the Colorado Search and Rescue Association. We're away from the phone right now. If you have an emergency and need search and rescue assistance, please hang up and call the San Juan County Sheriff's Department. They will assist you with instructions. If you would like to speak with Coffy Summerfield, please leave your name and number and she will return the call. Thank you."

Flint left his information and went to the kitchen to find something to eat. He found a couple of leftover pieces of pizza and decided they would be perfect. He loved cold pizza for breakfast. Rachael had always made fun of him for it. Before he could get back to the living room, his cellphone rang. He sat the pizza on the countertop and reached for the phone in his pocket.

"Hello?"

"Hello. This is Coffy Summerfield. Is this Flint Westbrook?" the voice on the other end asked.

"Yes, it is. Good morning, Ms. Summerfield," Flint said as he made his way back to his chair.

"Good morning, Mr. Westbrook, and please just call me Coffy. May I call you Flint?"

"Sure. Thank you for calling me back."

"My pleasure. Listen, I'm using a satellite phone at the moment so if I lose you, I'll call you right back?"

"Sure."

"Flint, I wanted to talk to you about something you may find a bit difficult right now. When I called your office yesterday, I didn't realize the memorial service for your K-9 was that afternoon. If it's too soon to discuss, we can talk about this another time."

"No, I'm good. I appreciate your concern, though."

"No problem. First of all, has anyone told you anything about me or my organization?"

"No, but I read one of your books on dog handling. I recall learning a lot from it."

"I'm glad to hear that. I run a not-for-profit organization called the Colorado Search and Rescue Association. Our primary purpose is to train animals for the search and rescue community and to provide dogs and handlers for search and rescue call-outs. But we also have another mission that we don't advertise a lot. We try to help handlers replace their dogs when they've been lost to accidents or tragic events on the job." Coffy paused for a moment. "I understand you suffered a bad experience while searching for a little girl who'd been kidnapped."

Flint sighed. "Yes, I'm afraid so. My dog was shot and killed by one of the kidnappers."

"I'm truly sorry to hear that, Flint. I heard about what happened from reading the Durango newspaper. Evidently the media picked up your story and it went all across the nation. You're quite the hero."

"Well, I don't know about that hero thing. It was my fault Bella got killed."

"I disagree, Flint. It was the act of a crazy man that got your dog killed, and she saved two lives in the process from what I understand."

"Yes, she did," Flint replied. "She was doing what she was trained to do. You know she was a police K-9 right, and not strictly a search and rescue dog?"

"Yes, I knew that. Your friend Troy gave me the details. While I don't specifically train police dogs, I know of some people who do and would be willing to help you get another dog when you're ready. However, your friend also told me that even though you're a park police officer, there isn't a lot of need for police K-9 work in the park. Is that right?"

"Yes, ma'am, that's right. I retired from a police department in Texas and moved out here to Pensacola to get my daughter away from all the bad stuff going on in town. My K9 Bella retired with us after my wife died. Out here, there's just not much going on that would warrant a police dog. However, I started working with her on search and rescue, and she got pretty good at it."

"Well, that's what I wanted to talk to you about. If you're interested in obtaining another search and rescue dog in the future, I'd be glad to help you with that. That is, if you think there's a need for it in your community, and of course, only if and when you're ready."

"That's a kind offer Coffy. I don't know what I want to do right now. I'm trying to concentrate on getting healthy again. I don't know if you read about it in the article, but I was shot, too." Flint was almost embarrassed telling her, but if he wouldn't be able to use his left arm much, she needed to know that going into it.

"I did read that, Flint. I hope you're doing well with your recovery."

"I am, thank you. It's been a bit difficult because I was shot in both arms, but the right one is healing well. The left one will take some rehabilitation work, but the doctor says I should be fine. I'm fortunate that my twelve-year-old daughter, who thinks she's thirty, is taking pretty good care of me." Flint chuckled.

"Oh, that's great. That's good to hear," Coffy said. "Well, listen, no pressure here. I just wanted to put the offer out there for you. There would be no charge to you or the Park Service for the animal, and my organization would pick up the cost for your travel up here and your training."

Flint wasn't sure he heard correctly. "My training?" he asked.

"I'm sorry, Flint, I got ahead of myself. You would need to come up to Silverton for a few days while we go over the correct handling and training techniques for yourself and the dog. It's important to know that you and the dog are going to be a good team before you get back home. Would that be doable for you?"

"Well, sure, at least I think so. That is, if it all works out," Flint said trying to think of the obstacles that might prevent him from traveling.

"Of course." There was a short pause. "Listen, Flint, unless you have any questions, I'm going to let you go. You take all the time you need to think about my offer. If you decide it's right for you, you have my number. If I don't hear from you, I'll understand."

"I appreciate it, Coffy. I'm sure I'll have another question or two, but I can't think of any right now. I'll call you if I think of any."

"Fair enough. And Flint--"

"Yes, ma'am?"

"I was a mother once. In case I don't hear from you again, I wanted to say thank you for what you did for that little girl. I can assure you that, in her eyes, you'll always be her hero."

"Thank you, Coffy. That means a lot to me," Flint said softly.

"Good. Take care. I hope to hear from you," she said.

"Goodbye," Flint said hanging up his phone. *Did she say a mother once*

CHAPTER THREE

The drone of the MD80 turboprop's engines lowered in pitch as the captain of the MD80 turboprop announced the plane's descent into Durango. It had been a pleasant flight thus far, considering how small the plane was. Flint left the Pensacola Regional Airport that morning on a 737 to Dallas, then caught a direct flight into Durango. It was already two-thirty, and he was hoping to have enough time to pick up his rental car and drive the seventy miles to Silverton before dark. He knew the sun would be setting early this high up in the Rocky Mountains.

It had been just over three months since he'd been wounded and, by all accounts, he was healing well. His left arm was still stiff, but getting better every day. His right forearm was doing fine, though he had a pretty ugly scar as a reminder of what happened. Gripping things like a water glass or the steering wheel of a car could be challenging, but he was steadily progressing. The injury had prohibited him from carrying his gun until he could pass the shooting qualification exam given twice a year. He was given twelve months to pass. He had done it in less than three.

The decision to take Coffy Summerfield up on her offer turned out to be easy. Bella's loss had been hard to absorb, and he missed the companionship of a dog that would go to work with him during the day and be part of the family at night. Just about any dog could be a companion, but he had finally decided a search and rescue trained dog was what he needed so he could carry on with what he'd begun with Bella.

As he stared out the plane's window, the rugged beauty of the mountains below was becoming more detailed with every foot the plane descended. Living on a barrier island for several years had conditioned him to living on flat, almost two-dimensional terrain. He had forgotten that the landscape could extend up and down, too.

After the plane landed, Flint took time to send a text to Sam and Troy that he had arrived safely. Sam would still be in school, and Troy no doubt would be wandering the park in his own police truck.

Troy hated the responsibility of being in charge of the park for any extended period of time while Flint was gone, which was why he didn't apply for the superintendent's job when it became vacant several years ago. Instead, Troy called his friend Flint and practically begged him to put in for it. He knew Flint was looking to get out of the dangerous side of police work after Rachael had been killed. Flint didn't want to leave Sam without a mother *and* a father, so Troy encouraged him to try. Flint didn't think he had the management experience needed to get the job, but he took a shot and was surprised when they offered it to him. Flint loved his new job and, even more so, the healthy environment it provided for Sam.

Flint was a tall man, six foot two, so he waited for most everyone to exit the plane so he could take his time getting out. Grabbing his only bag, a carry-on, he headed down the boarding ramp to the car rental kiosk where he was given the keys to a Jeep Wrangler, directions to Silverton, and a useless frequent driver discount card for half-off his third rental.

He took Highway 550 out of Durango and settled in for the drive to Silverton. Soon, he found himself mesmerized by the dramatic views of rugged granite mountaintops on one side of the highway and a narrow, tree-lined valley with spectacular glimpses of the Animas River far below on the other. He made a note to bring Sam up here before she graduated from school. Maybe next summer.

The highway made a steep decline into Silverton where he was forced to use the brakes more than the accelerator. Finally entering the small town, he felt as if he were the star of an old western movie. The tall, expansive wooden facades and small second story windows of the larger buildings blended with the post and beam architecture of the shops and art galleries. If Clint Eastwood had turned the corner on the next street, he wouldn't have been the least surprised. He followed the GPS directions to the Grand Imperial Hotel which Coffy had told him was the closest hotel to the train station where he would be meeting her tomorrow. It was a little after four-thirty now, and the tall mountains on either side of the city were casting their long, purple shadows into the valley as daylight faded. Flint wanted to get checked in and find a place to eat soon. The cool mountain air had made him hungry.

The hotel lobby was full of antiques and old ceiling fans matching the late 1800s motif of the city streets. A woman at the front desk welcomed him to Silverton and gave him the key and directions to his room. He couldn't help but smile as he opened the door. Two four poster iron beds sat in the room, painted white to match the vintage furniture. A ceiling fan with simple but over-sized wicker paddles graced the ceiling above, and two tall, narrow windows overlooked the main street below. The wallpaper was fresh, but had a small, delicate floral pattern that mimicked the nineteenth-century theme. The only thing that looked out of place was the television in the corner of the room. Flint was glad to see it. From what he'd seen driving into town, there might not be a whole lot to do after dark.

Flint didn't bother to unpack. He would only be in the hotel overnight, so he elected instead to set out just the items he was going to wear tomorrow. For the duration of his training, he would stay at the Colorado Search and Rescue Association's training facility somewhere south of town.

The mountains of Colorado were much cooler than Florida this time of year. Thankful that Coffy had advised him on what to wear, he grabbed his jacket, went downstairs, and asked the clerk at the desk for dinner recommendations. She directed him to the nearby Hungry Moose Bar and Grill where he enjoyed the best chicken fried steak he had ever eaten. The beer wasn't bad either.

He took his time walking back to the hotel. Feeling happy from the alcohol-induced, high-altitude buzz, he decided to take a different route. There were lots of museums and art galleries he would need to visit in the morning. He wanted to get something special for Sam. Before long, Flint realized he was lost. Fortunately, Silverton was a small town laid out on a grid. It didn't take long to find his way back to the hotel.

Entering his room, he laid on top of the green and white diamond quilted bedspread and turned on the TV. The Cowboys were playing the Philadelphia Eagles, but halfway through the first quarter, he was sound asleep.

The alarm on Flint's cellphone went off at seven-fifteen, but he'd been lying in bed awake since six-thirty. Between the time change and the excitement of meeting his new dog, he hadn't been able to get back to sleep. The plan was to meet Coffy at the Silverton Train Station which, when she first told him, he thought was a joke. This wasn't Chicago after all. Why would it be necessary to take a train in the middle of the mountains? When Coffy explained to him she lived off-the-grid, near the bottom of a canyon with no roads, it became apparent he was in for an adventure.

He had until two o'clock to get to the train station, but he wanted to get an early start on the day and see a bit more of Silverton on his own time. Eventually, he crawled out of bed, showered, then laid back down waiting for his coffee to brew. After his first cup, he put on his tan tactical pants, a black long-sleeved knit shirt, and the brown hiking boots he'd laid out the night before. He picked up his black, sleeveless down-filled vest and wondered if it would be warm enough to get him through the cool temperatures of early morning. He threw it back into his bag after deciding it was going to be wonderful to experience low humidity and cool air for a change. After another sip from his coffee, he was ready to go.

Coffy's organization had an account with the hotel, so check-out was easy. Outside, it was a beautiful sunny day with just enough chill in the air to cause his breath to freeze, but with the sun just peaking over the nearby mountain tops, the cold air would soon be warming up.

He drove around town until he found a small coffee shop, parked the Jeep, and went in to get some breakfast. Afterward, he decided to walk the main street and do some shopping. There were plenty of jewelry stores and art galleries to explore. He found a blue turquoise necklace for Sam in one store and a matching bracelet to go with it in another. He visited an art gallery that specialized in Native American artists and bought a beautiful John Nieto print of an adobe church with a dog standing at the front gates. He decided it would be the perfect gift for Troy and Liz as a thank you for helping take care of Sam while he was gone. The gallery volunteered to ship it to Pensacola.

He spent the rest of the morning visiting a few other stores and one fascinating mining museum before deciding it might be time to start heading back to the Jeep. It was going on twelve forty-five, and it would take at least twenty minutes to walk to where he had parked the car this morning. Halfway back, he found a bar that had interested him as he passed by earlier and decided it deserved further investigation. It was decorated like a western saloon with the swinging front doors and an antique bar on one side. Having a cold beer wouldn't be a terrible thing. He walked in and took a seat at the bar. It was obviously a tourist trap, but interesting none-the-less.

The bartender walked over, wiped a damp towel across the bar in front of Flint. "What can I get you?"

Flint smiled at the obviously rehearsed routine meant for tourists. "I need a beer, please. Whatever you have on draft is fine."

"You got it."

The bartender set the beer in front of Flint.

"You on your way to Durango or Ouray?" the bartender asked.

"Neither," Flint said after sipping his drink. "I'm here to meet someone about a dog."

"Coffy Summerfield," the barkeep said without hesitation.

"You know her?" Flint asked.

The man nodded. "Did you read the population sign when you came off the highway? Six hundred and one, on a good day. Just about everyone here knows Coffy, or if they don't know her, they know about her."

"Really," Flint said. "Because of the work she does?"

"Well, there is that. She's saved quite a few lost hikers around here. It has more to do with the reason she's in that kind of work to begin with."

"Really?" Flint said with a smile. "I'm supposed to spend several days with her. Is there something I need to know about her going into this?"

"I really shouldn't say. She's a good person and does good work. The reason why? That's a personal matter which is none of my business." The bartender was staring at his hands as he used his towel to wipe the bar top in circles. "It probably has something to do with her husband and her son. Has she told you anything about them?"

"No, not really," Flint answered, suppressing a laugh as the bartender suddenly changed directions on his moral compass. Small town gossip is the same across the country. People just couldn't resist it.

35

"Well, just keep in mind that you can't talk to her about it, or she'll tear you and me a new one."

Flint nodded his agreement.

"About fifteen years ago her husband and her son disappeared while hiking in the canyon south of here. No one knows what happened to them. Some folks think they just got lost and died. Some think her husband kidnapped the kid and moved off somewhere. Other's even think Coffy had something to do with it. All I know is, whatever happened, Coffy has never forgiven herself for it."

"That's terrible!" Flint said, his good mood suddenly turning somber. Flint thought back to their first telephone conversation. *So that's what Coffy meant when she had said she had been a mother once.*

"You must be pretty close to her to know all that," Flint said.

"Not particularly. We were high school friends, but really, all that I just told you is small town rumor. I shouldn't have said anything."

"Oh, I won't say anything to her. Trust me. That's good information to know, though."

"Yep. No sweat," the bartender said. There was a long pause in the conversation as the bartender stared at his now motionless rag. Flint downed the last of his beer and slapped a ten-dollar bill on the bar.

"My name is Flint. What's yours?"

"Scott," he said.

"Scott, you have a pretty nice place here. Thanks for the drink."

"Nice to meet you, Flint. Please tell Coffy I said hello."

"That, my friend, I'll tell her," he said as he turned and walked away.

Flint parked the Jeep in the nearly vacant train station parking lot and waited for a moment to scan the area for someone fitting the description that Coffy had given him of herself. It took only a few seconds to spot her. She was standing near the main entrance to the train station. Instantly he was ashamed of himself as he realized he was looking at a completely different woman than he'd imagined in their phone conversations. This woman was no tree-hugging earth muffin, or if she was, she wasn't like any of the earth muffins he'd ever seen.

Flint exited the Jeep, grabbed his bag, and began walking her direction. She was wearing a black leather jacket with silver accents, a black knit shirt, and black shorts. It was a lot of black, especially with her long, shiny black hair, but it was apparent to Flint that it worked for her.

She was taller than expected, even though she had told him she would probably be the tallest woman there. As he got closer, he noticed her angular cheekbones and a tiny cleft in her chin which gave her a strong Native American appearance. Her olive brown skin and brown eyes reinforced his opinion. She appeared to be in her mid to late thirties, though he was a terrible judge of age.

They locked eyes as she finally looked in his direction and smiled. Flint spoke first, "Hi, Coffy, I'm Flint." He stuck out his hand.

"Hello, Flint, nice to meet you in person finally." She shook his hand firmly. "I feel like I know you already with all the good things I've read about you."

"I wouldn't believe any of that stuff. I'm sure that if you ask my twelve-year-old daughter, she'll tell you there's no solid evidence I'm a good person." They laughed.

"Are you ready to go? Got everything you need?" she asked.

"I think so. I have everything you told me to bring."

"Good, let's go in and get our tickets. You're going to love this part of your trip." She reached over to a wooden bench beside her and picked up two reusable grocery bags that Flint had failed to notice until now.

"Would you like some help with your bags?" Flint asked after seeing they were full.

"Thanks. No. I'm good. I don't get to town that often so I thought as long as I was here, I might as well get us something to eat that isn't freeze-dried or comes from a can." Coffy led Flint into the station. Like his hotel, the railroad depot was a restored period piece giving homage to the late 1800s when Silverton was a silver mining boom town. It was well done, complete with wooden benches, extensive amounts of lavish wood molding, and an old ticket window behind which sat an older woman dressed in clothing that fit the times.

Coffy took care of the tickets and led Flint outside to the boarding platform. The train was spectacular. A late nineteenth-century black iron steam engine which, even while sitting idle, belched huge clouds of gray steam from somewhere underneath. Just behind the engine sat a black, open-top coal car filled to the brim with what Flint assumed was actual coal, followed by a long line of a dozen-or-so yellow and brown train cars refitted to carry tourists instead of the silver ore that came out of the surrounding mountain mines over a century ago.

"Wow, this is impressive," Flint said.

"Yes, it is. The entire train is original rolling stock. No new stuff built to look old."

"The whole town is amazing, Coffy. You must love it here."

"I do. But I don't actually live in town during the summer, which is why we need the train. Let's see if you still feel amazed when you see my place out in the middle of nowhere." She pointed to one of the passenger cars near the end of the train. "We're in this car down here."

The brakes squealed in several octaves as the train slowly ground to a halt. Coffy stepped off the train car's platform followed closely by Flint. They hadn't made it five steps before the steam whistle sounded and the train began to move again. The ride along the Animas River and into the canyon south of Silverton had been fascinating. Flint couldn't take his eyes off the scenery. As the train lumbered through the flats of the valley floor, Flint was treated to spectacular views of Kendall Mountain reaching 13,000 feet above sea level to the east and slightly taller Sultan Mountain to the west before finally entering the canyon where their world shrunk down to just what could be seen along the river.

Coffy stopped to let Flint get alongside, and together they walked westward, away from the tracks, to a trail cut into a dense grove of Ponderosa Pine. "The cabin isn't far from here. Just a few hundred yards or so up this trail."

It may not have been far, but it was a pretty serious climb, and after a minute or two, Flint started to get a little winded. He hoped the problem was the thin mountain air and being forty years old, and not because he had let himself go a little over the last couple of years. His lungs were used to the rich oxygen at sea level, not this thin wispy stuff nine-thousand feet up. He watched Coffy negotiate the climb with hardly any effort and felt a little embarrassed that he was breathing so much harder than she was.

The trail finally leveled out and curved hard right, revealing a wooden split rail fence with a large cedar sign above the gate that read Colorado Search and Rescue Association. Ahead, at the end of a well-worn path, sat a rustic but charming log cabin. The sun filtering through the wind-blown leaves of nearby trees produced clusters of sunlight that danced across the home's cedar logs and green metal roof.

"Here we are," Coffy said, whirling around to see his face.

Flint stopped and took a good look around. "Coffy, I have to say, this is something else. So this is where you train your dogs?"

"Yep, this is it. This is the headquarters and training facility for the Colorado Search and Rescue Association. Are you ready to meet your new buddy?"

"I am!" Flint said with excitement.

"Well, come on then. Put your pack on the front porch and I'll take you over to the kennels." They both turned to walk toward the cabin just as the train whistle blew once again. This time, coming from much farther away, it sounded lost and lonely as it echoed up and down the canyon walls.

The building didn't look like a normal dog kennel in the traditional sense. Instead, it was a one-story cedar log structure with a flat roof higher on one side than the other, giving the building a look of saltbox architecture. There was a single door on the front and lots of windows lining the right side wall. It looked to be in good repair, but still seemed rather old and quaint. Flint was a little disappointed. It didn't seem like a place that a professional organization could call a 'facility.' If this was indeed the place where she kept her dogs for training, it must be because she couldn't afford a proper kennel. It wasn't until he walked through the door that, he saw just how wrong he was.

Cedar planking covered the entire interior of the structure; floor, walls, ceiling, everything. The right side of the structure was entirely open with plenty of wall space where leashes, harnesses, and vests labeled Search and Rescue K-9 hung. Sunlight streamed through the windows brightening every corner of the structure, making it feel warm and clean. A chain link fence ran the entire length of the kennel on the left side. Behind it stood three German Shepherds, two all-black and one black-and-tan, happily wagging their tails.

Two more large German Shepherds, both black-and-tan, ran into the enclosure through a small opening in the barn wall. Flint realized there must be an outside dog run attached to the barn, though he didn't see it as they walked toward the building. The dogs were absolutely stunning. They looked well cared for and were obviously happy with Coffy's sudden appearance. This was no mom-and-pop shop. The lady knew what she was doing.

Coffy walked over to a chain link gate built into the fence separating the dog's quarters from the rest of the kennel.

"Are you ready?" she asked with excitement.

"You bet!"

Coffy opened the gate. "Sit!" All five dogs followed her command. "Apache! Come!"

One of the all-black Shepherds came forward and walked through the gate, immediately sitting next to Coffy.

"Good girl. Flint, meet Apache."

Flint couldn't believe how beautiful she was. He'd seen long coated German Shepherds before, but never one that was all black. He made his way over and knelt beside her. Apache looked him in the eyes as he buried his fingers into her silken, shiny black coat. He was silent for a moment.

"Hello, girl! Look at how gorgeous you are!"

Coffy smiled and watched Flint stroke Apache for a long while without saying a word.

"Coffy, this is some dog!"

"I'm glad you like her. She's one of the best I've had in a long while."

"How old is she?"

"She's a year-and-a-half. I've been working with her since she was a puppy."

"Wow. She's," His words trailed off as he searched for what to say. "Sensational."

"Let's take her up to the cabin so you two can get to know each other. I think I'll bring Argo, too."

"Argo?"

"Argo is my working dog. He's the one I take with me when I get called out."

"Do you get called out a lot?"

"Yeah, quite a bit actually. My organization doesn't just train dogs. We also provide personnel and dogs for mass casualty events in addition to regular search and rescue calls. I have several people around the state who work with me."

She let one of the black and tan Shepherds out of the gate. "This is Argo." Argo didn't hang around to meet Flint. He and Apache shot out the main kennel door.

"Let's go up to the cabin and let those two tire themselves out," Coffy suggested.

The cabin looked well cared for. The walls were made of logs painted dark brown on the outside. The dark green metal roof contrasted well with the brown, bringing in the colors of the forest surrounding it. The cabin's foundation was made of flagstone, and a covered, elevated porch stretched across the entire front.

Climbing the steps and walking through the front door, Flint was immediately struck by how masculine the furniture looked. Cedar logs and green cushions seemed to be the theme. As feminine as Coffy looked, he wouldn't have guessed this particular style to be her first choice. The walls on the inside were unpainted, but had an attractive satin gloss that brought out the cedar log highlights. The living room was large, taking up almost the entire front of the house. In the back, he could see the kitchen, which was open to the living area. There was no hallway, but there were two doors to the right. Flint figured one must be the bathroom and the other a bedroom. He surmised he would be sleeping on the couch tonight, which was fine with him.

"Welcome to my cabin, Flint. Please make yourself at home. You can put your pack in that room over there." She pointed to one of the doors on the right.

"Are you sure? I don't mind sleeping on the couch," Flint said. Coffy looked at him funny. "I mean, I don't want to kick you out of your bedroom."

"Oh, you won't. That's my bedroom right there," she said, pointing to the other door.

Flint laughed. "Sorry, I thought one of those was the bathroom."

Coffy echoed his laughter. "Sorry Flint. The bathroom is out back. So is the shower."

Flint looked at her and smiled. "Like an outhouse?"

"Not quite that bad. There's a composting toilet in a shed next to the back patio. I'll show it to you in a minute."

Flint walked into the bedroom, threw his pack onto the bed, and joined Coffy outside on the front porch.

"Let's go around back," she said.

Flint followed her around the house.

"This is the bathroom," she said, pointing to a small wooden shed covered with green moss and flowers. It sat adjacent to a rustic flagstone patio which showcased lots of flower pots and plantings. She opened the door to the bathroom. "Like I said, it's a composting toilet. Works just like a regular one, but since we have no sanitation hookups here, we compost the poop."

"That makes sense," Flint replied.

"Out here, on the side of the shed, is the shower. It's not extremely hot, but it's hot enough. I have a solar water heater on the roof."

Flint saw a shower-head protruding from the side of the bathroom building. "Not much privacy, but you really don't need to worry about that with trees this thick. The closest neighbor is about a mile farther down the canyon." She looked at him and smiled. "I promise not to peek." Flint smiled and thought, *I'm not sure I could make that same promise.*

"Would you like a cup of coffee?" she asked.

"Thanks. That sounds great."

"I'll be just a minute. Meet you on the front porch."

Flint walked around the house and sat on one of the large wooden rocking chairs on the front porch. The scenery around him was spectacular. The sun, lowering in the west just above the mountaintops, turned the rock formations across the canyon several different shades of red and orange. There were too many trees to see the river from the porch, but he could hear the water as it swirled along the granite boulders below. A clearing to the right of the cabin gave an unimpeded view south through the canyon where he could see the mountains on both sides of the Animas River. He delighted at the sight of Apache and Argo running through the meadow just below them. Suddenly, he felt a pang of guilt for taking Apache back to civilization and away from the beautiful home she had grown up in.

"Here you go." Coffy handed him a cup and sat in the chair next to him. "What do you think?"

"I think if I lived here I would never leave."

She laughed. "No. I mean Apache. What do you think about her?"

"Oh," he said with a chuckle. "She's a beautiful dog, Coffy."

"I'm sure you two will get along great. We'll see how you feel about her tomorrow after you've had a day to train with her."

Flint took a sip of his coffee.

"Let me know if you don't like it," Coffy said. "I'm on well water here, so it can affect the taste. I'm used to it, so I don't think about it."

"It tastes fine, thanks." He meant it. Having a cup of coffee in this storybook setting was a treat.

Flint looked down at Coffy's rocking chair. "Did you make these chairs?"

"No, my father did years ago. He's the one who actually built the cabin."

"Really?"

"Yeah. When I was little, my family and I lived in Silverton. During the summers, my mother and I would come out here and help my father build this cabin. He and my mother loved this place, and we would spend all of our summers here."

"Your father isn't around anymore?"

"No. Neither of my parents are living. My mother died when I was ten. He went into a deep depression and never came out of it. Things sort of went downhill until one day he committed suicide. He just couldn't live without my mother."

"Oh, I'm sorry to hear that," Flint said.

"Yeah. That's the way it goes sometimes. But he left me this cabin, so he made sure I was taken care of."

Flint didn't know what to say and was thankful when Apache and Argo thundered up onto the porch and collapsed next to them, worn out from their romp in the pasture. He leaned over and stroked Apache between the ears. "Did you have fun, girl?"

Apache's tail thumped against the wooden porch floor as she looked up at him. Her tongue was hanging, flat and wide. She looked tired and happy.

"How about you, Flint? Tell me something about yourself," Coffy asked.

"Well, I have a twelve-year-old daughter named Samantha, though she prefers to be called Sam. She's in the sixth grade and smart as can be. Fortunately for her, she looks just like her mother. My mother lives in Austin, Texas, and I have a sister who lives in San Francisco. My father passed away about the time Sam was born."

"I knew we had that in common. If you don't mind me asking, one of the news articles I read about you mentioned that you lost your wife several years ago."

43

"Yeah, she and I both worked for the Dallas Police Department. She was shot and killed about three years ago serving an arrest warrant."

"Oh, I'm so sorry," Coffy replied. "I didn't mean to--"

"It's okay," Flint interrupted. "I like talking about her. Her name was Rachael. Sam and I miss her terribly."

"I can imagine."

"Rachael is the one who got me interested in police K-9 work. I'd gotten bored with everyday police work so she suggested I try the K-9 unit. It turned out to be a good move for me. After she died, I decided I didn't want Sam to lose another parent to a dangerous occupation, so when my friend Troy called and told me about a position being a superintendent and police officer for a park in Florida, I jumped on it. I'm still a cop, but it's a lot less dangerous now. At least, that's what I thought until I got shot."

"How are you doing with that? Are you feeling better?"

"Yeah, I'm doing well. I've got good movement in my left arm now, but I still have an issue with my right hand. It's getting better with physical therapy, though."

"So you were shot twice?"

"I was actually shot four times. My vest stopped two of the bullets, but the other two got me pretty good. One went through my left arm and punctured a lung"

"Wow. So you were lucky and unlucky at the same time."

"That's a good way to look at it. I know I'm lucky to be alive. The irony of moving to a smaller city to be safer isn't lost on me."

"I would guess not," Coffy said.

The conversation carried on for some time, and Flint was enjoying every minute of it. It had been a long time since he'd been in the company of a woman other than Rachael, and Coffy made him feel comfortable. She made it easy to relax and say what was on his mind.

It was just getting cold enough to be disagreeable when Coffy said," Are you ready to go inside and get something to eat?"

"You bet."

Coffy made a salad while Flint shuffled back and forth cooking steaks outside on the grill.

"Do you have to get all your groceries in Silverton?" Flint asked.

"Yes, I have to go pretty much once a week, especially for the things that require refrigeration. As you can see, my refrigerator is pretty small, so I can't keep a lot of things in it. Sometimes my neighbor Frisco will bring stuff from town. He has more time than I do to go back and forth."

"Did you say Frisco?"

"Yeah, Frisco Bennett. He lives about a mile down the valley. He's an older man who helps me with the dogs quite a bit. You'll meet him day after tomorrow. He's a good guy."

"Does he help you take care of the cabin?"

"I may ask for advice on how to fix something, but I pretty much take care of all the handyman work around here. I'm pretty good with a hammer and a saw. Are the steaks ready? I'm just about through here."

"Yep, I'll bring them in." Flint returned with the steaks and set them on the table.

"Looks like you know your way around a kitchen, sir," she said, smiling at him.

"I've had to learn to do it. I'm not too bad."

She brought over the salad and had a seat at the table across from him. "I'm not used to having visitors. I hope my rustic lifestyle doesn't bother you too much."

"Not at all," Flint said, reaching for the salad. "I'm impressed with what you have here. Quite jealous actually."

"Thanks. It's different, but I like it." She pushed the steaks a little closer to him. "You know, I was married once, too."

Flint put down the salad and met her gaze.

"I was married for eight years. I had a son named Justin, and after my father died, we would spend summers here at the cabin. My husband wasn't that great with his hands, so I took care of most of the repairs."

"Really?"

"Yep, I built that patio out back. I put a new metal roof on the cabin, and I put the solar power system in. I've done a lot of the work around here. My father was a good teacher."

"Well, I guess so," Flint said. He thought about the conversation with the bartender that morning. He was curious as to how much she would be comfortable telling him. "If you don't mind me asking, did you and your husband divorce?"

"No. We came close a time or two, but we never divorced." Coffy reached for a steak.

"It's unfortunate, but I'll probably never know what happened to him. One day about ten years ago, Stephen took Justin down to the river to do some fishing, and they never came back."

Flint had no idea how to react. After a long moment, he said, "My Lord, Coffy! You must have been devastated."

"We searched for months, but never found any trace of them. It took a long time to get over it, and in some sense, I'm still not, but my search and rescue work has been therapeutic. I don't know if I could have stayed sane without my dogs to talk to." She looked at Argo, who was lying next to Apache on the living room floor, licking his paws. She looked back at Flint. "Now that I've brought the conversation down to an all-time low, let's eat before all this food gets cold." Flint could tell she had shared as much as she was willing to at this point.

Over dinner, they discussed their philosophies on search and rescue technique, life in the mountains versus the seashore, and how life can take sudden turns. It was nine-thirty by the time Flint and Coffy had finished with the dishes, and since there was no television in the house, they decided it was time for bed. Coffy wanted to be up early tomorrow to start the first day of training.

Flint changed into his tee-shirt and shorts, hung up his clothes, and looked down at Apache, who was curled up next to the bed. She looked up at him when she noticed his attention on her. It had been several long months since Bella died, and he remembered the dream he'd had the night he had been shot. He hoped to God it was real. There must be a place in Heaven for dogs. So bittersweet was the thought of Rachael taking care of Bella in the afterlife. It had given him great comfort during his time of mourning. He hoped like hell there would come a time they would be together again.

He knew it wouldn't be fair to compare Apache to Bella. The love and trust he had for Bella could never be replaced. Instead, he needed to find a new way to connect. Find a different path to the mutual respect the two had once had for each other. Time would help with that. For now, he just needed to open his heart again and let the dog live on its own terms. No comparisons, no disappointments.

"Apache, my name is Flint. I promise to keep you safe, warm, and fed. In return, I'd appreciate it if you'd help me find a few lost souls who need our help. Is that cool with you?"

Apache cocked her head sideways trying to understand what he was saying to her.

Flint walked over to her, gently picked her up, and placed her on the foot of the bed.

"Tomorrow's going to be a long day. You might as well be comfortable."

CHAPTER FOUR

The sound of rain outside the open bedroom window woke Flint from a deep sleep. He reached for his cellphone. It was five-fifteen in the morning. Not wanting the floor to get wet, he threw back the bedspread and stumbled to the window. When he parted the curtains, he saw it wasn't raining after all; it was Coffy taking a shower on the patio. He knew instantly he should look away, but he couldn't bring himself to do it. She was long and lean with curves he hadn't seen in years. An aura of steam from the warm water hitting the cold morning air surrounded her, softening her edges and gently muting the reflection of the early morning moonlight from the water cascading down her spine.

Something inside him stirred, something primal that had been buried deep inside since Rachael had died. She was beautiful. Eventually, decorum kicked in, and reluctantly, he let the curtains slide from his fingertips and crawled back into bed. Feeling guilty for his emotional betrayal, he closed his eyes, hoping to dream about Rachael. When sleep did come, the dreams came with it, but for the first time since the death of his wife, they were dreams of another woman.

Flint woke again, this time to the smell of bacon and eggs. Not having had that pleasure for a long time, he lay there, enjoying the moment. A few minutes later, the door to his bedroom slowly cracked open. Apache jumped off the bed and ran through the open door. The door closed gently behind her. Flint's short-lived bliss began to turn to guilt for being laggard. He rolled out of bed and got dressed.

Coffy had started a fire in the fireplace so the living room was much warmer than the bedroom. Turning the corner into the kitchen, he saw her staring out the window.

"Good morning," he said gently, not wanting to startle her.

"Good morning, Flint. I hope I didn't wake you when I let the dogs out," she said without taking her eyes off the window.

"Not at all. It was the smell of bacon that woke me up, and it was fabulous!" he said with a smile. "What's so interesting outside?"

"Oh, sorry!" she said. "I was watching Argo and Apache play. I wish I had their energy."

"I know what you mean. I apologize for not getting up as early as you."

"No problem. I thought you might still be tired from your trip so I didn't want to wake you. Besides, we have all day. You do need to eat, though. You'll need plenty of energy for what we have planned today."

"Yes, ma'am. I'm always willing to stuff my face."

During breakfast, Coffy and Flint talked about search and rescue methods and swapped stories about some of their most memorable searches. Their conversation made it obvious to Flint that Coffy had earned her reputation in the search and rescue world the hard way, though she never once bragged on herself. She certainly had the experience to back up her methods.

After breakfast, Flint started on the dishes while Coffy walked down to the barn. He caught himself staring at her through the same window she'd been watching the dogs through before. There was something about her that was different, something alluring. She was an attractive woman, for sure, but something about her struck him deeper than that. This woman had confidence. It was oozing out of her pores, and it made him a little nervous. A little *excited*.

Rachael had been confident, too. For any cop, showing weakness on the street meant a high probability of getting killed, but when cops come home, they are usually tired of being cops, tired of being street wise. Rachael always exuded confidence when others were around, but when alone with Flint, she didn't mind letting him see her be caring and vulnerable. Flint could be the same with her. He remembered entire Sunday afternoons devoted to trying to decide what restaurant to go to. Coffy, however, didn't seem to be the type of person who spent a lot of time second guessing herself.

Coffy returned to the cabin with Apache, who was all decked out in her search and rescue K9 vest and harness. She handed her over to Flint, gathered a few items from a closet, grabbed a small cooler from the front porch, and led them both down the main trail toward the train tracks.

Once they crossed the train tracks, they went another twenty yards toward the river where Coffy put down her gear. "This area will work fine for what we're doing today. It's full of distractions and smells, and the river will keep us all pointed in the right direction." She sat on a boulder facing Flint. "Today is all about you. I know a lot more about Apache and how she works during a search than I know about you."

"Okay. I'm ready," he said.

"I want to tell you a little about her first. She's one of less than a hundred FEMA-certified search and rescue dogs. She's able to search for people in a wilderness area as well as in an urban disaster. It may not be likely you'll encounter the complete collapse of a building, but you never know. I'm sure the people of Oklahoma City never thought it could happen, but look what happened with the bombing of the Murrah Federal Building. Should you ever join a team deployed somewhere for a disaster, you'll have a K9 with the skill set needed to get the job done. Just make sure you keep up on her training. Argo is certified too, but he has more training than Apache. I want you to promise that you'll continue her training after you leave here and you will do it correctly. Can you do that?"

"I promise," he replied.

"Good. Let's start by learning about what motivates a search and rescue dog. A lot of well-intentioned handlers think that dogs search for people out of instinct or some sense of honor. They don't. They're not capable of thinking that way. Do you have any idea why they do what they do?"

"Yep. To a dog, it's all a game. They're playing."

"That's right! Very good." Flint's self-esteem shot up a notch. "They're looking for that magic rubber ball. The more instinctively playful a dog is, the more serious it will be about finding that rubber ball. That's why you have to reward a dog every time it finds its target. Do you remember the search teams at the World Trade Center towers?"

Flint nodded.

"Several of those dogs had to retire early because they were only finding dead bodies. They got confused because they were accustomed to finding live people, and being rewarded for it. So, even when your victim is found deceased, you should reward your dog. If you don't, it's no longer a game to them. I've had cases where we found a deceased person and the family was right there with us. I had to walk away to reward my dog with a game of tug of war just to make sure they saw some fun in it. It's a hard thing to do, but you have to do it."

"Understood," he answered.

"The first thing we're going to do is the standard 'Seek' command. I'm going to lay a scent track for about a hundred-and-fifty yards. Give me about five minutes, then give her the command. Why don't you take her upstream a bit so she won't see which direction I'm taking."

"All right."

"Oh, one thing I forgot to tell you. She's trained to find a subject, then return to you with an object of some sort. A stick, article of clothing, something. She'll drop it at your feet and sit."

"Bella was trained that way, too."

"Good."

Flint and Apache walked north along the stream for about twenty yards and waited. Of all the places he had ever had to kill time, whether it was sitting in a squad car in the barrio or standing over a body waiting for the county coroner to show up, being in the middle of a tall canyon near a stream surrounded by mountains wasn't the worst of them. He sat on a large rock and passed the time talking to Apache and looking at the scenery. After several minutes had passed, he stood, released Apache from her lead, and commanded, "Okay, girl, Seek!"

Apache shot off, headed south along the river. Flint lost sight of her within the first fifty yards, the rocks between the river and the railroad tracks making it difficult to keep up. Every now and then he would catch a glimpse of her as she returned to make sure he was still behind her. After several minutes of searching along the edge of the river, she turned west, heading across the tracks and into the woods. It wasn't long before she returned to Flint with a stick in her mouth.

Flint enthusiastically praised her. "Good girl! Good girl! Now show me!"

Apache dropped the stick and led him several yards to a boulder that lay next to a huge pine tree. They found Coffy on the other side.

Coffy leaped to her feet and instantly rewarded Apache by bouncing a rubber ring on the ground, and then playing a quick game of tug-of-war.

"That was easy enough!" Flint said. "She went right to you."

"Yep, nothing to it. She had a good trainer," she said, never taking her attention away from Apache.

Most of the morning was spent acting out search and rescue scenarios with Coffy playing the part of the victim and Flint learning how to read and handle Apache. He was pleased to find out that Apache had been trained with many of the same techniques that had been used with Bella. Though he wasn't the one who taught Bella as a puppy, it was evident that most of the techniques they were using were pretty much universal. It wasn't as foreign to him as he had feared.

Near mid-morning, the lonely whistle of the Durango-Silverton train echoed through the canyon announcing its morning journey north toward town. As it got closer, they decided to take a break and watch it go by. It wasn't every day that a flatlander from Florida got to see a steam engine train pass by in the mountains. A few minutes before the train arrived, a small, diesel-powered rail car motored past them on the tracks.

"That's the safety car," Coffy explained. "It makes sure the rails are clear for the main train."

"How do I get that job?" Flint asked.

"I'm sure a lot of people are standing in line for that one."

Finally, the billowing clouds of black coal smoke appeared wafting out of the trees and drifting over the Animas River well before the train got close enough to see. When it arrived, Flint felt like a kid seeing a train for the first time. Even though he had ridden the train from Silverton just yesterday, it was nothing compared to seeing it from the ground, churning and groaning as it climbed the steep grade back up the canyon to Silverton.

The massive black and silver steam engine numbered 486 was a ghost from an old western. The smokestack mounted atop the old behemoth belched rich, dark smoke high into the sky where the wind caught it and brought it back down the hill, covering Flint and Coffy in small specks of coal dust. The smell was unforgettable, like old machine oil and sulfur. Apache barked with excitement at the iron horse passing by. The engineer waved and let loose with a quick burst of the steam whistle when he saw Coffy standing below. Behind the engine, the coal car with Durango & Silverton written in old English style text rumbled by.

Passenger cars with rustic yellow and gray paint schemes followed next. They were full of happy tourists waving to every living thing they saw on their journey. Some of the passenger cars were fully enclosed with windows that protected the passengers from the elements. Others were open cars with no windows. Only a half wall and a roof separated the passengers from the elements. Flint couldn't help but smile as the sight of the tourists standing in the open cars passing by reminded him of the old cattle cars that used to take cattle to the market. It would be where he and Sam would ride if they were on the train. Sam liked to smell, taste, hear, and feel everything. Just like her mother. As the last car passed by, he suddenly realized how much he missed his daughter.

"Now in about ten minutes, another rail car will come. That's the fire car that follows to make sure the coal cinders blowing out the smokestack of the engine don't catch anything on fire," Coffy explained.

"Has that ever happened?" Flint asked. "I mean, the train starting a fire?"

"No, not since I've lived here, thank God."

As predicted, the fire car came through a few minutes later with two jubilant looking old men on board. It resembled a little fire truck on train wheels.

After running a few more search scenarios, Coffy finally called for a lunch break. The three of them walked back to the area next to the river where they had started this morning's first training run. Coffy pointed out a couple of boulders perfect for sitting on and watching the river roll.

Coffy opened the top of the cooler and asked Flint if he wanted water or bottled tea. He chose the tea. She handed it to him and pulled a large insulated bottle from her pack along with several foil packages.

"I brought these freeze dried meals, and I'm not sure which you would prefer. There's beef stroganoff, lasagna, and spaghetti. Hopefully one of them might work for you," she said, handing the packages to him so he could choose.

"I think I'll take this spaghetti."

"Pour in two cups of this hot water and let it sit for four or five minutes," she said handing him the water bottle.

"Got it." Flint mixed the water into his food packet, set it on the rock next to him, then leaned back to take in the beauty of his surroundings while he waited for his food to rehydrate. He wasn't used to seeing the horizon tower above him. Living on a barrier island meant there were few trees to break the skyline and certainly no mountains to entertain the eye. On an island, the horizon was always somewhere, out there, far away, not high above as it was here in the bottom of a canyon. There were certainly no rivers on the island. The sound of the water rippling through the rocks was nirvana for Flint. *How easy it would be to just to lay down and go to sleep right here,* he thought.

"What do you think?" Coffy asked, interrupting his daydream of living in the mountains someday.

"About what?"

"This place. Pretty awesome, huh?"

"I'm thinking about bringing Sam up here and moving into your barn. It's been a long time since I've felt so at peace."

"Well, I guess that's high praise coming from a man who lives on an island. I would think being able to sit on the beach whenever you wanted would be the ultimate."

Flint leaned forward and shook his head. "Most people would agree with you, but I don't get much of a chance to enjoy it. There are so many knuckleheads I deal with on a daily basis that being on the beach is nothing more than a job."

"You don't get much time to enjoy it?"

"No, not really. The winters are great, but spring, summer, and fall are pretty tough. I'm always getting called out for drunk tourists, fights, lost kids, loose dogs. It's like being a cop in a small city, mostly minor stuff, but it's constant. By the end of the tourist season, I despise people and don't want to be around them anymore." Flint looked at Coffy, who had started eating her lunch. "Do you ever get that way? I mean, just not wanting to be around people at all?"

Coffy smiled and looked up at the canyon walls. "Why do you think I live out here? I don't trust people. Out here, I get to choose who I deal with, and unless they have four legs and a tail, I usually don't have anything to do with them."

Flint picked up his spaghetti and stirred it again. It was nice not

54

having a politically correct conversation with someone. "I don't have a choice. I have to deal with people. It's my job."

"I'll bet, being a police officer, you've seen some of the worst of humanity."

"Yes, I have. People can do horrible, unspeakable things to one another. It gets tiresome and debilitating to see it day in and day out. I'd like to say that there's enough goodness in people to balance it out, but in my line of work, you don't get called out often for situations where people are being kind to one another."

"How do you keep it away from your daughter? Surely you don't share all the bad things with her?"

"Good God no. My wife was good about that. She never brought her work home. She was all Disneyland and puppy dogs when she walked through the front door. She had this amazing ability to separate her life from the evil things going on, and she refused to believe in a world that was otherwise. She was my inspiration and still is to this day. If I have a bad day at work, it stays at work. I don't bring it home. She was the one who taught me how to do that."

"Sounds like she was an amazing woman."

"She was. Is. She still is."

Coffy looked at Flint, obviously confused by what he said.

"When I got shot looking for the girl in Florida, Rachael came to me and intervened. I was near death and at the time, actually preferred it to going on. I was ready to give up. To 'go to the light,' so to speak. But Rachael came to me. Told me to breathe, to fight to live. She convinced me to stay for the sake of my daughter. So I did. I didn't want to, but I did, because of Rachael."

"That's amazing," Coffy said, reaching out, and placing her hand on his shoulder. "To feel love from the other side. I can't say there are too many people lucky enough to experience that." She looked at him until he smiled back at her.

They finished their lunch in silence and got back to work. Running so many different exercises during the afternoon was tiring, but interesting for Flint. The physical challenge of working in thin air at high altitude and the muscle burn of climbing up and down steep terrain did little to diminish his excitement for learning new techniques in search and rescue from one of the world's best. The fact that she was awakening feelings in him that he had forgotten long ago was a welcome bonus.

As Flint made his way to the cabin, every muscle in his body ached. He was in pretty good shape, but the day's events had worn him out. He'd been spending too many hours behind the desk at his office, and he knew it. He vowed to himself to get out more and exercise his body. Coffy opened the door and went in, followed by Flint, who headed straight for the leather couch.

"Uh-uh!" she teased. "What is it about men? You come home from work and sit on the couch for the rest of the day. We're not through yet. We still need to feed the dogs and put away the equipment."

Flint sighed; she was right. He needed to take care of business first. He followed her to the barn and helped her feed the dogs. Apache tagged along while Coffy showed Flint the evening routine. She let Argo out of the kennel, and after he and Apache had eaten their dinner, they ran out into the pasture to play while Coffy and Flint went back to the cabin.

"Now you can take a seat. I'm going to start dinner," Coffy told him.

Flint had fallen into that trap before with Rachael. He knew what she really meant was, *You're off the hook if you choose that option, but it would be nice if you helped me with dinner.*

"I'm good. What can I help you with?" he asked.

Coffy smiled at him. "Why don't you take those potatoes over there and start peeling them? That would be great."

After working together for about an hour, they finally sat down to enjoy their meatloaf and mashed potatoes. Flint was especially happy for the fact there were no green vegetables to eat. Rachael had been relentless in making him eat vegetables with every meal. He didn't like them and was grateful that they were evidently not that important to Coffy.

After dinner, Coffy surprised him by pulling out a chilled bottle of red wine and leading him to the front porch. She poured them both a glass, and they toasted the last remnants of yellow sunshine still painting the canyon walls high above. Before long, Apache and Argo joined them on the front porch.

"Coffy, I think if I lived here, I'd become the world's most useless human being. I could just sit here and do nothing all day long."

"I have those days, too. And you know what? Some days, that's what I do. Nothing. But, believe it or not, too much of that gets old. I can't sit for too long or I get restless. You have to strike the right balance."

"I suppose so," he said. "I just get so tired of dealing with assholes all day. The petty stuff is what really gets to me. I honestly enjoy helping people when they need help, but it's those who bitch about every little inconvenience that get to me. At the park, we deal with people who choose to go camping in the middle of July, then complain about there being too many mosquitoes, or the humidity is too high. *Those people.* The people who don't know what it's like to deal with genuine heartache, like living with cancer or the death of a loved one. Once you have an experience like that, the little stuff just seems so unimportant." Flint suddenly felt a little guilty for bringing down the conversation.

"I know what you mean. It's hard to feel sorry for people who complain about rush hour traffic while the guy in the car next to them is driving his wife to the hospital for her chemo treatment." Coffy took a sip from her wine glass. "It's all about perspective. A person who hasn't dealt with true tragedy won't have a point of reference to judge what is and what isn't important. For someone like you or me who's felt the pain of losing someone, then living life with the emptiness it leaves afterward, rain on your birthday just doesn't feel like the end of the world anymore."

Flint looked at Coffy who returned his glance. "Amen, sister! Well said." They both took a sip from their glasses. Flint was amazed to find someone who felt about people the way he did. Interesting.

"Do you ever get lonely up here by yourself?" Flint asked.

"Sometimes I do, but my dogs are pretty good company. They never yell at me or get upset. They entertain me, and the only thing they ask in return is to be loved and fed. It's a pretty good trade, and then there's Frisco. You'll meet him tomorrow. He's quite a character. He and I will work on a project around here, and by the time we're done, I always feel better. He keeps me laughing."

"Sounds like a good guy."

"Yeah, he can be when he applies himself. How about you, Flint? Do you ever get lonely raising a child by yourself?"

He took a moment to think about how to reply. "Yes, I do sometimes, but having a twelve-year-old daughter who loves life as much as she does keeps me pretty happy. I'm so lucky to have Sam. She's the reason I'm still here. Well, that and the fact that my dead wife insisted that I stay here." He chuckled at his morbid comment.

"You mentioned that at the river today."

"It's a true story. But I know deep down I would have done everything I could to stay alive for my daughter. She's the only real joy I have in my life."

Coffy looked at Flint who was staring at Apache. "I knew that joy once. I loved my son more than life itself, and when he went missing, well, my life pretty much ended that day. The only reason I'm still walking this planet is to keep that from happening to someone else. So they don't lose their reason for living, too."

Flint met her gaze, suddenly understanding the immensity of what she had just shared. It was heartbreaking. He would never be able to understand the pain she was talking about. Losing a child was the worst emotional pain a human could feel, and he hoped to God he would never know the depths of it. He had never really thought about the impact his search and rescue work could have on someone until now. The parents of Abigail Day, as bad as they were, didn't deserve to lose their daughter that way. No one should lose a child.

Coffy was surprised and grateful at the same time when Flint reached across the small table between them and wrapped his hand around hers. They sat for a little while, not speaking, just enjoying the presence of another human being who understood them.

The cool air began to settle at the bottom of the canyon, and Flint decided he needed to shower off the day's sweat and grime before it got too cold.

"I'm going to take a shower if you don't mind," he said, releasing his grip from Coffy's hand.

"Sure. Everything you need is back there. Soap and towels are in the cabinet on the side of the shed."

"Okay, thanks."

He headed to his bedroom, retrieved a fresh set of clothes from his bag, and walked out to the shower. When he arrived at the patio, he looked around to make sure he was alone. It was a strange feeling to be taking a shower outside, but then he had never lived in the country either. He undressed, laying his clothes on a wooden bench next to the shed. Finally finding the soap and a towel, he turned on the shower. Surprised at how warm the water was, he looked up and saw the large black plastic water container on the roof of the shed that warmed the water during the day. He decided it was a pretty nice setup and stepped into the water. It felt great.

As soon as he was wet, he realized he had forgotten his shampoo. After finding none in the cabinet, he decided he had no other choice than to use the bar of soap on his hair instead. He lathered his hair and stood motionless, allowing the water to wash it out. The warm water felt wonderful on his aching muscles. The altitude combined with the wine was making him feel pretty good. but just a little light-headed. He reached out to steady himself against the rock wall of the shed.

Feeing her hand brush across his hip, he turned to see her standing behind him, nude. She looked up at him with a smile and moved closer to embrace him. He was surprised even though he had hoped for this from the moment he saw her in the shower this morning. He welcomed her embrace. They stood there for a moment enjoying the warmth of each other's body until she leaned back and looked up at him.

"You were right. I do get lonely sometimes," she said softly. "I hope you don't mind.

He answered her by bringing her back into his arms, guiding her around him so she could enjoy the warmth of the water coming from the showerhead. He stroked her long, black hair until the water completely saturated it. He put his hand under her chin and tilted her head back. With her hair wet, the angular outlines of her face became more apparent. Her large, brown eyes begged him for kindness and comfort. He didn't want to disappoint.

Flint gently rubbed soap into her hair and helped her rinse it out. He started rubbing her shoulders with the bar of soap, gently moving it down along her back. She was stunning in the low light of the evening. He soaped her legs, then with his hands, encouraged her to turn around and face him. He started at her feet and slowly worked upward. Coffy grabbed the top of his head and locked her fingers into his hair. Taking his time, he worked the lather around her upper thighs causing her to tremble. Rising to his feet, he soaped her belly and slowly made his way to her breasts. She shuddered as he lingered there.

Coffy rinsed off and took the soap from Flint. She returned the favor, making sure she cleaned every inch of his well-muscled body. When she finished, they stood toe-to-toe, staring at one another with obvious excitement.

Flint leaned down and kissed her lips softly at first, which she countered with hunger and desire. Flint put his arm around her waist and pulled her closer, tracing her spine with his fingers until he found the nape of her neck. He intertwined his fingers into her hair and held her there for a long while, enjoying her moans. He hadn't held a woman since Rachael died. He wanted to enjoy every moment of it.

Not wanting to take her to the cold patio ground, he did the only thing he could think of. He placed both hands on her bottom and lifted her up to him. She supported herself by wrapping her long, tan legs around his waist while he leaned her back against the wall of the shed.

Kissing him passionately, she reached down and guided him into her. He held her there, against the wall, careful not to hurt her, gently thrusting into her body. He was careful at first, letting her indicate when the time was right to be more passionate. Coffy soon let him know through her soft groans that she was ready, and he did everything he could to make her feel that he understood her, what she needed. What they both needed. He wanted it to all be for her, *and a little for him, too.*

Flint made sure to take care of Coffy's needs before himself. It was comforting to the ego of both that they climaxed together, each caring more about the other than themselves. As they finished, Flint continued holding Coffy against the wall for several minutes as they continued to kiss.

The warm water began to turn cool, so Flint gently helped Coffy back to her feet. Flint, not knowing what to say or do, followed Coffy's lead as she shut off the water and led Flint by the hand through the cold night air back into the cabin to the warm comfort of her bedroom where they both had full intention of making up for lost time.

CHAPTER FIVE

The next morning, Flint woke once again to the smell of eggs and bacon. Coffy left their bed quietly, allowing him to sleep a while longer. He had no intention of lying around in bed this time. He had plans to get up and enjoy every moment he could learning about this fascinating woman. The only problem, all of his clothes were still on the patio. Coffy had seen to it that he was too busy to retrieve them last night.

He peeked out the bedroom door and saw Coffy sitting at the kitchen table reading a book with her back facing him. The door leading to the patio was accessed through the kitchen, but he thought it best to quietly make his way through the living room and exit through the front door, which was wide open, then he could sneak around the cabin to the patio to get his clothes.

He didn't understand why he felt embarrassed. After all, he had showered with the woman and made love to her several times the night before, but his modesty and decorum for the moment seemed to indicate desperate measures were necessary. The front door was his only option.

Carefully opening the bedroom door, he tip-toed quickly through the living room. Looking back as he made his escape, he saw Coffy still concentrating on her book. He was on the front porch and home free.

As he reached the bottom of the porch steps, he froze. Something didn't feel right. Slowly, he turned his head to the left to see Grizzly Adams himself sitting in the same rocking chair that Flint had used the night before.

"Howdy," Grizzly said.

"Hi," Flint replied, not moving a muscle.

"What are you doing?"

"Nothing." Flint felt like a six-year-old caught doing something wrong. He didn't know what to say. "I ah, ah, left my clothes around--"

"You know, if you thought you could come in and dilly dally my daughter, then sneak out, you didn't think it through, son. Next train doesn't come through for three hours, and they might not like having a naked man amongst all the tourists."

"Oh no, sir. I wasn't leaving, I was--" Flint abruptly stopped talking and stood silent for a moment. The man wasn't making sense. "Wait a minute. Your daughter? I thought--"

"You thought wrong, my friend. You wait here while I go get my shotgun." Grizzly rose to his feet.

"Now wait just a damn minute! There's no reason to--"

"What's going on out here?" Coffy suddenly appeared in the doorway. "Flint! Why are you naked?"

"Coffy, I'm afraid I gave your father the wrong impression. I was just going to get my clothes from the patio when I ran into him, and I think--"

"My father?" She looked at Grizzly and started to laugh. "What the hell did you tell him, Frisco?"

Frisco Bennett smiled. "Nothing! I was just telling this young man that the next train don't leave for a while. He might want to get dressed before he heads down to the tracks."

"Frisco?" Flint said. He looked back at Coffy. "As in your neighbor Frisco?"

"Uh-huh," she replied, trying to stifle her laughter. "Did he tell you he was my father?"

Flint suddenly felt very naked. "Yes."

"Flint, I told you my father died a long time ago." She turned to address Frisco. "Frisco, dammit, it's hard enough finding a decent person around here. You don't need to be scaring them off."

All three of them stared at one another until laughter took over.

"I'm sorry, young man. I couldn't miss an opportunity like that,"

Frisco said.

"Coffy said you were a funny guy. I guess I should have listened better. Now if it's all right with the two of you, I'm going to get my clothes now."

"I put your clothes in your bedroom," Coffy said, pointing back into the house. Flint averted his eyes to the ground and let out a heavy sigh as he began the walk of shame up the steps and back through the front door.

"He's got a cute ass, Coffy." Flint ignored the comment and kept walking.

"Frisco, stop it!" Coffy yelled. "If you do something like that again, I'm going to use your dead body for cadaver training."

Training during the morning had been intense. It was warmer today than yesterday, and some of the search scenarios required long treks through dense forest with steep elevation changes. Air movement in the woods was nothing like it was down by the river, and Flint was having a hard time gauging scent patterns. He felt like he had quarterbacked four quarters of a football game and was facing double overtime.

Frisco played the search victim for them all morning while Coffy tagged along as Flint's assistant, guiding him through the critical thinking required from the human half of a K-9 search and rescue team.

Coffy set up the training base for the day just south of the cabin in the woods. The spot overlooked the river, about seventy-five feet below them. The train tracks were somewhere between them and the river.

"Flint, let's run one more scenario before we break for the morning." She removed Apache's short lead and replaced it with the long line. "Frisco, you doing all right?"

"You worry about yourself. I may be old, but I ain't dead yet, dammit!" He sounded insulted.

"All right, let's do the jailbreak scenario. Go ahead and take off." Frisco took off into the trees headed south.

"We're going to give Frisco a twenty-minute head start," Coffy explained. "You and Apache are searching alone this time. You're looking for an inmate who just escaped from a road crew and was last seen entering the woods off the highway. He's young and mobile."

"Have you done a lot of inmate searches?" Flint asked.

"No. Most Colorado prisons have their own bloodhounds for that type of search. But remember, Apache is cross trained in air-scenting and ground tracking. Even so, she's not as naturally gifted at ground tracking as a bloodhound, so she'll need a lot of guidance and decision-making help from you, but she can do it when she needs to. That makes her an especially valuable dog."

The conversation shifted to technique while they waited for Frisco to lay a scent track. Coffy was all business this morning, which unsettled Flint a little considering the intimacy they shared the night before. Deep down he knew it might be because there was little time to waste while learning how to best utilize the four-legged gift she was giving him. Still, he hoped last night wasn't a meaningless exercise in biology when lonely people find themselves in the right place at the right time.

"It's about time for you to get started," Coffy said. "Remember, trust your dog. Dogs never lie. They tell the truth, and when they get confused, it's usually not their fault. It's the handler's fault. You have to be smarter than the dog. The dog is a tool. You are the user of that tool. Understand?"

"Yes," Flint replied.

"Go ahead and take off. I'll catch up to you somewhere along the way."

Flint leaned down and grabbed Apache by the shoulders. She whined with excitement. "Are you ready, girl? Are you ready? Find him!" Apache took off into the trees with Flint close behind.

The path had been used many times and was well worn. Flint thought it might be the route that Frisco used to get to Coffy's cabin when he would visit. The trail would be saturated with his scent, and it might be difficult for Apache to discriminate between what had been laid down by him previously, and what was new. Coffy's warning to 'trust your dog' kept replaying in his mind. He hoped Apache was smart enough to figure it out.

After only a few minutes, Apache slowed down and turned off the trail into an area that had been cleared of brush and rocks, leaving the ground smooth and covered with brown pine needles. In the middle of the small clearing was a large granite boulder with two homemade, pine slab benches, one on either side. Flint could see something carved into the boulder, but was too far away to make out what it said. The area was probably a meditation garden of some kind created by someone who liked

64

walking through the woods. Perhaps Frisco had built it.

He wanted to take more time to investigate, but Apache reversed direction and pulled him back toward the trail. Not wanting to slow her down, he decided he would ask Coffy about it later.

The train whistle surprised Flint. It sounded close. He must have been so distracted by the training exercise that he hadn't heard it when it was farther down the canyon. The trees blocked his view of the track, but he could hear the rhythmic clicking of the steel wheels getting louder below him. Another load of tourists headed to Silverton.

Apache led Flint down the trail for at least another half-mile before she stopped cold. With little to no wind, Flint knew it would be difficult for her to ascertain where the scent was coming from. It didn't help that Frisco had probably been down this trail a hundred times.

Suddenly, Apache left the trail, bushwhacking through the trees toward the river below them. Flint knew Frisco must have left the trail at this point. *At least he went downhill instead of uphill,* Flint thought. He followed Apache down the hill until she came to a stop near the train tracks. She began to alternate between sniffing the ground and putting her nose to the sky. Flint didn't like this new development. *She's gotten confused. There must have been a hundred people on that train, and with those open windows and the cattle cars, all their scents have mixed with Frisco's.*

Slowly at first, she led Flint north along the tracks. Knowing she'd lost the scent and was confused, trying to locate it again in the midst of hundreds of other new smells, he allowed her to take him up the tracks a bit. With no success, he decided the best course of action would be to reverse direction and possibly reacquire Frisco's scent farther south. No luck. Apache was determined to follow the train tracks in the direction the train had passed. It was hopeless, too difficult for an air-scenting dog to separate one scent from a hundred. A ground-tracking bloodhound could do it, but then like Coffy warned, Apache was no bloodhound.

Flint decided it best to end the exercise and head back toward the cabin. He hated the thought of Apache feeling as if she had failed, so he rewarded her with a game of tug-of-war for her efforts. He knew it probably wasn't the best idea to reward her for failure, but it wasn't her fault the train came through and ruined everything. They roughhoused for a few minutes before beginning the walk back. Flint decided to follow the tracks north to the trail that led to the cabin.

Keeping Apache on the long line was difficult during the walk back. Unwilling to give up as easily as Flint had, she kept straining at the lead. He decided to turn her loose and watched as she continued air-scenting for Frisco the entire way back. She was dedicated to her work; Flint would give her that. He felt sorry for her.

As they got closer to the main trail to the cabin, Flint saw Coffy sitting on one of the boulders near the river. Apache's nose went high into the air, and she began pulling Flint toward her.

"So how did it go? Did you find Frisco?" she asked him.

"No, we didn't, but it wasn't Apache's fault." He wanted to make that clear.

"It wasn't? What happened?"

"The train came through. Frisco must have crossed the tracks somewhere down there either just before or just after the train passed. His scent got all mixed up with the others coming out of that train. Apache got confused and started to follow the train."

"What did you do when that happened?"

"I took her back to where we lost the scent and tried to reacquire, but she kept trying to follow the train."

"You didn't let her follow the train?" Flint noticed a little tension in her voice. He figured Coffy didn't like her dogs to fail.

"No, of course not. I mean, yes, we followed the train tracks, but only because I wanted to get back and let you know about what happened. Really, it's not Apache's fault."

"Oh, I know it's not her fault. Do you want to know how I know it's not her fault?" Coffy sounded a bit angry now. She didn't wait for Flint to answer. "Because it's your fault!"

Flint squinted as his focus changed from the ground to Coffy. "Why the hell is it my fault?"

"Frisco, come here!" Coffy never took her eyes away from Flint. Frisco appeared from behind one of the larger boulders near the stream.

"Ah, shit!" was all that Flint could muster.

"That's right," Coffy said. "She led you directly to him, and you didn't even know it. What did I tell you up there before we started this exercise?" she said, pointing up the hill.

"Trust your dog," Flint said, breaking from her gaze and looking at the ground.

"You didn't trust her, did you?"

"I did trust her. I guess I just didn't believe she could do it."

"Well, she did it. I told you, she's cross-trained to air scent and ground track. Frisco walked those tracks *after* the train came through. Yes, his scent was mixed with others, but Apache can sort it out. She's not as good as a bloodhound, but she's still pretty darn good."

Flint remained silent for just a moment to let his anger at himself subside a little. "Coffy, I get your point. I should have believed in her more than I did. But answer me this; if she was so hot on his trail, how come she didn't alert when we got here? I mean, Frisco was right there," he said, pointing to him.

"Did you tell her the search was over? Did you in any way tell her that her task was done?"

"No, I--" He fell silent.

"What did you do?" she asked him.

"I rewarded her with a game."

"Yeah, well, there's your answer. You told her that the search was over. There was no need for her to alert you that Frisco was here. She found him out of her own interest. She knew he was behind that rock, but you told her you weren't interested anymore."

Flint felt like an idiot. Never had he failed so miserably with a search and rescue mission, and it embarrassed him.

"I'm sorry, Coffy. I screwed up," he said sincerely.

"Don't be sorry, Flint. Learn from it. Remember what I said, trust your dog but, be smarter than it is. Look at me."

Flint looked up at her.

Coffy leaned over and touched Apache on the head. "Instinct in here." She then placed a finger on Flint's forehead. "Intelligence in here. The two can work together or work against each other. It's your choice." She smiled at Flint to let him know she was no longer angry. "All right guys, lunch break. I'm going to run up to the cabin and get some sandwiches made. I'll be back in a few minutes. Frisco, behave yourself!" She took off up the trail.

Flint took a seat on one of the boulders. Frisco sat beside him.

"I'm sorry for what I did to you this morning, Flint," Frisco said, trying to fill the uncomfortable silence. "I don't know why I do stuff like that."

Flint chuckled. "It's all right. It was pretty funny once I got over the shock." Flint took a sip from his water bottle.

"Coffy told me you were a pretty good fella and that I shouldn't give you a hard time," Frisco said, throwing a pebble toward the ground. "It's just what I do."

"Really, Frisco, it's okay. I got a good laugh out of it, too." Both men watched as Apache wandered to the edge of the river for a drink of water. "Coffy is a talented dog trainer, isn't she?" Flint said, trying to change the subject of the conversation.

"Oh yeah, she really is, but she's even better at search and rescue technique. She's accomplished some pretty amazing things."

"Really? Like what?"

"Well, like when she and Argo found a young couple who had driven their car over an embankment during a snow storm. They survived the crash, bloodied and injured, but took off on their own trying to find help. No one had any idea where they had gone because the snow storm covered their tracks. The sheriff called off the search when it got dark, but Coffy, being Coffy, knew they wouldn't survive the night. She and Argo stayed out all night in two feet of snow till they had tracked them down. She found them huddled up in a ravine nearly frozen to death. No one else could have done that."

"That's pretty amazing," Flint said earnestly.

"Yep. She was given an award for that one, though she never told me about it. I found out about it from someone else when I went into town one day."

"That doesn't surprise me. She seems like a pretty private person," Flint said.

"She is. She would never brag on herself."

"Well, I can see she's good at what she does."

"She thinks you're good at what you do, too."

"Me?" Flint said, incredulously. "No, I'm nowhere near her caliber."

"I don't think anyone in the world is as good as she is, but she told me you did a pretty miraculous thing saving a little girl who had been kidnapped. She said only someone with instinct could have done what you did."

"Shoot, that wasn't me, that was my dog. If I had been paying more attention to my K9, she might still be alive."

"I heard your dog saved your life. Is that true?" Frisco asked.

"Yes, sir! Every bit of it. My dog died taking a bullet meant for me."

"I'm sorry to hear that, but I'm glad you survived," Frisco said, looking at Flint. "Still, Coffy was pretty impressed by what you did. That's one of the reasons she picked you to give one of her best dogs to."

"One of the reasons?"

"Yeah," Frisco said, casting his glance back at his feet.

"I have to ask. There were other reasons?"

Frisco kept staring at the ground. After a moment he spoke. "She told me you had lost your wife a while back."

"Yes, I did." Flint was curious where this was going.

"You have to get to know Coffy a little better for anything she does to make sense."

"I'm not following what you're saying," Flint said.

Frisco looked up at the trail to the cabin, then said in a low voice, "Coffy has been through a lot in her life. Not much of it good. Because of that, let's just say there aren't a whole lot of people she gives a damn about." Flint looked at Frisco who briefly met his gaze before looking up at the canyon wall across the river. "Coffy doesn't respect too many people who've never lost something or someone important to them."

"Really?" Flint didn't want to tell Frisco that he had already known this about Coffy.

"Yeah. Has she told you anything about her son?" Frisco asked.

"She told me that she and her husband argued one day and that he took their son and neither were ever heard from again."

"Well, since you already know, I don't feel so bad telling you this. When she lost her son, she lost her sanity for a while. She didn't know how to handle it."

Flint remained silent.

"You have to understand, and I think you do because you lost your wife, when people lose someone who means more to them than life itself, it creates a huge hole in their soul. Some people can start filling in that hole with love and care from others. It never gets completely full, but over time, it's not as deep and dark as it was."

Flint thought back to his own loss. When Rachael died, it felt like the end of the world for him. Had it not been for Samantha and Bella, he might not have made it back from that dark place himself.

Frisco looked toward the trail head one more time before he continued. "Then there are others, like Coffy and myself."

Flint looked at Frisco, who was staring at the river again.

"I lost my son in Afghanistan twelve years ago," Frisco said softly.

"Oh God, Frisco, I'm sorry," Flint said, suddenly finding an emotional connection with this man he barely knew.

"Me, too. But like I was saying, in some people, the hole just gets bigger, deeper, and darker with every passing day. Some people try to fill that hole with alcohol, sex, drugs, whatever they can find to ease the pain. But no matter what you try to fill it with, it's never enough. For me, it was solitude. I wanted to get the hell away from people. I moved out here so I didn't have to be around others. That's how I deal with it. Now Coffy, she figured out something decent to help her cope. She trains dogs to help people. It's the salve she needs for a wound that never heals."

"She throws herself into her work because she lost her son. Is that what you're saying?"

"No. Not exactly. With Coffy, and I don't know how to say this so it doesn't sound crazy, it's more like restitution. Something she has to do as punishment. For some reason that only makes sense to her, she feels responsible for losing her son. She feels as if she has to cleanse her soul by saving others from that same fate. But, no matter how many times she's able to save someone, or no matter how successful she becomes, it's never enough. It's her drug of choice. I'm afraid one of these days it's going to kill her."

Flint was trying to process what he was hearing. Frisco wasn't describing the same woman he made love to last night, but, he reasoned, he barely knew her.

"So to answer your question, Coffy chose you for a number of reasons. First, she felt you had a natural talent for this type of work. She also knew you were a brave person after nearly giving your life for that little girl. But, I think deep down in her soul, she may have also chosen you because you're a survivor from your grief. She admires people who can reclaim their lives and carry on after a loss because she hasn't been able to. I think she wants to learn from you as badly as you want to learn from her."

Flint caught movement out of the corner of his eye and looked up to see Coffy coming down the trail. "Coffy!" Flint shouted rather haphazardly as more of a warning to Frisco than anything else.

Coffy stopped cold on the trail. "Were you expecting someone else?" she said as she looked behind her mockingly.

Frisco spoke loudly, "So anyway, the guy was born with no eyelids, so the doctors decided to use his foreskin to create some. They said he would be all right; he would just be a little cockeyed!"

"Frisco!" Coffy yelled.

The rest of the day was spent chasing Frisco through several different types of search and rescue scenarios. Flint took to heart Coffy's suggestion that he needed to trust his K9's instincts more. He and Apache did much better during the afternoon. The runs were shorter and more technical than the morning missions, which Flint greatly appreciated. Coffy finally called for an end to the day's training activities, and everyone retired to the cabin. Frisco stayed long enough to enjoy a beer with Flint and Coffy on the front porch, then walked home. Flint was amazed at the older man's stamina. He looked old, but he certainly didn't act it.

Coffy and Flint worked on dinner together while discussing the day. Afterward, they walked to the barn to feed the dogs and let Argo out so he could run with Apache. Making their way back to the front porch, Flint assumed the position he liked most, sitting in the rocking chair.

"Tomorrow I've got a little something different planned for us," Coffy said. "You and I are going to take the train about ten miles south of here, then take Elk Park Trail a few miles up into the mountains."

"That sounds interesting." Flint was already worrying about the climbing part.

"It will be. You're going to learn a lot about how wind speed and direction can influence a search. Down here in the canyon, you don't get as much variation in wind conditions as you do up in the mountains. It'll also give the dogs a chance to get out of their usual training area."

"Will Frisco be coming with us?" Flint asked.

"No, not tomorrow. But he'll be back on Friday for our final day."

"I have to tell you, that man is something else. How old is he?" Flint asked Coffy, who had taken the rocking chair next to him.

"I don't really know. I think he's in his early seventies, though I'm not sure. I've never asked him."

"Well, he's in great shape for being in his seventies. He can outwork me on my best days."

Coffy laughed. "He's been up here for a lot of years. I think he's pretty well acclimated to the thin air." She paused for a moment to watch Apache and Argo playing in the open field next to the cabin. "I apologize for what he did to you this morning. He doesn't know how to act normal with people." She laughed.

"No apology needed. Besides, he already apologized to me. I can take a joke."

"Good. You know, I rent a house in Silverton for the winter, but that old man spends winter out here by himself. I worry about him sometimes, but he seems to do fine."

"I bet he's glad to see you when you come back in the spring."

"He sure is. He comes over almost every day when I get back. Drives me nuts, but he helps me a lot. He makes me laugh, too. It's good to have him around."

"Where does he live?" Flint asked.

"He lives about a mile south on that trail over there," she said, pointing to the trail head they had trained on earlier in the day. "You almost made it to his house before you bushwhacked down to the river this morning. He lives in a UFO." Flint looked at Coffy thinking she was making a joke. "Really, he lives in a UFO. Have you ever seen those flying saucer-shaped buildings on the side of the road?"

"Yeah, I guess I have. There's a house on Pensacola Beach that has one on top of it. It looks like a UFO landed on their roof."

"Frisco told me they were mass produced in the sixties to be used for ski huts, cheap housing, and all kinds of other weird stuff. Now you usually see them on the side of the road as used car lot offices or some sort of tourist attraction. He found one down in New Mexico somewhere, Roswell I think. He bought it and had it flown up here by helicopter and set in place. It's a nice setup. Maybe we can walk over there before you leave and look at it. I know he would love to show it to you."

"Yeah, I've got to see that." Flint thought about the conversation he and Frisco had that morning. "He told me he lost his son in Afghanistan."

"Yes, he was killed by a roadside bomb. He doesn't like to talk

72

about it much. I'm surprised he told you. He must like you an awful lot."

"Is that boulder on the path a memorial to his son?" Flint asked.

Coffy looked at Flint with a sad smile. "No, that was something I did for my son." She looked off in the distance to the other side of the canyon.

"Oh, I'm sorry, Coffy. I didn't mean to bring--"

"It's all right. I don't mind. If Frisco likes you enough to tell you about his son, the least I can do is talk about mine."

"I guess you two have a lot in common when it comes to losing someone close." Flint knew he was close to betraying what Frisco had told him in confidence. He would have to tread lightly.

"Yes. Losing a child is a difficult thing. We actually don't talk to one another about it much. It's just an understanding we have, if you know what I mean."

"I can only imagine." Flint let a couple of minutes go by. He wrestled with whether or not it was appropriate to ask, but decided Coffy was handling the conversation well. "If you don't mind me asking, what does the inscription say on the boulder?"

"I don't mind, but you have to understand, I was in a bad place when I carved it into that rock." She thought about it for a moment. "It says, *I WOULD WALK THROUGH THE FIRES OF HELL TO SPEND ONE MORE MINUTE WITH YOU.*"

"You wrote that for your son?"

"I wrote that for me. At the time, I didn't know if I would ever see him again. I was lost without him, so with Frisco's help we built that little garden down there. I know it means as much for Frisco as it does for me."

"Do you think there's still a chance you'll see your son someday?"

Coffy took a moment to answer. "No, I don't think so. It's been so long, and no one has seen nor heard from him or my husband. I just know something bad must have happened. It took a long time to accept that."

"Is that why you got into the search and rescue business?"

"Yes and no. I didn't start training rescue dogs just because my child and husband went missing. I did it because I wasn't there for my son when he needed me most." Coffy reached over for Flint's hand and looked into his eyes. "You have to understand. For a long time, I didn't want to live. Carrying the guilt of losing my son made me feel as if I had no right to carry on without him. There was a time in my life in which I prayed for death. It never came. But as time went on, with Frisco's encouragement, I began getting a little better. When I finally got my head screwed on straight, I figured I'd be better off helping other parents who might be going through what I had gone through rather than wasting what was left of my life. It took a while to decide how to do it, but I finally found a way. I do it with my dogs."

"That's an amazing story, Coffy. Amazing."

Coffy squeezed his hand. "Come with me. I have something I want you to see."

Coffy led Flint around to the back of the cabin and up a trail that climbed along the side of the canyon wall. After only ten minutes of climbing the steep trail, they arrived at a place that, like the thin Colorado air, took Flint's breath away. They stood atop a flat outcropping of rock which jutted from the mouth of a shallow depression in the canyon wall. From their vantage point, Flint could see the Animas River below snaking along the bottom of the canyon. The entire eastern wall of the canyon was awash in deep hues of purple, orange, and red.

"What do you think?" Coffy asked, reaching for Flint's hand once again.

"It's beautiful. Absolutely beautiful. Do you come up here often?"

"As often as I can. It's kind of a spiritual place for me. I like to watch the colors of the canyon change when the sun starts to set."

"Well, I can see why," Flint replied. They stood hand-in-hand for several minutes watching the colors deepen on the canyon wall.

"Do you see that mountain to the right over there?" She pointed to a mountain peak just visible over the east wall.

"Yeah."

"That's Electric Peak. That's where we're going tomorrow."

"Really? It looks pretty far away."

"It's actually not. The train will carry us most of the way south. We'll have to hike a few miles to the east, but you'll love it, trust me."

"If you say so," he said purely to make her smile.

"Come here, I want to show you something else." She guided him to the back wall of the overhang. "What you read down there, on the boulder, was something I wrote to help me cope when I felt I had nothing to offer this world anymore. This is me now," she said, brushing her hands across something carved into the rock wall.

Flint looked at the lettering which read, *I MUST WALK ALONE, IN DARKNESS, TO LIGHT THE PATH FOR OTHERS*. He took a moment to fathom the pain that these words must have been written with.

"You don't have to walk alone, Coffy."

"Yes, I do. But not tonight. Not now." She reached her hand up to the back of his neck and gently brought his mouth to hers. They kissed for a long while and made love high up on the canyon wall in the last vestiges of the setting sun.

CHAPTER SIX

Coffy waved down the train just below the cabin. It stopped just long enough for Flint, Coffy, and the dogs to jump onboard before it rumbled off again. The train was full of tourists headed back to Durango after spending the day shopping in Silverton, making it difficult to find a seat. Finally, they found one which Flint insisted Coffy have. He stood in the aisle next to her. Apache and Argo wore their search and rescue vests, which caused the passengers to be inquisitive about why they were on-board. The barrage of questions and requests for pictures made the hour-long trip pass by quickly.

The train slowed to a stop at Elk Park where Coffy and Flint disembarked along with several backpackers planning on hiking the same trail. They waved at the passengers as the train departed, crossed the tracks, and walked to the trail head, which was marked with a simple gray, weathered board on a wooden post labeled Elk Park Trail.

"This is it," Coffy said with excitement. "Let's see, it's three forty-five. We need to be at our campsite by six-thirty to set up before dark. Are you ready?"

"I'm ready!" Flint replied.

"Okay, let's go, kids," Coffy said to the dogs.

The first hour wasn't too painful. It was a climb, to be sure, but nothing Flint couldn't handle. The trail wound its way through tall, thin pine trees situated along a meandering stream. The water bubbled its way over and around the rocks, making a tranquil sound. Every now and then, Coffy made it a point to stop and enjoy the view, though Flint knew she was doing it just to be kind and let him catch his breath. He was careful never to ask for a break himself. He did have some pride after all.

It wasn't long before the terrain started a steep incline straight up. The dogs handled it like they were out for a walk in the park, and Coffy was barely breathing. Flint tried hard to muffle his gasps for air so Coffy wouldn't hear his labored breathing. Of course, that required trying not to breathe deeply, which just made things worse.

Finally, the trail leveled out and led them to an open area surrounded by silver-trunked aspen trees with leaves of gold and red that seemed to vibrate with the slightest breeze.

"This is it, Flint. You made it! We camp here tonight."

"Oh really? I was just getting warmed up," he said as he unbuckled his pack and dropped it to the ground.

Coffy laughed. "There's another spot about two miles farther down the trail if you'd like to continue? It's about twenty-five hundred feet higher."

"That's all right. We should take advantage of what light is left." He knew he'd been had.

"I thought you might say that. It's beautiful here, isn't it?"

"Yes, it is. Thank you for bringing me up here," he said, reaching out and pulling her close.

She leaned in to kiss him and laughed when he had to end the kiss early so he could breathe again.

After setting up their tent, Coffy lit a tiny camp stove to boil water while Flint started a campfire. They sat next to each other on a fallen log and took in their surroundings. As the sun began to lower, the peaks of nearby mountaintops turned bright yellow against the deep blue sky. The aspen meadow was darkening by the minute, and the temperature was beginning to drop. Flint retrieved both of their jackets from the packs.

"I love coming up here," she said. "There's a lot fewer people up here in the early fall than there is in the summer. This really is the best time to be here."

"It's the same way in Pensacola," Flint said. "For some strange-reason, people visit the beach in July when it's hot and miserable. I refuse to

77

go to the beach when it's like that. But in October, oh man, it's something else altogether. There's hardly anyone there except for locals. That's the time I enjoy it most."

"Maybe I'll come visit you and Apache sometime. I've never been to the ocean."

"You're kidding, really?"

"Nope."

"Well, you have an open invitation."

Coffy walked over and retrieved several foil packages from her pack. She handed them over to Flint.

"Your choice."

"I'll take the spaghetti."

"That's what you had the other day!"

"I know. I happen to like spaghetti. I haven't had freeze dried spaghetti since I was a Boy Scout."

"I knew it!" Coffy shouted.

"Knew what?"

"That you were a Boy Scout."

"No, you didn't."

"Yes, I did! I totally did. I could tell by your hair cut."

"My haircut?"

"Yep. No offense, but your haircut screams God, country, and guns."

"Ouch!" Flint laughed.

"Don't worry, big man! I happen to find that extremely attractive at this point in my life."

When dinner was eaten and the dogs taken care of, they sat together on the log and began scanning the night sky. Flint had never seen stars like this before. Thousands of them twinkled brightly through the thin atmosphere. The thick, humid air at sea level and the light glow of city lights from Pensacola would never allow for such a show. The Milky Way glowed brilliantly across the entire span of the night sky as they made a game of seeing who could spot the most satellites slowly making their way across the background of stars.

Flint was first to notice a couple of small clouds to the north which appeared to be a light shade of orange. *Probably some artifact of the sunset or a reflection of lights from Silverton.* The more he studied them though, the stranger they became. The clouds were actually flickering.

"Coffy, look up at those little clouds to the right of that mountain peak," Flint said, pointing so she could see where he was looking. "Notice anything strange about them?"

Coffy studied the clouds for a few seconds. "Uh oh. There's a fire somewhere to the northeast. The light from it is reflecting off those clouds."

"That can't be good," Flint said.

"It looks like it's pretty far off, but let me text the sheriff and see if he knows anything about it." Coffy slid out from under Flint's arm and walked over to her pack. When she returned to the light of the campfire, he recognized by the shape of the antenna that she had a satellite phone in her hand. "This thing comes in handy. I can talk to anyone directly, but I can also just send a text." After it booted up, she typed a short message.

A minute later, it beeped, and she read the message aloud to Flint. *Fire sixteen miles east of Silverton moving south. Crews responding. Lite winds at 3 miles-per-hour from the northwest. No threat to town at this time.*

"Well, that sounds pretty far off. We're south of town, right?"

"Yep. Twelve miles southeast, so it's nowhere near us right now. You're not getting out of final exams, mister."

"I wouldn't dream of it! Besides, I have a final exam of my own I need to give you."

Flint reached out to Coffy and pulled her close. He caught a glint of moonlight in her dark brown eyes as he leaned in to kiss her. Her lips were cold, but her tongue was warm as they embraced. She wrapped her arms around him, under his jacket, and pressed her body against his. Flint felt her shiver with anticipation. Together they laid next to the campfire and enjoyed each other until the moon set below Electric Peak. Sleep came easy.

The alert tone from Coffy's satellite phone woke her instantly. It was a message from the San Juan County Sheriff's Department.

Fire shifted overnight and is now moving west. We need your help locating an autistic child separated from family while escaping. Please contact us ASAP.

Coffy quietly unzipped her sleeping bag, rose to her feet, and began fumbling through her pile of clothes. She dressed, sat on the log to put on her shoes, and quickly typed a reply.

I'm fifteen-miles southeast of Silverton on Electric Mountain about nine miles up on Elk Trail. I can hike down, catch the train, and be in Silverton around noon.

While waiting for the reply, she walked over and knelt next to Flint, who was still asleep. "Flint, wake up."

Flint rolled over and looked up at her.

"I think we're going to have to change our plans for the day. The Sheriff's Department needs me for a search and rescue this morning. That fire we saw last night shifted, and now someone is in trouble. We're going to have to hustle and get down the mountain in a hurry so we can catch the train."

"Uh, okay, I'm on it," Flint said sleepily. "What time is it?"

"Six thirty-five."

He threw the sleeping bag off and stood. The sight of him nude and standing there caused Coffy to yearn for more time like they had last night, but it wouldn't happen. There was no time for it. Her satellite phone beeped as another message came through.

Time is critical. If you have K-9 with you, we will send helicopter to you.

She typed the response while Flint quickly dressed and checked on the dogs.

K-9 is with me. Will have second K-9 and passenger. She tried to think of a safe place she and Flint could meet the helicopter. *Have helicopter meet us just above timberline, Electric Peak, Elk Trail. Think it is near eleven-thousand three-hundred feet. Should be there by nine a.m.*

"Flint, I hate to tell you this, but it looks like we're going up, not down, and we have to run. They're sending a helicopter for us, and the only place it can land is above timberline."

"That's not so bad, is it? We're pretty close to timberline now, aren't we?"

"Well, we're two-thousand feet below timberline as the crow flies, but we have four miles of trail to go, and it's up *and* down most of the way."

They scrambled to take down the camp and make sure the campfire was completely out. There was no time to feed the dogs, though Coffy found some dog treats in her bag. They would have to do.

Her satellite phone beeped again.

'Again, time critical. Helicopter leaving now and will be waiting on you. Please hurry.'

"Shoot! We've got to go, Flint. *Right now!*"

Flint and Coffy helped each other with their packs, hooked the dogs to their long-lines, and hit the trail at a fast walk. There wasn't much talk along the way because neither had the breath for conversation. Two-thousand feet up was tough enough, but spread out over four miles when it was two-hundred feet up followed by one-hundred feet down, they had to make the two-thousand foot climb several times over.

Finally, after an hour and forty-five minutes of half-running, half-walking, they broke out of the tree line and into the green, treeless terrain that signaled they were above timberline. Few trees grew above eleven-thousand feet, so it was perfect for landing the helicopter that was meeting them. After negotiating another sixty-foot rise on the trail, they spotted the helicopter on a rock-free spot of ground just below them. They were there in seconds.

Coffy recognized the pilot standing near the back of the helicopter as the Sheriff's Deputy she had flown with on many occasions before. She shook his hand.

"Flint, this is Deputy Tom McNeil. Tom, Park Police Officer Flint Westbrook. He'll be riding with us."

"Okay," the pilot said. "We need to get going. Flint, help me put the packs into the cargo hold."

With the equipment loaded, humans and dogs climbed aboard. Coffy took the front seat next to Tom while Flint and the two dogs squeezed into the back. Coffy pointed to two pairs of headphones hanging from the ceiling and signaled to Flint to put one of them on. In less than a minute, they were airborne.

The helicopter took off headed south, but as it made a sweeping turn to the north, the smoke from the fire became visible. They were ten miles away, and it still looked huge.

"So what's going on, Tom?" Coffy asked. "Who are we looking for?"

"You'll be looking for a sixteen-year-old autistic, nonverbal male named Jason Greene. He was last seen near his home farther down the mountain. His mother thinks he ran off after the family dog when they were evacuating their home. He's shy and scared of strangers, so he's not likely to reach out for help."

"Well, at least he likes dogs," Flint said. "We have that in our favor."

"The family was forced to leave him behind when the fire overran

81

their house, but they're hoping he ran up the mountain away from the fire. If he's still alive, he's somewhere between the front of that fire and the top of the mountain we're about to set down on. Hopefully, you can find him before the whole mountain goes up."

The helicopter lowered closer to the ground and swung to the east to land on a small peak to the south of the main fire. There was another, much larger helicopter already there unloading a fire crew.

"Coffy," Tom said, "that Huey down there is a hotshot crew out of Ft. Collins. They're going to help you look for the kid. Their goal is to keep you safe."

"I'm better on my own, Tom."

"Take my advice for once, Coffy. Let them help you. This fire is unpredictable. It's coming up the side of this mountain, and if it overruns you, you're dead. These guys know how a fire moves; you don't."

"It's not rocket science, Tom. I can handle it. Besides, the more people we have running around, the harder it is for my dog to locate the right scent."

"Damn it, Coffy, this *is* rocket science. You need those guys to stay alive. If you aren't going to use them, I'm not landing this helicopter."

Coffy thought about calling his bluff, but decided now was not the time to argue. "All right, but they had better stay the hell out of the way."

Flint, Coffy, and the dogs disembarked once the helicopter landed. Tom shouted to be heard over the blades, "I'll be overhead looking for any sign of him. I can communicate with the fire crew, so stay close to them in case I see something. Be careful, Coffy. Flint, watch her! She doesn't take instruction well." Once they were clear of the helicopter, Tom took off.

Coffy and Flint walked over to the fire crew and introduced themselves. The leader, an older man named Robert Creasy, seemed to know his business. There were seven other members of the fire crew, each covered in smoke and suet. No doubt they'd been on the fire line all night and were just recently called to the top of the mountain to help handle this new situation.

Creasy quickly gave them a short course in wildfire safety and handed them each a set of red field packs with water, maps, radios, and an emergency fire shelter in case they got caught and couldn't get out. "If shit hits the fan and you can't outrun the fire, find an open spot away from trees if you can, pull this Mylar tent out of the box, throw it over your back, and lay down on the ground. Keep your face near the ground so you don't breathe the hot gasses and hang on to it tight. Winds can reach fifty miles an hour when the flames are coming through. You'll still get burned, but you just might live through it. Understand?"

"Yes," Coffy replied. Flint nodded.

"Let's go!" Creasy said.

The group took off down the mountain toward the smoke and flames.

Twenty yards before entering the tree line, Coffy stopped everyone. "Flint, we need to split up. You take the area to the right of a line drawn straight down. I'll stay left."

Creasy spoke up, "We're not going to split the group."

"We have to," Flint said before Coffy could. "If the fire is coming as fast as everyone says, we don't have the luxury of time to find this kid. We have two dogs, and we can cover twice the area."

Creasy didn't appear happy with the new suggestion, so everyone was surprised to hear his new orders. "All right, Gates, Thompson, and Andrews go with her. Spencer, you and Rhodes come with me. Check your radios everyone."

While radio communications were checked, Coffy walked over to Flint. "Hell of a final exam, Flint. Don't get my dog killed."

"Your dog? I thought she was my dog," he said with a smile. He loved how this lady had no fear.

"Not until I say so. And by the way, it would be just fine with me if you didn't get yourself killed either. I'd like to pick up where we left off last night."

"Deal," he said. "See you back on top of the mountain."

The crews split and set off in different directions with the dogs leading the way. Flint and his crew headed due east along the elevation line hoping that winds generated by the fire below would bring the boy's scent up the mountainside. If Apache gave him even the slightest indication, he would turn her loose to track back and forth until she found the scent cone and followed it to back to its source. It was a long shot, but the only chance they had. There was one big caveat to the plan. Without a scent article containing the boy's unique scent, Apache wouldn't know what the boy smelled like. If anyone else was down there, fire crews, search and rescue personnel, anyone, she could pick up their scent and lead his crew straight to them.

"Are there any other fire crews below us?" he shouted to Creasy, who was twenty yards or so behind him.

"No! No one else should be down there. We have crews on the other side of the fire, but they should be in the burned areas only, not in front of this thing."

Coffy chose to descend straight down the mountain thinking that if the kid was still alive, he would be closer to the fire line and would eventually be forced upward toward the top of the mountain. She knew he would be scared and most likely would hide from rescuers if they came near him. Once she was satisfied with their starting point, she released Argo from his lead and gave him the 'seek' command.

Coffy kept the crew moving down the mountain in a straight line, until after descending another two or three-hundred feet, Argo alerted, but as quickly as he acquired it, he lost it. Running from side to side with his nose as high in the air as he could get it resulted in nothing. The wind was becoming turbulent as they got closer to the flames, and at times, Coffy couldn't tell which direction it was coming from, but deep down, Coffy knew it wasn't a false alarm. She trusted her dog and knew he had something even if it was ever so brief. When she directed everyone to proceed farther down the mountain, one of the fire crew shouted at her. "Check your radio!"

Coffy stopped, dropped her pack, and pulled out a handheld radio. "Summerfield here. Go ahead."

"Coffy, Deputy McNeil. I have the helicopter about two-hundred yards north-northeast of your location. I'm catching glimpses of a small dog running back and forth along a ridge. I don't see anyone with it, but if it's the kid's dog, he may be nearby."

"Ten-four, Tom. I'll check it out. Two-hundred yards north-northeast."

"Confirmed," he answered back. "Coffy, I can't stay here. The smoke is shifting, but you need to hurry. The fire front is moving fast, and you don't have much time."

"Understood, Tom." Coffy called Argo back, hooked him to his lead, and set off down the mountain.

84

Flint heard the radio conversation and decided to stay away from the area Coffy was headed to. Putting too many people in the same area was a sure way of confusing a dog. Instead, he took his crew wide to the east in case the kid was trying to escape the smoke.

A loud tone blared from all the radios simultaneously, followed by a voice that demanded authority. "Incident Command to all fire and rescue crews, clear channel two for emergency traffic only. Crews south and above the fire line need to evacuate immediately. The fire has jumped the fire break at nine-thousand four-hundred feet and is moving rapidly up the mountain. Winds have shifted to south-southwest at twenty. Repeat, we've lost control of the south line, and all crews south of that line need to evacuate now!"

Flint looked back at Creasy, who keyed his radio. "Eight-fifty to Incident Command, understood. Evacuating now." He clipped the radio back to his belt and shouted to the crew, "All right guys, let's go. Back to the top."

"We can't, Creasy. We still have to find the kid." Flint couldn't help himself. Being a police officer, he knew following directions was paramount, but this time, it felt different. It felt *wrong*.

"It's not up for a vote, Westbrook. We go to the top and wait for instructions. Now let's go!"

Creasy turned around and started walking back up the mountain. His men followed. Flint thought about the consequences of ignoring the man, but he was out of his element here. He didn't understand the mechanics of wildfire, wind direction, and fuel loads. There was one thing he knew for certain; the climb down had been slow and difficult. The climb up would be far worse. If the fire caught up with them, he wouldn't stand a chance of outrunning it. The clincher was the thought of leaving Sam alone, with no parents at all. He had to go.

"I'm not leaving until we find this kid," Coffy shouted to the crew behind her as soon as she had heard the order to leave.

"Miss Summerfield, you have to. You'll die if you don't!" one of the crew members shouted down to her. She was twenty yards further down the mountain showing no signs of slowing down to consider the options.

"Summerfield! Stop!"

She continued.

"Creasy to Thompson, are you on your way up?"

Thompson pulled the radio off his belt. "No, sir, not yet. We're having a bit of an issue with Miss Summerfield. She won't turn around."

"Summerfield, this is Creasy. You need to turn your ass around and get the hell off this mountain. If you don't, you'll be killed, and I'll have a lot of freaking paperwork to fill out."

There was only radio silence.

"Do you copy me, Summerfield?"

More silence.

Creasy tried a softer approach. "Summerfield, my men there will not leave you. They're under orders to protect you no matter the cost. That means they will die trying to save you from yourself. Do you understand what I'm saying?"

Coffy stopped walking, but didn't turn around. Creasy was most definitely a jerk, but what he said caused her to think about the consequences.

"Summerfield, answer me. Do you understand?"

The thought of leaving someone behind was overwhelming for her. How could she live with herself if the child was killed and she was only moments away from finding him? Thinking of the boy's mother and what she must be going through right now, she decided she would rather die than take a chance of leaving someone behind. Taking off down the mountain without answering Creasy, she had to find the boy no matter the consequences

"Coffy, I know you hear me. Think about what you're doing. You're going to get my men killed."

She didn't answer.

"Coffy, my men have families. They have children, for God's sake."

She reluctantly stopped and hung her head. She hadn't thought about that. No matter what she did, there would be dire consequences. It was a no win situation. After pausing for a long moment to get her thoughts together, she knew what she had to do.

"Argo, come." Coffy turned around and looked up at the tired, smoke-covered faces of the three firefighters above her and sighed. After a moment of contemplation, she reached for the radio. "All right, Creasy. I'm on my way."

The climb was difficult for both crews. The constant needling over the radio from Incident Command to pick up the pace was no help. Evidently, the fire had blown up and was making people at the I.C. nervous. Flint's crew was first to reach the top. The Huey was already there waiting on them. The helicopter pilots helped the fire crews take their field packs off and rushed everyone on board. Like Incident Command, the pilots were obviously nervous.

The sky darkened as smoke began to block the sunlight. Like a blanket of fog, the smoke moved in overhead and slowly lowered over the helicopter. A yellow-orange haze covered the mountaintop and grew thicker with each passing moment. They needed to get out of there quickly.

It was an agonizing ten minutes before Coffy's crew finally appeared. Flint, worried they might show up without her, was relieved to see her and Argo outside the open helicopter door. One of the pilots helped the newly arrived crew out of their packs while the other sat in the cockpit getting the helicopter ready for a quick liftoff. Coffy helped Argo on-board and found an open seat next to Flint. She looked up at him and smiled disappointedly. Instantly, he felt something wasn't right. He grabbed her hand and held it while the rotors spun up, making it too loud to talk. She leaned over and kissed him.

As the helicopter blades came to full rotation, she looked into his eyes and mouthed the words, Thank you, for everything. She stood up, and kicked one of the field packs sending it sliding across the helicopter floor and out the door. Before anyone realized what she was doing, she gave Argo a silent command with her hands and leaped with him out the side door of the Huey. Everyone in the helicopter was stunned. Flint unbuckled and stood to see what she was doing in time to see her and Argo sprinting down the mountainside, and disappearing into the thick, orange smoke.

The helicopter had already left the mountaintop before Flint could get the pilot's attention.

"We need to go back. Coffy just jumped out of the helicopter."

"Who?" the co-pilot responded.

"Coffy Summerfield. She just jumped out. We need to go back to get her!" Flint shouted.

"Sorry, buddy. We can't do it. Taking off in this smoke is bad enough, but there's no way in hell we're going to land in this stuff. I'll radio

I.C. and tell them she's on the mountain, but she's going to be on her own for a while."

Flint looked over at Creasy, who shook his head and shrugged. There was nothing he could do.

Coffy and Argo raced down the mountain. She started to feel the heat radiating through the forest below. The fire must have moved a considerable distance up the mountain during their retreat. The smoke might be able to mask the flames, but it couldn't contain the heat.

Adrenaline pushed her down the mountain without stopping to rest. She could hear the fire crackling and pine trees exploding in the distance. The wind flowing from the base of the fire and up the slope of the mountain was starting to get hot, but so far was tolerable. She unleashed Argo and shouted, "Seek, Argo. Seek!"

Argo ran right, then left, jumping over downed trees and racing around large boulders with ease. He was good at this, born for it. The smoke was thick, but hardly a distraction for him. It didn't smell like humans. If there was someone down here still alive, Coffy knew Argo would find them.

Argo finally vanished into the smoke, though Coffy wasn't worried. He would often disappear, returning after a few moments to explore another area or to give her the signal that he had found something. After several minutes, however, the smoke began to dramatically thicken and the sound of exploding trees was getting closer. She was ready to retreat back up the mountain to a safer position when she caught a glimpse of Argo to her right. He was carrying a stick in his mouth. When he approached her, he laid the stick at her feet. He had found something.

"Show me where he is, boy!" Argo took off down the hill with Coffy close behind struggling to keep sight of him in the smoke. Coffy yelled the boy's name several time, but got no response. Instead, she heard Argo barking and followed the sound until she found her dog near the trunk of a large aspen. Sitting with his back to the tree was the boy, staring down the mountain and ignoring the large barking German Shepherd.

"Oh my God, Jason!" She ran toward him, stumbling several times in her haste. "Jason!"

As she got closer, she intentionally slowed her approach and circled to face the boy in order not to scare him. She had no experience with autism and was worried that he might try to run from her.

She knelt in front of him as Argo approached and sat next to her.

"Hi, Jason. My name is Coffy, and a lot of people have been looking for you. I'm so happy you're okay!"

Jason's gaze met hers, but he didn't respond. She was tempted to reach out to him, but wasn't sure he would find it reassuring.

"You know what, Jason? Your mother and father are sad you're not with them right now, and they would very much like to see you. Will you let me take you to them?"

There was no response at all. She knew he was nonverbal, but nothing in his eyes told her he was listening. She took a moment to assess. He was big enough that she couldn't physically carry him up the mountain if he didn't want to go. She knew he was scared and had no idea what to do. Unfortunately, she didn't know what to do either, but she needed to figure something out fast. The roar of the fire was close now, and the heat was starting to get uncomfortable. Somewhere below them, a tree exploded causing Jason to jump.

"Jason, I'm going to help you get up? We need to find a safer place to get you to." She reached out and gently put her hand on his arm. He was fine with that, but when she tried to help him to his feet, he jerked from her grasp and let out a sound that instantly told her this approach wasn't going to work. Out of desperation, she sat next to him with her back to the tree, trying to think of a way out of this situation. One thing she knew; she was going to die here with him rather than leave him behind.

The Huey landed at the bottom of the mountain on a two lane highway close to the Incident Command Center. Flint was in a hurry to get to whoever was in command and explain what happened on top of the mountain. Before he could exit the helicopter, Flint saw a familiar face from the morning. Tom McNeil was waiting for him to disembark.

"Hi, Tom," Flint shouted over the still rotating blades of the Huey.

"Hello, Flint. Come with me."

Tom led Flint and Apache away from the Huey where they could talk without shouting.

"What happened up there, Flint? Did Coffy refuse to come down?"

"No. She came back to the helicopter with the crew, but just as it was taking off, she grabbed Argo and jumped. The helicopter pilot didn't want to risk landing the helicopter in all that smoke."

"That sounds like Coffy all right. Why don't you come with me and let's see what we can do?" Tom said.

"Lead the way," Flint replied.

Tom led them to the sheriff's helicopter stationed a little farther down the highway from the Huey. They loaded up and took off for the top of the mountain.

Coffy turned the radio on and keyed the mike. "Summerfield to Incident Command. I've located Jason Greene on the north slope. I'm unable to get him to leave this location, over."

The response was immediate. "Summerfield, this is Captain Bayden of the Colorado Forest Service Fire Command. We've been trying to get in contact with you for some time now. What are your coordinates?"

Coffy gave him the numbers off her GPS unit.

"What's the situation?" he asked.

"I've found Jason Greene. He's alive, but I'm not able to get him mobile, and the fire is getting close."

"Can you carry him out?"

"No, he's too big."

"All right, standby."

Coffy looked down the slope and saw a massive wall of fire breaking through the haze of smoke. The God-awful roar coming from it as it consumed every ounce of fuel in its path made it hard to hear the radio.

"Summerfield, are you there?"

"I'm here, Captain," she answered.

"Listen to me carefully. Your options are limited. The southern edge of the fire is climbing the slope fast, and you have to get out of there. We're not going to be able to get to you in time. Your best option is to head for the top of the mountain as fast as you can. Once you get there, head west until you're out of the smoke, and we'll send someone up to get you. Do you copy?"

Coffy thought about the implications of what the captain just said. He was telling her to leave the boy and save herself, something she wasn't willing to do. She wasn't there when her son needed her the most. She wasn't about to make the same mistake again.

"Understood, Captain."

She sighed and resigned herself to her fate. It seemed fitting after all. She had known all along she would die a violent death some day. After all, her father killed himself violently. Her son died an unnatural death, so why not her? It was proper punishment for what she had done. She hoped for Jason's sake, though, that the smoke killed them first.

"Coffy, this is Flint. Can you hear me?" The radio shook her from her morbid thoughts.

"I'm here Flint. Where are you?"

"I'm with Tom McNeil. We're in the helicopter west of your location. We're going to hover until you can get to us."

"Glad you two are all right. You may have to wait a while, though."

"Coffy, you need to get a move on. The flames are getting close to you."

"Oh, I'm very much aware of that, Flint. Problem is, I can't get young Master Jason here to budge. He's a big boy."

"Coffy, you need to leave now. You'll die if you don't get out of there."

"Can't do that, Flint. I'm not leaving him behind."

"Coffy! You have to!" Flint yelled into the radio.

After a moment of silence, Coffy keyed the radio. "Flint, tell Frisco to take care of my dogs until someone can get over there to get them."

"Coffy, no! You need to get out of there. There's no sense in you doing this."

"It's okay, Flint. This has been coming for some time now. I've been lucky so far, but now it's time to pay my dues. I should have paid them a long time ago."

There was a long moment of radio silence.

"Remember, Flint, this was my decision. I had a lot of fun this week. I wish you and your daughter the best. And take good care of Apache. She's a good dog."

"Coffy!" Flint yelled into the radio. "Coffy, no!"

Coffy switched off the radio and looked at Jason, who was surprisingly calm. She was certain he had no idea what was about to happen. Mercifully, he had gone somewhere deep inside himself. She looked down at Argo, who stared back into her eyes. Coffy reached out and pulled him to her. She hugged him tight, burying her face into his long black fur.

91

"Argo, I'm going to need you to go up the mountain, sweetheart. I don't want you here with me. I want you to run as fast, and as far as you can." She knew he didn't understand. When the time came, she would make him understand by sending him off with the search command. It wasn't his fault he was here, and he shouldn't pay for it with his life. She hugged him again and then reached for her pack to get some water for him. He had to be thirsty, and he would need it for the climb out. She opened the pack and looked inside. What she found gave her a glimmer of hope. It was the fire shelter she had been given before they started the search for Jason. She had completely forgotten about it.

She opened the case and quickly pulled out the foil-covered fabric. It really wasn't a tent at all; it was more like a silver-coated quilt to throw over one's self in case the fire was moving faster than the person could run. When she saw the size of it, her heart sank. She remembered during the quick training she was given at the top of the mountain that it was only suitable for one person. She knew she and Jason couldn't use it together. He was a pretty large kid, and the shelter was too small for both of them. She looked back at Jason and was stunned by what she saw. He was hugging Argo. He had reached out to Argo and Argo nestled up to him. *The power of a dog* she thought.

"Jason, sweetheart, I need your help, and you know what? My dog needs your help, too." She stood, then knelt in front of him. "I need you to save my dog's life. Can you do that for me?"

His eyes connected with hers, though she wasn't sure if she was getting through to him.

"Jason, I need you to lie down and cover up with this blanket. It's a magic blanket with special powers. As long as you wear it, you'll be safe. I need you to cover my dog with it so he'll be safe, okay? He can't do it without you."

She scanned the area around her, looking for a spot safe from falling branches. Finding nothing, just getting him away from the base of the tree would be better than nothing.

"Argo, come." Argo left Jason's arms and walked over to Coffy.

"Jason, sweetheart, listen to me. Argo needs you to come over here and cover up with this blanket. We don't have a lot of time right now, honey."

The fire was close now, just yards away. The radiant heat was beginning to burn the back of her neck and thighs. Shouting more than she wanted because of the roar of the approaching fire, Coffy did her best to encourage Jason to get up. Finally, she was overjoyed to see Jason rise to his feet and slowly walk toward her. She thought about trying to coax him up the mountain, but knew it was too late. The fire was going to overrun them now no matter what they did.

Jason sat next to Argo and reached out for him again. "Argo, lie down," Coffy commanded. Argo stretched out next to Jason. "Jason, I need you to lie down next to Argo here. I'm going to put this blanket over you so you two can rest for a while."

Surprisingly, he did as she asked, lying on his stomach while still holding on to Argo. "No matter what happens, Jason, no matter what you hear, don't peek out from under the blanket. If you do, Argo will get scared. He needs you to be brave right now. Will you do that?"

She knew now that he could understand her instructions, but could only hope that he would follow through with what she told him. She was betting Argo's life on it. She hoped she wouldn't regret not sending Argo up the mountain, but, she would soon be dead anyway so regrets weren't a problem anymore.

She looked around for a place to spend her final moments. She wanted to stay close to them, but she didn't want Jason or Argo to hear her suffer if it came to that. She scrambled upslope, trying to stay ahead of the fire, but soon found that it was no use. The fire was gaining on her. Looking around, she spotted a cluster of boulders in a depression and raced toward them. She cleared out as much of the dirt and leaves as she could from under the base of the largest one. The boulders would block some, but not all of the radiant heat, and they would be useless in preventing her from breathing the hot gasses as the fire passed over her.

It didn't matter now; she was out of options. The heat had begun to blister her skin. She crawled under the rock as far as she could get and tried to cover as much of herself as she could by scraping the dirt with her hands. Finally, with the flames just yards away, she pushed her face into the dirt. Hopefully, it would muffle her screams

CHAPTER SEVEN

The drive to Aurora outside of Denver was long, almost three-hundred and thirty miles. The University of Colorado's Burn Center was located there and was where rescue crews had flown Coffy after they found her badly burned but alive the day before. The time driving alone provided ample opportunity for Flint to think about what happened, and more important, what he could do to help, which was next to nothing. Even though he'd only met her less than a week ago, he found himself doing things that only couples or extremely close friends would do for each other.

Once Coffy had been transported to the hospital, he and the dogs flew back to Silverton in the helicopter with Tom. There was a veterinarian's office there who agreed to look at Apache's burned paws and check both dogs for any smoke inhalation problems. They would also look after them while Flint was gone to Aurora. Tom volunteered to get word to Frisco to watch after Coffy's dogs while she was in the hospital.

Flint sorted out his new plans by getting his flight moved back a couple of days and calling Troy to tell him he would be late returning home. He spoke with Sam, too, who was fine with his change of plans. She had always been someone who was independent, though he could tell by the sound of her voice that she missed him. She was no doubt ready to get back home after being with Troy and Liz all week. He missed her and was ready to get back to Pensacola, but he couldn't just leave, not yet. He needed to ask Coffy some questions, face-to-face.

Yesterday's events had brought him to the realization that he needed her more than she needed him. The last several days had been full of mystery, laughter, and lovemaking, which he was hoping to continue, but he wasn't sure how. She lived so far away, and she was happy with what she had. He was happy with his life, too, for that matter, which made it all so complicated.

Yesterday, after he thought he'd lost her, he was shocked at how hard it was to control his emotions. Maybe he was just getting more sentimental as he got older, but whatever it was, he was confused about how much he cared for Coffy. He wasn't sure if he was ready to call it love, but he was damned sure that whatever it was, he liked it. Of course, it wouldn't mean anything if she didn't survive her injuries.

It had taken the fire rescue crew almost two hours to reach the area after the flames had passed. Flint felt useless the entire time as he and Tom could do nothing from the helicopter except guide the crews to the general location they thought Coffy's body might be. He and Tom watched helplessly from above as the fire overran Coffy's position. He knew from her radio silence afterward that she, Argo, and Jason were most likely killed. There was no way they could escape the flames.

There was some solace to be had when the rescue crew radioed back to I.C. that they had found Argo alive and that the dog was leading them somewhere, hopefully to where Coffy and Jason had made their stand. He knew a dog could outrun the flames, but there was no way a human could do it. It wasn't until he heard over the radio that Jason was found alive, though with burns on his arms and hands and a suspected case of smoke inhalation, that he began to hold out some hope for Coffy. The boy had been found wandering the burned and blackened forest alone. Radio chatter soon began about the boy who miraculously survived the flames.

The rescue crew informed I. C. that Argo was leading them to another area farther up the side of the mountain. About two-hundred yards upslope from where the boy was found, they found Argo again, this time sitting next to a large rock, barking and pawing at the ground. That was when Flint got the surprise he dared not hope for. Crews found Coffy dug in under a boulder, alive but badly burned. After discovering the empty fire shelter nearby, crews could only surmise that she successfully coaxed Jason inside of it, which had saved his life. She'd done her best to survive by digging in and crawling as far under a granite boulder as she could, but without a way to protect her backside, she was exposed to the radiated heat of the wildfire as it passed through. The pain must have been excruciating.

Tom landed the helicopter at the bottom of the mountain where he and Flint rushed to the Incident Command Center for an update on the rescue. Ground crews called in a rescue helicopter, which lowered a litter and lifted Coffy out of the blackened and still smoking forest and flew her to the bottom of the mountain. Flint watched as she was transferred, bandaged and unconscious, to a medical helicopter which flew her to the burn unit in Aurora. Rescue crews later carried Argo down on foot with severely burned pads on the bottom of his feet. The still burning coals from the fire had burned them, but he bravely endured the pain until he could lead rescue crews to Coffy.

Flint pulled into the parking lot at the hospital around three in the afternoon. Stopping at the information desk downstairs, he learned she was located in the intensive care unit upstairs on the third floor. After lying to the nurse at the nurse's station that he was family, he was allowed into her room.

The flashing lights of the medical equipment and the dim light of the room took him back to several months ago when he was in the same situation. Coffy was lying face down on the hospital bed. The sheet covering her couldn't hide the bulky bandages that covered her shoulders, back, and upper thighs.

Her beautiful, long black hair had been cut short, no doubt because the heat had burned most of it off. She was asleep. Not wanting to wake her, he sat in the beige, vinyl reclining chair next to her bed and stared at her.

After being alone with his thoughts, he was caught off-guard when a nurse walked in.

"Oh, hello," she said to him.

"Hi," he said, trying hard to smile.

"Are you family?" she asked as she walked up to the far side of Coffy's hospital bed.

"Yes," he lied.

"I understand we have a hero here," the nurse said, looking at her watch as she checked Coffy's pulse.

"Yes, she is," Flint replied. "She risked her life saving a young man from a forest fire."

"That's amazing." She checked some of the medical equipment and Coffy's IV drip. "Has anyone filled you in on her condition?"

"No, not yet."

"I tell you what. I saw her doctor a few minutes ago checking on another patient. I'll find him and ask him to talk to you."

"Thank you. I appreciate what you're doing for her," Flint said.

"Anything for an angel like her," she replied. It touched Flint somewhere deep inside when he heard her say that.

A half-hour later, the doctor walked and introduced himself. Hoping the doctor wouldn't ask who he was, Flint stood, shook his hand, and said, "Nice to meet you, Doctor. My name is Flint."

"Hello, Flint. It's nice to meet you, too. My name is Dr. Clark. Has anyone talked to you about Ms. Summerfield here."

"No sir."

"Are you related to Ms. Summerfield?"

Dammit. "Yes, sir," he lied again. He was starting to feel bad about it.

"Well, Ms. Summerfield has been through a lot. She has a lot of second-degree burns on her neck, shoulders, and back, as well as the back of her thighs. Some of them could almost be considered third-degree and are serious, but we're going to stick with second-degree for now. Second-degree burns come in two types, partial and full thickness. She has both types. Most of the burns are partial, meaning there's damage to the entire epidermis and some of the upper layers of the dermis, the deeper part of the skin. While painful, they'll usually heal on their own with minimal scarring. Unfortunately, about twenty percent of her burns are of the full thickness type. They're located on her back and will most likely require skin grafts. It will scar, and it'll take her several months to recover."

Flint's heart sank. "That sounds pretty serious."

"Yes, sir, it is, but from what the medical crew who brought her in told me, she saved her life by trying to dig in, *under a rock?* Is that correct?"

"It is," Flint responded.

"That's one smart lady. It could have been so much worse. I understand she saved another person's life by giving up her emergency fire shelter?"

"Yes, she did. She saved the life of a sixteen-year-old kid."

"That's amazing. She knew the risk to herself and helped the kid anyway," the doctor said, shaking his head. "Well, she's sedated at the moment. She most likely will be unresponsive tonight. Why don't you go home, get some sleep, and come back in the morning? You should be able to talk to her then."

"Thank you, Doctor. Home is a long way away. If it's all right with you, I'll stay here with her tonight."

"You can do that, but I'm afraid you won't be getting much sleep. We'll be checking on her every thirty minutes or so. Not that the chair there is very comfortable anyway."

"Thank you." Flint shook the doctor's hand again and watched him leave. He looked down at Coffy, thankful she was sleeping through the pain. He couldn't imagine what she was about to go through with recovery. He sat in the chair and reclined it as far as it would go. It was going to be a long night, but he had nowhere else to go, and he wanted to be here. She nearly died saving someone's life. The least he could do was be there when she woke up.

True to the doctor's words, Flint barely got any sleep. It was clear that the staff at the hospital wanted to make sure she was well taken care of. All night people were making their way through her hospital room checking this and that, checking her vitals and administering all kinds of drugs through her IV. He was happy to know she was receiving good medical care.

He woke not too long after midnight. Taking a moment to remember where he was, he looked at Coffy and was surprised to see her awake and staring at him. She smiled at him.

"My God, Coffy! How long have you been awake?" She didn't answer him. "Are you all right? How are you feeling?"

"I'm doing okay," she said weakly. "How are you?"

"How am I? Really? You nearly died, and you're asking how I am?"

She shrugged her eyebrows, which caused Flint to laugh out loud. "Are you in pain?" he asked.

"Well, I don't feel great, but they have me on some good stuff I guess. It hurts, but I don't care that it hurts." She smiled at him again.

Flint stood, walked to her bedside, and began stroking the remains of her once beautiful hair. "Coffy, do you remember what happened?"

"I remember. I remember every bit of it," she said, closing her eyes. "I'm surprised I'm here. I thought I had died."

"You almost did."

"How bad am I burned?"

"Well, you're burned pretty good."

"My face?"

"No, just your back and your legs. The doctor said you have second-degree burns and that most of them will heal just fine."

"Most of them?"

"Yes, you'll need some skin grafts, but not a lot."

She opened her eyes, but couldn't move her head far enough to see his face now. Flint knelt beside her so she could see.

"Sounds like I'll be pretty scarred up."

Flint looked into her eyes and smiled. "Even angels have a few scars, my dear. You saved a young man's life. I would call them battle scars, and there's nothing more beautiful than a scar received when saving a human life."

She closed her eyes again. Flint could tell she was fighting to stay awake.

"So he lived?"

"Yes, Coffy. You saved him."

"Argo?" she said softly.

"Argo is alive and well except for some sore paws. He's being treated for them in Silverton, and the veterinarian there said he'll be just fine. You should know he led the rescue crews to you, so he's a hero, too."

"He was born to be one," she said as she faded off to sleep.

Coffy slept most of the next day, allowing Flint to get out of the hospital for a while. He was exhausted, but he didn't want to spend his last couple of days sleeping his time away, so he decided to drive around and see what was in Aurora.

He spent time thinking about the previous week and the excitement that had returned to his life. It was a strange situation to be in. He felt such a strong attraction to Coffy, but he had no idea how she felt about him. He wanted to ask her, but now, while she was in the hospital, was not the time. But if not now, would he ever get the chance again?

Flint stopped to get something to eat, then found a florist. He wasn't sure what type of flowers to get, so he asked for help from the lady in the shop. He walked out with a bouquet of white and yellow daisy spray chrysanthemums, carefully placed them in the floorboard of his Jeep, and headed back to the hospital.

When he walked into Coffy's room, he was surprised to see her awake again. "How are you feeling?" he asked, walking up beside her bed and placing the flowers on the table next to her.

"I'm still in a lot of pain, but I'm hanging in there. Thank you for the flowers. They look like the flowers in the field beside my cabin."

Flint stroked the top of her head. He was afraid to touch her anywhere else.

"Why are you here? I thought you'd be on your way back to Pensacola by now."

Flint felt a bit of disappointment at her assuming he would leave her like that. He was hoping she would have been happier about him being there.

"I couldn't leave you like this, Coffy. What kind of friend would I be if I just took off like that?"

"Thank you."

"Do you remember me being here this morning?" he asked.

"I do, but I thought maybe I was dreaming."

"You weren't dreaming but, to be fair, you were pretty drugged up."

"Yeah, better living through chemicals, I always say." They both laughed. It was good to see her sense of humor returning. Flint took a seat in the chair beside her bed.

"Well, how many folks did I make mad this time?" Coffy asked.

"What do you mean? No one is mad at you. Hell, you're a hometown hero."

"Yeah? I guess despite my screw-ups, I'm still alive."

"Yes, it beats the alternative any day of the week."

"I guess."

"You guess? What do you mean by that?" Flint asked.

"Nothing. Do you know if anyone has talked with Frisco? I need to make sure someone is taking care of my dogs."

"It's all been handled. Tom McNeil flew the helicopter out to your place yesterday morning and made contact with Frisco."

"Thank you, Flint. I appreciate everything you've done."

"You're welcome," Flint said, smiling at her. "Do you feel like talking about what happened on the mountain?"

"I guess so. There's not much to tell, though. Argo found the boy, the kid wouldn't budge, so I broke out the fire tent and covered them up. Problem solved."

"You're something else," Flint said, shaking his head. "I believe you're minimizing the fact that you risked your life for someone you didn't even know."

"Um, excuse me. Isn't that what brought you to Colorado in the first place? I mean, isn't there a little girl alive in Florida somewhere because you did the same thing? You're being rather hypocritical, aren't you?"

Flint wasn't sure if she was kidding or really angry, but he couldn't let it stop right here.

"No, absolutely not. What happened to me was different."

"How so?" Coffy demanded.

"I walked into that situation not knowing what was going to happen. I had every expectation of walking out of that situation alive."

"So did I!" She tried to lift her head, but the pain wouldn't allow it. "I took a calculated risk. One that I thought was worth taking only because Argo found the boy's scent before we were ordered back. I wasn't going into it blind."

"And I didn't know I was going to be shot. If I had known, I might not have gone back to the diner that night. I would have just called it in."

"That's some major league horse-shit, Flint. You're going to sit there and lie to my face about what you might have done? I know you well enough to be able to tell what kind of man you are. You would have gone back to save that girl's life no matter the consequences."

There was no doubt in Flint's mind that she was mad now. He didn't like this side of her. "I don't know what I would have done. But I do know I wouldn't have gone in with some kind of death wish. I have people I have to take care of." As soon as the words left his mouth, he regretted saying them. He didn't know where they'd come from, they just *happened*. It was too late to take them back now. It was clear from Coffy's silence that she was about to go off on him with a vengeance.

Finally, in a low, slow growl, Coffy spoke. "How dare you insinuate that because I have no one to take care of, I have some sort of perverted desire for death!"

"Coffy, that's not--"

"You're just like every man I've ever known. Just because a woman takes the initiative to be brave and do something others wouldn't do, you have to find fault with their intent."

"No, Coffy! I didn't say that." Flint was confused and on the defense. This wasn't turning out at all like he was expecting, but he didn't know how to turn it around.

"You know, Flint, I liked you. I really did. I thought maybe you were different, but now I see you're not different at all. My husband was like that. Always critical of everything I did. My motives were always questioned and were never for the right reasons. I hated that about him, and I hate what you're saying to me right now."

Flint tried to speak calmly. "Coffy, please listen to me. On the radio, you said this had been coming for some time now. You said you'd been lucky so far, but now it was time to pay your dues. What the hell would that sound like to you if you heard someone say that?"

Coffy went silent for a long moment.

"You know, I like you, too. A lot. I want the same thing as you. I'd love to work something out, but I need to know that you want to stay around long enough to make it work. To me, you sounded on the radio as if you preferred to die over saving yourself. I want to know that you enjoy living."

Coffy slowly turned her head and stared at the ceiling. Flint instantly knew he had pushed too hard.

"Flint, I've had a wonderful week. I hope you and Apache save a lot of lives. Thank you for being here and for bringing me flowers, but I think it's time for you to go."

"Coffy, no! Let's discuss this," Flint pleaded.

"Goodbye, Flint. Take good care of my dog."

Flint stood and stared at Coffy's face. How had this conversation gone so wrong?

Coffy closed her eyes as Flint saw a tear run across her nose and drop to her pillow. He stroked her hair one more time.

"Goodbye, Coffy. I could have loved you." He turned and walked out of the door.

CHAPTER EIGHT

It had been a long week at the park and Flint was tired. Fridays were always the hardest because it was when everyone checked in at the park for a weekend campsite. Campers were often grumpy after being on the road all day, locked up in an RV or a small car for hundreds of miles with a family that hated road trips. They always took their frustrations out on the first person they encountered, which was usually the ranger at the front desk. No one in the office looked forward to Fridays.

Flint was in his office working on his weekly reports when Troy Burnside walked in and sat in the chair across from Flint's desk. Not saying a word, he sat there with a grin until Flint was forced to look up from his work.

"What do you want?"

"Nothing," Troy said.

Flint went back to his paperwork while Troy continued to sit in silence. The awkwardness was reaching a crescendo, neither man willing to give in to the other. Flint was first to cave.

"Troy, what in the hell do you want?" he said, throwing the pen down and leaning back in his chair. He hated letting Troy win these little contests.

"Well, since you asked. I was just up front with the clerks, and Barbara told me you have a date tonight. Is that true?"

"Yes, I guess it is," Flint said with a heavy sigh.

"How come I'm the last to know?" Troy said, folding his arms and overacting his disappointment.

"Because when I tell you things, Troy, the whole world finds out about it. It's like you're some kind of central data hub for the planet. Information goes in, then becomes available for every living person on Earth within seconds. It's amazing."

"It's a gift I have. Will Liz and I be taking care of Sam tonight?"

"No, she's spending the night with one of her school friends."

"You know, I'm beginning to think you don't love me anymore."

Flint smiled. "I love you, Troy. I just didn't want to broadcast my personal life to the world just yet."

"Well, who is she? I should at least know who the unlucky lady is, don't you think?"

"She's a new teacher at the elementary school. I met her at one of Sam's soccer games. She's probably a little young for me, but she's looking to make friends, and I couldn't refuse."

"So she asked you out?"

"Sort of. She seems nice, and I wouldn't mind talking to a woman every now and then rather than having to put up with you all the time."

"So does this mean you're finally over that Colorado fling? I don't believe it for a second."

"I got over that a long time ago, Troy. You're the one who kept pushing me about that."

"Me? Really? I seem to remember you making everyone's life miserable around here for the first six weeks after you got back. It's been almost a year now, and you still don't want to talk about it."

"I choose not to talk about it because there's nothing to say. There never was."

"Say what you want, but I know whatever happened up there messed you up. You were a different person when you came back. I noticed it, Liz noticed it, the entire park staff noticed it. You can keep lying to us about it, but those of us who give a shit about you know better." Troy stood and left Flint's office without waiting for a reply.

Flint was stunned at how quickly the lighthearted conversation had turned. It wasn't like Troy to say anything serious to anyone, let alone Flint. It took a few moments to try and decipher what Troy meant by his words.

THE SCENT OF REDEMPTION

It was true Flint was a little melancholy when he first returned from Colorado. He chalked it up to his feelings of being helpless during Coffy's rescue on the mountain rather than actually missing her. It could have been a little of both, he supposed. He'd been on Coffy's turf while in Colorado, and he wasn't used to not being in charge. To stand by and watch someone else do the dirty work, well, that just wasn't in his DNA, yet he was drawn to her independence, her mastery of living alone, her expertise. It was a quandary.

Flint always loved women who had a strong sense of independence, starting with his mother. She was a divorced mother of three and knew of no other way to be. Raising children while working full-time to support them demanded no less.

God knows Rachael was independent. Her life as a cop depended on it. To shoot or not to shoot wasn't a decision debated with others and voted on. Coffy, however, brought self-reliance to a whole other level. She was the type of person who could make it through a zombie apocalypse singlehanded, and to Flint, that kind of independence was a complete turn on.

Flint had a stubborn independent streak as well, one of the reasons he hadn't contacted Coffy since he'd left Colorado. He would rather die than allow Coffy to think he needed her, especially with the way she dismissed him. In the end, though, it was mostly pride that prevented him from writing or calling to check on her, even if it was just to let her know how Apache was doing. He had come close several times, but his anger at how things ended never allowed him to go through with it.

He reached for the computer keyboard and typed 'Coffy Summerfield' into the search engine just as he had done so many times before. He didn't like doing it and always felt ashamed afterward, but it helped him remember her. Yes, maybe he really did love her, or maybe he *wanted* to be in love with her. Whatever he was feeling, he dared not share it with anyone, especially Troy.

There were the usual hits he'd seen countless times before. News alerts praising her heroic rescue of Jason the year before. Blogs and articles about her Colorado Search and Rescue Association events and accolades for her donations of trained search and rescue dogs to other agencies. This time, though, something new caught his eye. He clicked on a link to the Durango Herald newspaper and an article popped up about her recovery from the fire and how much progress she had made.

Scrolling down a little further, he found a picture of her standing in front of the Durango-Silverton steam engine with a man in an old train engineer's uniform handing her an over-sized train ticket. The caption read that the Durango-Silverton Railroad line was going to allow her to ride free of charge back and forth to Silverton, Durango and her home in the Animas Canyon as a reward for the work she had done conducting search and rescues for the community.

She looked fantastic. Her hair had grown longer, and her smile seemed genuine. Flint smiled, too, when he realized that he was truly happy for her. *Maybe I should call her to congratulate her. No, maybe not. She thinks I'm such a weak person. The last thing she wants is some milk-toast hanging on to false hopes for something that will never happen.*

His work done for the day, Flint drove home, showered, and changed clothes for his night out. It was a well known fact that he had no fashion sense and was often made fun of by Samantha for wearing old man clothes. Rachael had always advised him on his attire. It had been a long time since he'd gone out on a real date, so to avoid creating a fashion faux pas, he asked Sam to help him pick out some clothes the night before. He put on a new pair of dark blue denim jeans, a long sleeve cream colored button down shirt, and a dark brown sports coat. He drew the line with Sam at not wearing socks with his brown suede shoes. He wasn't twenty years old, for God's sake.

He walked into the living room and called Sam from his cellphone.

"Hey, kiddo, what's up?" he asked when she answered.

"Hi, Pop! Not much. Are you getting ready to see Christine?" She sounded excited.

"Yep. I thought I would check in with you first and make sure you're having fun."

"We are. Alexa and I are making a movie with her cellphone and her parents are taking us out to eat after while." She paused for a moment. "Are you nervous?"

"No, honey, I'm not nervous. I'm too old to be nervous."

"Not even a little?"

Flint thought about it for a second. "All right, you win. Truth is, I'm terrified."

"Aw, you'll be okay," she said with genuine concern. "She's a nice lady, and you'll have a good time. I know it. What are you going to do?"

"Well, I thought we'd go to Allison's for dinner, then to The Blue Diamond for a drink."

"Ooh, The Blue Diamond. Fancy!"

"Yeah, yeah, whatever, kid. Hey, listen, you be good tonight. I don't want to hear about any late night shenanigans. You go to sleep when the Mitchells say it's time to go to bed, okay?"

"I will, Pop."

"Promise?"

"I promise," she replied.

"All right, have fun and I'll come get you in the morning."

"Good night, Pop!"

"Good night, Sam." Flint shoved the cellphone into his jacket pocket, grabbed the truck keys, and made his way toward Pensacola.

Traffic going over the Pensacola Bay Bridge wasn't bad for a Friday night, so the trip into town only took twenty minutes. Finding Christine's house took a little longer. His personal truck, a 1967 Chevy he rebuilt himself after Rachael died, didn't have GPS, and he found the map app on his phone too frustrating to bother with, so he did it the old fashioned way, with his eyes. He hadn't counted on it being dark, though, and he was having trouble seeing the addresses of the older homes in the East Hill section of town.

Finally finding her home, he parked his truck, walked up to the front door, and rang the doorbell.

Christine smiled at Flint as she opened the door. "Hi, Flint!"

She hastily stepped out onto the porch. A man's voice from inside yelled, "Good night, honey! Have a--" Christine quickly shut the door before the man could finish. Flint raised an eyebrow after hearing the man's voice.

"That's my dad," she told him before he could ask. She sounded almost embarrassed.

"Oh, is he visiting?"

"No, I live with my mother and father. This is their house. Are you ready?"

"Sure. Let's go."

Walking to the truck, Flint started to question why he was doing

107

this. Christine was, as near as he could tell, eight or nine years younger than he so that would put her in her early thirties. *Why was she still living at home with her parents?* This did not bode well.

In the ten minutes it took to get to Allison's, Flint realized that he had made a huge mistake. For sure, Christine was an attractive woman. She had blonde hair, blue eyes, and still had a shape that she must go to great lengths to maintain. At the time, he was pretty pleased with himself that she had taken the initiative to ask him out, but with great beauty sometimes comes great social responsibility, as was made painfully evident by her nonstop texting the entire trip to the restaurant. He never asked who she was texting with; not because he wasn't curious, but because she never gave him a chance to. He was amazed at her skill of texting with both hands while at the same time totally dominating a verbal conversation. He couldn't get a word in edgewise. He hoped she was just nervous and the texting and talking would subside if he could somehow make her feel more comfortable.

Inside the restaurant, things went from bad to worse. The hostess escorted them to a booth in the back and gave them each a menu. Small talk ensued, punctuated every couple of minutes by an annoying whistle every time Christine received a text. After a while, Flint had finally had enough.

"Please don't think I'm being rude, but who are you texting with?"

"Oh, I'm sorry. Is it bothering you?"

"Well, I--"

"It's my best friend Karen," she interrupted. "She's curious about you."

Flint wasn't sure how Christine could know anything at all about him. She hadn't given him a chance to tell her anything.

"You don't know much about me. I can't imagine what you're telling her."

"I know more about you than you think. The teachers I work with at the elementary school all have a crush on you. Since you rescued that little girl last year, you've become quite the catch."

Flint was shocked. "Really? That's pretty bizarre. How come I'm the last to know about it?"

"Maybe you don't pay enough attention when you're at the school. Or it could be most of the teachers are married so there isn't much they can say out loud. But I know for a fact that you're a pretty popular guy there."

"Well, I'll be damned." He sat back in silent disbelief.

"Did I embarrass you?" Christine asked.

"No. I just have a hard time believing it."

"It's true. You're a good looking man raising a daughter on his own. You save children in danger and you live in a home in one of the most beautiful places in the state. I mean, there's not a whole lot to dislike about you. At least not from what I know about you so far."

Flint never felt he was particularly attractive, so this news was a welcome salve to his wounded self-perception. He couldn't help feeling pretty good about what she had just told him, at least until her phone went off again.

"You know it wasn't me who found that girl right?"

She looked up from her phone. "That's not what I heard. I heard you were nearly killed trying to save her."

"I did get shot, but only because I was being stupid. It was my dog who figured out who kidnapped the girl. She died saving me, and it seems like I'm the one always getting all the credit."

"Oh, I'm sorry about your dog. I think I knew that, but still, wasn't she doing what she was trained to do?"

Flint was stunned at what Christine had just said. He was afraid to respond because the words about to fly out of his mouth were not going to be pleasant. He decided to keep his mouth shut. Christine went back to texting her friend, oblivious to what she had just said. Fortunately, the waitress showed up to take their order.

Flint did the best he could to salvage the rest of the evening. He tried to be kind to Christine, but she exhausted him. It was obvious she was disconnected from having any empathy or feelings toward others, caring mostly about herself and what her friends thought about her. Small talk was the rule for the rest of the evening.

As they were waiting for the check, Flint's phone vibrated in his jacket pocket. He ignored it because he didn't want to give Christine the satisfaction of seeing him on his phone, but after it buzzed a second time, he thought he should check it just in case it was Sam. The caller ID showed it was an unknown number. He decided to answer it; he needed the break.

"Christine, would you mind if I answered this? It might be my daughter?" He could at least be polite about it.

"Sure. Go ahead." She began looking at her phone again.

"Flint Westbrook," he said, putting the phone up to his ear.

"Hello, Officer Westbrook. This is Corporal Jennifer Haynes with the Ft. Walton County Sheriff's Department. I'm sorry to bother you, sir, but I was hoping to get your assistance in locating a lost elderly patient here in Ft. Walton Beach. Are you in a position to help us tonight?"

"I might be. Tell me what's going on."

"At about five-thirty this evening, an eighty-two-year-old male with dementia wandered away from a senior facility. Officers have been unable to locate him. I was hoping you and your K-9 could help us."

Flint didn't have to give it a second thought. "I'd be glad to. I just need to go home to get my dog. It may be about two hours before I can get there."

Christine's head popped up from her phone when she heard what he said.

"Do you have something to write with?" the corporal asked.

Flint grabbed the pen the waitress had left with the check and wrote down the address.

"I got it. I'll see you as soon as I can." He hung up the phone and looked at Christine, who was already glaring at him.

"I'm sorry, Christine. That was the Sheriff's Department in Ft. Walton Beach. They need me to help find someone. Can I get a rain check on the rest of the evening?"

"Wow, I've heard of date rescue calls before, but you really went overboard on this one," she said, picking up her phone.

It was a little after ten in the evening when Flint and Apache pulled into the parking lot of the Naval Oaks Retirement Village. During the day, the drive was usually spectacular along US 98. Also known as the Blue Water Highway, it followed the Gulf of Mexico along Santa Rosa Sound between Pensacola and Ft. Walton Beach and was gifted with dense populations of Naval Live Oak trees, vast expanses of sugar white sand, and plenty of scenic blue water overlooks, however, in the darkness of night, it was just another four-lane highway.

The sodium lights of the parking lot gave off a disconcerting yellow-orange light which barely penetrated the salt mist hanging in the lot. There wasn't the slightest bit of wind, and sea fog was beginning to move in from offshore. Flint parked his police truck near the front of the one-story brick building and went in to find Corporal Haynes. She wasn't hard to find.

Standing at the front desk talking to a building employee, she looked up at him when he walked in the front door. She was almost as tall as Flint, at the most an inch shorter. Flint smiled and stuck out his hand.

"I'm Officer Flint Westbrook with the National Park Service. You must be Corporal Haynes."

She shook his hand. "I am, and I'm sure glad to see you. Thank you for coming."

"Absolutely. Tell me what's going on."

"This is what we know so far," the corporal said, pointing to the report she'd been filling out on the desk. "At about five forty-five this evening, building staff noticed that Mr. Rex Henshaw, a resident of the facility, wasn't in his room. He's an eighty-two-year-old male with moderate to severe dementia. Staff conducted a building and grounds search, but were unable to locate him."

"Any chance the family came by and picked him up?" Flint asked.

"Doubtful. Management contacted us when they reviewed their video," she said, pointing up to a camera on the wall. "It looks like Mr. Henshaw followed a staff member out the back door of one of the hallways when she was dumping the trash. She had no idea he was behind her."

"What's behind the building?" Flint asked.

"A small paved area for maintenance access and after that, unfortunately, lots of woods and swamp."

"Okay, let me get my gear and my dog, then, if you would show me to his room, we'll get started."

When Flint reentered the building with Apache, Corporal Haynes escorted them to Mr. Henshaw's room. Flint let Apache walk through the entire room, memorizing the man's scent. She took a particular interest in the man's bedsheets. There would be millions of the man's dead skin cells on them.

"All right, I think we're ready. Take us to the door he exited out of," Flint asked the corporal.

Apache kept her nose to the floor as they left the room and walked down the long hallway to an exit door.

It was still locked, so Flint and Apache waited while Corporal

Haynes tried to find someone with the keys. Apache was eager to get started, whining and pawing at the door while they waited.

Corporal Haynes returned with an employee who opened the door.

"Do you want me to go with you?" she asked Flint.

"No, I'm good. The number you called me from earlier, is that for your cellphone?"

"Yes."

"I'll call you if I find anything."

"Good luck," she said, shutting the door behind them.

Mr. Henshaw had a four-hour head start, but Flint was hoping that because of the man's advanced age, he might be moving a little slower. Hopefully, if he got confused, he would sit down and rest. There was no telling what the man was thinking. He could be thinking he was just out for an evening stroll, or he could simply be trying to find someone he recognized.

Flint followed Apache past the utility drive to the edge of the woods. He swapped her short lead for the long one, switched on his flashlight, and gave the command.

"Search, girl! Let's go!"

Apache shot off into the woods with Flint close behind. The understory beneath the oaks was thick with chokeberry and waist high sawgrass making movement difficult at first. Soon, however, Apache found a narrow trail which made travel much easier except for one major obstacle; spiderwebs.

Hundreds of huge Banana Spiders had made their webs just about face high across the trail. Flint hated spiders. He knew this particular type of spider was harmless, but the thought of doing a face plant into one of them was terrifying. *Dammit!*

The reflection of his flashlight from the large glistening dew drops clinging to the webs made them look twice as big as they actually were. Apache had no issues with them as she was traveling well below them, but he wasn't as lucky. He had no choice but to duck under each of them. It was exhausting.

After several long minutes of making slow but steady progress, Apache led them to a small crescent-shaped pond filled with dark brown water. Flint couldn't tell if it was a brackish water pond that periodically appeared with a high tide or a natural fresh water pond more typically found behind sand dunes in coastal areas. Regardless of its origin, there were possibly fish in it because several trails coming from different directions all led to it. Flint knew the trails were most likely created by people who would come back here to fish.

Apache sniffed around the edge of the dirty water before leading Flint down another trail that terminated at the pond but originated from another location. They hadn't traveled many yards before Flint told Apache to hold up. The spider webs had become intolerable. They were everywhere now, in every direction, up high, down low. Everywhere Flint looked, there was a huge, dew-dripping orb with an enormous spider in the center. It was creepy. Even Apache was distracted, constantly stopping to find a way around them.

Apache suddenly shifted from ground tracking to air scenting, a sure sign to Flint that she had lost the track. He was actually happy about it because backtracking to reacquire the scent meant getting away from this infestation of spiders.

"Let's go back this way, girl," Flint said, tugging on Apache's lead. She turned around with her nose still in the air.

Walking back the way they came, Apache began alternating between the ground and the air. Because the air was dead calm and laden with moisture, it wouldn't be easy for her to find Mr. Henshaw's unique smell by air scenting. There was a slim chance of any breeze blowing the scent particles across her nose. The best thing would be for her to find the ground track again, but she was, after all, primarily an air scenting dog. She would naturally do what she knew best.

Returning to the pond's edge, Apache seemed confused. It was obvious she smelled something, but was having a hard time telling from what direction it was coming from. If Mr. Henshaw had taken one of the other trails out of the area or doubled back on the trail they had initially searched, the lack of air movement would make it difficult for her to figure out which direction he took. Flint decided to let her off the lead so she could roam until she got a better sense of which direction he took.

She bolted out of sight, though Flint could hear her scrambling through the brush. After several moments she returned to the pond, sniffed around, and darted off again in another direction. Several times she would disappear, seemingly on scent, only to come back with her nose in the air. She was trying hard to define the scent cone. She was trained to follow the smell one direction until the scent concentration became stronger or weaker, then reverse direction until she could pinpoint the source.

It appeared to Flint as if she couldn't tell which direction led to the stronger concentration. It was as if the smell was everywhere. There was no doubt she was smelling something, but with no air movement to move the scent particles, they were just hanging there. She couldn't determine their origin. This was a big problem.

Flint decided to take the trail back to the retirement village and head east to see if he could find the origins of any of the other trails leading to the pond. From there, Apache might pick up the ground scent at the location from where Mr. Henshaw exited the woods.

He shined his flashlight around to get his bearings. The reflections from hundreds of spider webs made him shiver. *How was there even enough food for these damn things?* He could see the webs on the way back had been pretty much cleared out except for those he'd had to duck under.

"Oh crap!" he suddenly shouted to the trees. He reached for his cellphone and called Corporal Haynes.

"Corporal Haynes," she answered.

"Corporal Haynes this is Flint Westbrook. Tell me, how tall is Mr. Henshaw?"

"Hang on," she answered. He could hear her talking to one of the staff members.

"Staff here thinks he's about five-five or five-six. Why? Did you find him?"

"No, not yet. I'm still looking. I'll call you back in a few minutes," he said, hanging up the phone.

"Apache! Come!" he shouted. She was by his side in seconds. He clipped her back to the long lead and led her back to the original trail where it intersected with the pond, then backtracked about fifty yards toward the building. Unhooking Apache again, he shouted, "Seek!"

Apache put her nose to the ground and began walking toward the pond. When she reached the pond, she paused and immediately started air scenting again.

"Good girl!" Flint shouted, reaching down to pet her. "I'm so stupid!"

He reached for the phone again.

"Corporal Haynes," he said, not giving her a chance to speak. "I think we're going to need a dive team."

Flint cracked an egg and dropped it onto the hot skillet. He shouted to Samantha, who was busy brushing Apache in the living room, "How many eggs do you want, sweetheart? One or two?"

"Just one, Pop, but I want three pieces of bacon!"

"You got it!" he answered. *The girl loves her bacon,* he thought, smiling.

"What did you guys get into last night? Apache is filthy!" she shouted back to Flint.

"Just a minute, honey, I can't hear you very well." Flint cracked the last egg, wiped his hands on a kitchen towel, and turned down the heat. Walking into the living room, he asked her to repeat herself.

"What did you and Apache do last night after your date? She has all kinds of twigs and dried mud in her hair."

"I told you, I got called out on a search and rescue."

"I know, but what happened? She's really dirty."

"Well, it was swampy where we were, and there were lots of spiders, too. You don't see any of those on her, do you?"

Sam gave Flint an evil look while hugging Apache. "Poor baby. Daddy doesn't take care of you, does he?"

Flint smiled and went back into the kitchen.

"Did you find whoever you were looking for?" she yelled.

"Yes, we found him." He didn't know what else to say to her about it. There was no sense in starting her day off with bad news. His cellphone rang at the perfect time. The caller ID told him it was Corporal Haynes.

"Hello, Corporal Haynes."

"Good morning, Flint. How are you this morning?"

"I'm good. Did you find him?" he asked walking to the far end of the kitchen so Sam wouldn't overhear.

"Yes. They recovered his body about an hour ago right where you said it would be."

"I feel bad for his family, but I'm glad they found him. I'm sorry it came to that."

"Yes, me, too. I have a question for you, though."

"Okay."

"You told me last night that your search dog had a lot of trouble because of the weather conditions. How did you figure out that Mr. Henshaw was in the pond?"

"It was the spider webs. When we took the trail to the pond, I didn't notice at the time, but most of the webs on the trail were located face high or higher, at least for me. Once we left the original trail and explored the area around the pond, I noticed that the webs were all over the place. Some were just off the ground, some waist high, and of course there were some up around my face. I finally realized that someone of shorter stature had already been down the trail. Mr. Henshaw couldn't have gone anywhere else without disturbing the spider webs located closer to the ground. When you told me how tall Mr. Henshaw was, it all made sense. There was nowhere else he could have gone but into the pond."

"Interesting. So you found Mr. Henshaw before your dog did?"

"Not exactly," Flint said. "My dog correctly led us down the trail that Mr. Henshaw had taken. Once she lost the scent on the ground and resorted to air scenting, I thought we'd lost him. We explored another trail, but I was so distracted by the webs that I didn't pay enough attention to what she was trying to tell me. I brought her back to the pond, but the air was so still she couldn't figure out where the scent was coming from. The problem was, she was smelling the scent particles rising out of the water. The stagnant water diffused the scent enough that it confused her. To her, he was everywhere. If I had read her correctly the first time, we would have figured it out sooner. It was my fault, not hers."

"Interesting. Well, however it happened, you and your K9 found him and I appreciate your help. I know his family would like to express their appreciation, too, but they're pretty broken up about it right now," she said.

"I'm sure they are. It's an awful thing to lose someone so suddenly."

"Let me ask you, Flint, can we call on you again if we need similar help in the future?" she asked.

"Sure, I'd be glad to help. Especially if it gets me out of the office now and then."

"Great! I'll keep your number in my contact list. Have a good weekend, and thanks again for your help."

"You're welcome." He hung up the phone and went back to cooking breakfast.

Sam and Flint spent the rest of their Saturday morning combing the beach for shells. They didn't have a whole lot of luck, though they did find lots of broccoli, lettuce, and onions on the beach. Flint supposed they were dumped from a passing cruise ship or maybe from the kitchen of one of the off-shore Alabama oil rigs. In any case, it made for a lot of laughs as they spent a good deal of time throwing soggy vegetables at one another.

That evening, Sam decided she wanted to go fishing, so they loaded the cooler and walked down to the pier with Apache following closely. Flint brought his folding chair and laptop with him to pass the time. Once they got Sam's pole baited and in the water, Flint sat back, opened his computer, and began searching for information about training dogs to search for objects in water. He was unhappy how the search had gone last night and didn't know if it was a lack of training for Apache or a lack of training for himself. He'd never done a water search before, and he wanted to learn more about it if he was going to continue doing them.

He was surprised to find out there was little online information about the technique. During his time with Coffy, she had told him there was nothing with human scent on it that a dog couldn't find, but she had never specifically mentioned if Apache had been trained to search water for human odor. If he could only call her to ask, but that wouldn't be possible. He was sure she had moved on to other projects by now and had put him far behind her. It would be up to him to train Apache and himself.

CHAPTER NINE

It was a beautiful late September day, and Flint was enjoying the drive along the park road with the windows down and the air-conditioner off for a change. Sam was busy telling him about her day at school and how well she did at soccer practice. She was a natural. Flint decided long ago that he would convince her to try out for the boy's football team when she got to high school.

The rush of the summer season had slowed considerably, and Flint was enjoying spending more time with his daughter. She made him laugh like no one else could. This year's tourist season kept him busy, and it was rare when he didn't get a call in the middle of the night to handle a loud drunk in the campground. Sleepless nights and the demands of the park visitors kept him exhausted. He lived for the off-season.

They pulled into the driveway and made their way into the house.

"What time is Christine coming over?" Sam asked.

"Sometime around seven." Flint invited Christine over at Sam's insistence. He wasn't sure if it was because Sam liked her so much or if she was just trying to find someone for her father. Probably a bit of both.

They had been going out on occasion, nothing serious, but he had to admit, even after their disastrous first date, it was better than sitting at home every night. Once he convinced her to put down that damn phone and be present in the moment, she had turned out to be a nice person. In turn, he learned to dial down his expectations and be more patient. She was, after all, quite a bit younger with a different frame of reference. He didn't hold much hope for a long-term relationship, but it was at least comfortable for the moment.

Flint went to the bedroom and changed out of his uniform. Afterwards, he went to the back yard, loaded the grill with charcoal, lit it, and went inside to get a beer.

Sam was flipping through the channels as he entered the living room and sat beside her. He was reading through the email on his phone when she flipped through a news channel and he heard the reporter say "one hundred and twenty-seven were aboard when--" before Sam went to the next channel.

"Whoa, whoa, honey, back it up. I want to hear what that lady was talking about."

Sam flipped back to the news.

"Twenty-seven of those aboard were from an elementary school in Houston on a field trip to Washington D.C. So far, rescuers have been unable to get into the area where the plane went down. Let's go live to Jason Edwards in Baton Rouge, Louisiana where the rescue efforts are being coordinated. Jason, what can you tell us so far?"

A young man obviously recently graduated from college took over. "Right now, Colleen, not much. All officials can confirm at the moment is that the plane went down into the Atchafalaya Swamp some thirty-five miles west of Baton Rouge at three-fifteen this afternoon. Officials are trying desperately to get to the site, but reports are coming back that wreckage is strewn out for miles across one of the toughest landscapes in the US. The swamp is proving difficult to navigate, and there aren't enough rescue vehicles that can get out to the crash site. Private air boats are being commandeered, and officials are requesting help from anyone with a boat. They're hoping that if anyone was able to survive the crash, they could find them before nightfall."

The news-lady interrupted him, "Jason, is there any word yet on what caused the crash?"

"No, not yet, Colleen. All officials know is that there were one hundred and twenty-seven people on board and there was no communication from the aircraft beforehand that indicated that they were in any sort of trouble."

The conversation continued back and forth between the two newscasters until they had repeated the same conversation several times.

"Sam, you can turn it to whatever you want to watch. I have to put the burgers on."

"Pop?"

"Yeah, baby?"

"Promise me you won't ever fly again."

Flint was touched. "I can't promise that, but how about I pack a parachute next time?"

"Deal," she answered.

The evening with Christine was pleasant enough. She and Sam connected, which made Flint happy. They spent the evening watching a movie and playing a dice game called Farkle which Flint could never get the hang of. The girls beat him mercilessly. Christine left around eleven, and soon after, Flint and Sam went to bed. He was beat and looking forward to sleeping late in the morning.

That rare luxury flew out the window around one-thirty in the morning when Flint's cellphone woke him from a deep sleep.

"Hello?" He could barely get the word out.

"Hello. Is this Officer Sterling?" said a male voice on the other end.

Flint knew the routine. Someone was being a knucklehead in one of the campgrounds, and he was going to have to take care of it.

"Yes, it is. What's the problem?"

"Officer Westbrook, my name is Jeff Landry. I work for the Louisiana Governor's Office of Emergency Preparedness. I'm sorry for the late hour, but can you talk for a minute?"

"Yeah," Flint said, still groggy. In his half-asleep state, he thought a camper from Louisiana was calling to bitch about something in the park.

"Sir, have you heard about the plane crash west of Baton Rouge earlier this afternoon?"

Flint struggled to sit up. This sounded more serious than dealing with a drunk. "Yes. I saw it on the news tonight. It's awful."

"Yes, sir, it sure is. What you're not hearing on television because it's being withheld from the news outlets is there's a good chance that it's terrorist-related. We're basing this assumption on the fact that at this point, it looks as if the plane broke up in midair. Unfortunately, there are bodies and pieces of wreckage scattered for several miles across the swamp. The plane didn't go straight in." The man paused either for dramatic effect or to let the news sink in. "We're hoping to utilize the services of you and your K-9 to help us search for, well, bodies. Would that be possible?"

"Certainly it's possible, but I need to tell you, I'm not sure how effective my dog and I will be for a water search. I haven't had good luck with that lately."

"Well, I can tell you that you and your dog come highly recommended," the man countered.

"Really? From who?"

"I'm not sure about that, sir, but someone high on the food chain said to get you here as soon as possible."

Flint surmised someone in Louisiana probably heard about his search for Abigail Day last year. It was the only thing he had ever done that was in the news.

"I'd be glad to help. What do I need to do?"

"How soon can you be ready to go?" Mr. Landry asked.

"I need to find someone to take care of my daughter, and that might be difficult at this hour of the morning. If I pack now, drop my daughter off at my friend's house in the morning, I could be ready to leave around seven-thirty or eight. It would take about six or seven hours to drive there, depending on where you need me to go."

"I have another option. I'm going to text you a phone number. When you get your daughter taken care of, call it. You'll be given instructions on where to go to meet a Navy transport aircraft at the Pensacola Naval Air Station. We'll fly you into Baton Rouge, then transport you to the crash site. Will that work?"

"Sure," Flint said, surprised at the urgent offer. "I'll start getting ready."

"Thank you, Officer Westbrook. We truly appreciate your help."

Flint made a strong pot of coffee and packed for the trip. He had no idea what to wear for work in a swamp. He threw in a pair of shorts, but knowing there would be mosquitoes, threw in his work pants as well. National Park Service regulations required him to be in uniform while working and traveling, but his Class A uniform wasn't practical for a swamp environment. He took the pants back out and replaced them with his tactical uniform instead. He had forgotten to ask how long he would be gone.

Flint sat on the side of his bed, sipped his coffee, and thought about what else he needed. Apache had been asleep in Sam's room, but the activity made her curious. She wandered into Flint's bedroom and sat down as if to ask what was going on.

"Come here, girl," Flint said, reaching out to rub her head. "We've got a hell of a job ahead of us, Apache. Are you up to it?" Flint knew he should be asking himself that question. Performance anxiety began to creep into his mind as he wondered whether either of them was up to the task. He didn't feel good about how they had worked together looking for the old man in Ft. Walton this summer. They accomplished what they were asked to, but the way they accomplished it was pure luck. He had difficulty reading Apache around water, and with his lack of experience with water search and rescues, it was definitely something that needed improvement.

Flint waited until about six to call Troy to ask if they could take care of Sam. Surprisingly for a Saturday morning, he and Liz were already awake getting ready to walk their dogs. They accepted, of course, the way they always did. Flint made a mental note to get something nice for Liz while he was in Louisiana.

He woke Sam around six-thirty. While she was getting ready, he busied himself with feeding Apache. He loaded his work truck with his duffel bag, rescue kit, and Apache's equipment.

Sam slept all the way to Troy's house, so the ride over was quiet. By the time Flint finished apologizing to the Burnsides for the last minute notice, it was seven-thirty as he got back into the truck and headed to Pensacola Naval Air Station.

Flint waited until he was across the causeway into Pensacola before pulling over into a parking lot and using his cellphone to dial the number he was instructed to call. The young woman who answered gave him directions from the station's front gate to the terminal building where his plane would be waiting. She would notify the pilot that he was on his way.

It took Flint another thirty-five minutes to drive through South Pensacola and make it to the front gates of the naval station. The young Marine at the front gate called the air terminal office to tell them Flint had arrived and sent him through. Arriving at the terminal, Flint parked his truck, hooked Apache up to the short lead, gathered his gear, and went inside.

He was surprised to see the small military terminal lobby looked much like any civilian terminal he'd ever seen, marble floors, vinyl upholstered seats with padded metal arms, and a tiny little ticket counter. He walked up and told the man behind the counter who he was.

"Yes, sir, Mr. Westbrook. We've been expecting you. Sir, we have coffee in the corner over there. If you would just make yourself at home, I'll notify the pilot that you're here, and he'll be here shortly to escort you to the plane."

"Thank you." He put his luggage on one of the lobby chairs, hooked Apache to another, and made his way to the coffee.

In a few short minutes, a sharp looking young man in a tan flight suit came through the door leading to the tarmac.

"You must be Flint Westbrook," the pilot said, reaching out his hand. Flint stood and shook it.

"I am."

"Sir, I'm Lieutenant Johnson, and I'm going to be flying you to Baton Rouge. Are you ready to go?"

"Yes, sir," Flint replied.

The pilot helped him with his luggage and led him out to the plane. Flint didn't know what type of plane it was, but he could tell it was a twin-engine turboprop, and it looked like it could hold ten or twelve people. *Man, this is big league now. I better not screw this up,* he thought.

The ride to Baton Rouge was comfortable. Flint tried to sleep, but couldn't force himself to do it. Apache had no trouble with it, though. She acted like this kind of stuff happened all the time. Arriving at the Baton Rouge Airport, they were met by a Louisiana State Trooper dressed in a flight suit. He escorted Flint and Apache across the tarmac and through a hangar to a helicopter emblazoned with the Louisiana State Highway Patrol logo on the side.

Flint and Apache loaded up in the back of the helicopter and took off for the short fifteen-minute trip to the staging area at Whiskey Bay in the Atchafalaya Swamp. Flint was already exhausted.

The helicopter circled the landing area before coming in from the northeast, an approach that would keep it away from the majority of the people milling about below them. Flint knew at first sight where he was. He and Sam had been at this exact spot several times on their trips back and forth to Texas to visit family. They were about to land at the Atchafalaya Welcome Center, a large, conveniently placed rest stop for travelers along the eighteen mile I-10 Atchafalaya Basin Bridge that ran through the heart of the Atchafalaya Swamp. Judging by the number of rescue vehicles, trailers, and boats below, it was serving as central command for the search and rescue.

As the helicopter settled, the pilot told Flint to report to the central command area inside the visitor's center. He would be glad to escort Flint if he wouldn't mind hanging on a minute until he got the aircraft shut down.

"Don't worry about that. I know where it is. Thanks!"

"Good luck, sir," the pilot replied.

Flint and Apache disembarked, gathered their equipment, and made their way to the visitor's center. Walking through the concrete parking area, Flint saw emergency vehicles with logos from every agency imaginable. There were vehicles from local EMS, FAA, Louisiana State Police, Federal Transportation and Safety Administration, even the FBI. As he approached the building, he passed several federal haz mat personnel exiting the front doors, which confirmed his feeling that this wasn't going to be the standard search and rescue. He felt the adrenaline begin to pump through his veins.

He entered the building and was immediately stopped by a police officer just inside the front door, who directed him to the back of the main lobby to a table with a hand-drawn white placard labeled Search and Rescue Check-In. Two men in military garb seated behind a white plastic table stood when they saw Flint and Apache approach.

"Hello. I'm Officer Flint Westbrook with the National Park Service," Flint said, sticking his hand out. "And this is Apache."

"Hello, Officer Westbrook. We were just informed you had arrived. Thank you for your assistance," one of the men said, shaking Flint's hand. "I'm Corporal James Gebhardt with the National Guard, and this is Corporal Dave Moreland. We're going to get you checked in."

Flint stood at the table while Corporal Gebhardt began putting papers together. Corporal Moreland picked up the phone. "This is Corporal Moreland at the check-in desk. Officer Westbrook has arrived." Flint assumed the corporal was arranging his transportation to the crash scene.

The paperwork seemed like the standard waivers and emergency information. Basically, if Flint was killed on the job, he would receive little more than a 'thank you for his service' call to his family. Flint filled it out and handed it back to Corporal Gebhardt.

Apache stood and tugged hard on her lead. Flint could tell she was ready to get to work.

"Apache, sit!" he said in a firm voice. She sat, but kept her attention on the front doors. A few seconds later she rose and tried to pull away again.

"Apache, what is wrong with you?" he said, wondering why she was acting this way.

"There's nothing wrong with her. She just misses her mama," a familiar voice from behind said.

Flint turned around and was speechless. Coffy Summerfield stood there smiling at the both of them.

She looked fantastic. Wearing jeans, a black, long sleeve tee shirt, and a black baseball cap with Colorado Search and Rescue embroidered across the front. She looked as beautiful as the first day he saw her in Colorado. Her jet black hair was almost shoulder-length now. The last time he'd seen her, she was in a hospital bed with second and third degree burns, her hair singed off, and she was mad as hell at him. He could see time had healed her physical wounds, but he wasn't sure about the emotional ones.

He instinctively reached out to hug her. She hugged him back. "My God," he whispered into her ear, "I had no idea you were going to be here. It's so good to see you."

"It's good to see you, too, Flint." She looked at Apache and went down to one knee. "And how are you, young lady? Oh, how I've missed you." Apache wiggled her way into Coffy's arms and sat reaching up to lick her chin. It was obvious Flint wasn't the only one who had missed Coffy.

"Have you eaten?" Coffy asked, looking up at Flint.

"No, not yet. Things happened kind of fast overnight."

"Come on. I'll show you where the mess tent is."

Coffy led Flint and Apache outside to a tent near the back of the main building. They were between breakfast and lunch, but Coffy was able to muster up a couple of sandwiches. They sat together at one of the tables under the tent so Flint could eat. He gave one of his sandwiches to Apache.

"When did you get here?" Flint asked.

"About five this morning," she told him.

"How in the world did you get here so fast? I only live three hundred miles away, and you still got here hours before I did."

"I got the call pretty soon after the crash. My organization has a contract with FEMA, so we get called quickly on the big stuff."

"Really. With FEMA, huh?"

"Yep. Considering that everyone in Louisiana was angry with FEMA after Hurricane Katrina, they broke records responding to the governor's request for help with the crash. Tom McNeil picked Argo and me up in the helicopter and flew us to Peterson Air Force Base near Colorado Springs. We took an Air Force plane down to Baton Rouge, then flew in on the same helicopter that brought you over."

"Wow. You must be tired."

"A little. Not as much as you probably. I was able to sleep some on the flight down."

"They waited a while before they called me. I got a late start."

"I know. I'm the one who requested you."

Flint looked at Coffy. She smiled at the surprised look on his face.

"Why would--"

She reached out and grabbed his hand from across the table. "I did it because I think you're one of the best dog handlers I've ever seen. You're a little hard on yourself, but that's what makes you good. You know you don't know it all and you want to learn. I knew you would be a tremendous asset to our search and rescue team."

Flint took a few seconds to absorb what she just said. "I appreciate that, Coffy. I really do, but I'm afraid my skills with water search and rescue are lacking."

"Why would you say that?" she asked, still holding his hand.

"First of all, I don't know if Apache has any experience with water searches. We never discussed that when I was in Colorado. And second, we did a water search earlier in the summer, and while we found the man's body, it was pure accident."

Coffy let go of Flint's hand. "I doubt if what you did this summer was an accident. You'll need to fill me in on the details, but I bet that whether you know it or not, you and Apache worked as a team to find what you were looking for. You should also know that Apache is one of the best water search and rescue dogs I've ever trained. We didn't have time to practice it in Colorado because of the fire, but she is."

"If that's the case, then I'm afraid I'm woefully inadequate to be her handler."

"That's garbage, Flint. You just haven't had the opportunity yet. I tell you what, you and I will partner up today and use this operation as a training opportunity. I'll prove to you that you have what it takes to use Apache to the best of her ability. Do you trust me?"

"Of course I do. I just--"

"Nope, you 'just' nothing. We need to be at the eleven-thirty briefing at the command tent, and I still need to get Argo. Come with me."

Flint followed Coffy to a blue tarp-covered shade shelter containing individual dog pens lined with hay. It looked like a comfortable space for the search and rescue dogs when they were off duty. Coffy walked up to one of the pens and opened the gate. Argo came out and immediately ran to Apache. Both owners smiled at the reunion. Flint unleashed Apache, and the dog party got underway. The humans were filled with joy as the dogs rolled together on the ground in complete and utter happiness at seeing one another again.

Flint noticed the lack of other dogs under the tent. "Where are the other dogs?"

"There are a couple of teams out on the water now. I have two other team members flying in tonight. Other than those on the water, you and I are it."

The K-9 homecoming put both dogs and owners in a good mood as they walked together to the command tent. Flint couldn't get over how good Coffy looked. He began remembering old feelings which led to a few pangs of sadness as he looked at her. He was glad she was here. He was also heartbroken she was here.

"Hello, folks," the man in military fatigues said to the dozen or so people assembled at the command tent. "My name is Major Vincent Cooper with the National Guard 256th Infantry Brigade Combat Team based in Lafayette, Louisiana. I'm in charge of operations until the FBI can get their shit together." Everyone laughed.

"I'd like to thank each of you for being here. Welcome to our eleven-thirty briefing. This is what we know so far. Yesterday at fifteen-thirteen hours, flight controllers lost contact with Flight 254, a Commercial Airlines 737 with one-hundred and twenty-seven people on board flying out of Houston. The flight never made it to its destination of Atlanta, Georgia. Reports came into the Lafayette Police Department of debris falling out of the sky east of town. Radar tracks confirm a debris field of approximately three-miles in length going north-northeast over the Atchafalaya Swamp approximately two-miles north of our present location. First responders have reported bodies and wreckage strewn out across inhospitable terrain inside the interior of the swamp."

The major reached back and brought forward a map on a tripod so all could see. "The area outlined here in red is our best approximation of where the debris field lies. Now the following information I'm about to give you is confidential, so do not share it with anyone. Especially the press. The plane appears to have broken apart in midair, which is the only explanation for the large linear debris field. The plane did not just fall out of the sky. It exploded. Other than a major fuel problem, we are not aware of anything else that could have caused this other than a terrorism-related event."

Flint saw several people in the crowd shaking their heads. Someone behind him muttered, "Bastards."

Major Cooper continued, "Those of you in a search and rescue role will be looking for bodies. I hate to say it, but you probably won't find anyone alive. It just doesn't seem likely given our present scenario. Your job over the next several days is to mark the location you find bodies and parts of bodies and to inform the haz mat teams of their locations. Keep in mind, if you find any wreckage from the plane, mark its location as well. We need to find every bit of evidence we can to determine exactly what happened here. Understood?"

Several people nodded.

"All right, search and rescue crews, head down to the boat launch. We have several airboats waiting to take you out to your assigned spots to meet with your area coordinators. Your coordinator will give you further information. The rest of you stay here with me for further instructions."

"Do you know the way to the boat launch?" Flint asked Coffy.

"I do. Let's stop at the visitor center, though. I would imagine it will be a while until we see another restroom."

"Good idea. I'm following you."

Coffy rejoined Flint behind the building, and together they made their way to the boat ramp. At least four airboats with pilots sat waiting for their passengers. Not knowing which to board, Flint asked one of the pilots. The pilot pulled a notepad out of his vest pocket, flipped through a couple of pages, and pointed to an air boat marked Louisiana Game Warden. Flint was impressed with the organization of the rescue effort shown so far. Flint and Coffy introduced themselves to the game warden. "Are we in the right place?" The warden nodded.

The trip to the search area started out fast and loud. At full throttle, the propeller on the back of the air boat created so much noise that talking was impossible. The pilot had given ear muffs to Flint and Coffy and soft foam ear plugs for the dogs which muted the roar to a more tolerable level.

The water channel they traveled along was narrow and deep, evidently built for barge traffic coming from the oil fields located farther north. Bald cypress draped in Spanish moss towered over the murky green waterway on both sides. The hardwood forest canopy allowed little sunlight to reach the bottom, giving the appearance of a dark and mysterious world beyond the banks of the channel. It was creepy and fascinating at the same time.

About two miles upstream, the game warden throttled down the propeller, and the airboat came to a slow crawl. The acrid smell of jet fuel hit them suddenly, overpowering the musty odor of swamp decay they had gotten used to. The warden tapped both of them on the shoulders.

"You can take the ear muffs off now," he shouted, removing his first. The whump, whump, whump of the helicopters circling above wasn't as loud as the propeller on the back of the airboat, but it still made it difficult to hear. "We're beginning to enter the debris zone now. I'm going to take us over to the search supervisor," the warden said, pointing upstream to an old, weatherbeaten houseboat that had seen much better days as someone's floating fishing cabin.

Two large rubber Zodiac boats tied up alongside the cabin forced the warden to negotiate the air boat to an open spot on the backside. Two men came from the front to help the warden tie off.

"Hello, Bob, this is Coffy Summerfield and Flint Westbrook from the Colorado Search and Rescue Association. Where do you want them?" the warden asked.

"We've been looking for you two," one of the men said. "If you would, please come on up. We're going to be using one of those," he said, pointing to the Zodiacs. "They're a little less noisy than what you've got there." Both of the men helped Coffy up onto the deck. Flint handed the dogs and the gear up to her, and then made his way up.

The tall, thin man who had done the talking so far offered his hand and introduced himself to Coffy. "I'm Captain Bob Spears. I'm with Lafayette Fire and Rescue and am acting as the Search Coordinator for the crash." He shook hands with Flint and Coffy and pointed to the man standing next to him. "This is Lieutenant Clay Cullum. He's also with Lafayette Fire and Rescue and will be working with you during your search."

"We're just about ready to go," Lieutenant Cullum said after shaking their hands. "Follow me and we'll get loaded up. I need to get a little more drinking water for us, then we can get underway."

After receiving an endless list of safety instructions and warnings from Captain Spears, the crew loaded up in the rubber rescue boat and took off for their assigned search area.

The Zodiac was just large enough for the three passengers and two dogs to spread out a bit, and the engine was much quieter than the air boat. It was much easier for the group to speak to one another.

The boat came to a stop in the middle of the waterway, which at this location was almost as wide as a football field.

"We're entering the southern edge of the search zone," Cullum said. "The red stakes you see in the water and on shore are where bodies have been found. The white stakes mark aircraft parts. We're primarily looking for bodies, but if we come across part of the aircraft, don't touch it. Just put one of these white stakes next to it," he said, pointing to the pile of plastic stakes stacked in the back of the boat. "Parts of bodies get a red stake just like a whole body. If you see something, or if your dog finds something, call out. We'll stake it, and I will mark it with my GPS. Any Questions?"

Flint and Coffy shook their heads.

"We'll start with the middle of the waterway and zigzag north to south while moving steadily to the west. The area to the north of us hasn't been searched," Cullum said as he added a small amount of throttle to the boat.

Coffy stood and walked Argo to the front of the boat. "Flint, I'm going to take the point so I can show you how these dogs locate scent under water. It's different than on a mountain somewhere. Swamps emit methane gas naturally, so combine that with jet fuel, and we really have some issues to work with. It's not impossible, though. These dogs had a good trainer." She looked back and smiled at him.

Coffy laid down over the bow, holding Argo by the collar. Argo's nose immediately went up into the air. She continued with the lesson. "Human scent particles, even after death, continue to shed from a victim's body. Just because the body is in water doesn't mean it stops emitting an odor."

"But it's the decomp, right? Aren't they smelling the decomposition gasses?" Flint asked.

"No, not necessarily. There's probably not a lot of decomp smell at this point since it's so soon after the crash. They should be able to pick up on any human odor just like the person is still alive."

Flint thought back to the search for the old man this past summer. Though the man was already dead when they were looking for him, his body hadn't had enough time to start decomposing. *Apache was searching for human scent and not decomp, so why wasn't she able to pinpoint the source of the smell?*

"How do the scent particles leave the water? I mean, I know decomp produces gasses that are water-soluble and can exit in water vapor, but how do skin cells make it into the air?" Flint asked.

"It depends on the air currents. While a gas will rise and mix with the air, scent particles have to be lifted from the water by air movement. We're lucky to have a bit of a breeze today."

So that was the problem! he thought. *The air was dead calm that night and heavy with fog. There wasn't a mechanism to lift the scent particles from the surface of the pond. That's why Apache couldn't pinpoint the source. There wasn't enough decomp to send gasses up through the water column. And what little she could smell near the water had no origination point to narrow down to. It made perfect sense now. Air movement was everything.*

"Lieutenant!" Coffy shouted. "Slow down and come about one-hundred and eighty degrees. I think we've found something."

Cullum turned the boat around and slowly began backtracking their route. Flint watched Argo as he began to get agitated. At one point, Argo actually bit at the water. "Stop!" Coffy shouted. "Mark this spot."

Cullum handed Coffy one of the red poles and went back to his seat to record the location. Coffy stuck the pole into the mud. It wasn't very deep, perhaps three feet at the most, but the swamp water was too dark and murky to make anything out. She gave it her best shot. A diver would have to confirm it.

"Your turn, Flint," Coffy said as she switched places with him. The boat turned around and continued on its original path. Flint laid across the bow of the Zodiac like Coffy had shown him, holding Apache's collar. After several minutes, Apache started to get excited, but just as Flint was convinced she was on scent, she calmed down. Flint looked at Coffy.

Coffy returned Flint's gaze. "She hit on something just then, but I think the boat carried us past it. Lieutenant, if you would turn us around like last time, let's see what she does."

The boat turned about and retraced its path. Apache soon acted uneasy again and pawed at the side of the boat.

"Stop!" Flint shouted. "Let's mark this spot."

Cullum handed him the marker and Flint placed it into the murky water. "That was a little easier than I expected," Flint said to Coffy.

"You just have to have the right conditions and trust your dog. You have a good one right there. Why don't you go ahead and try it again?"

Flint, Coffy, and Lieutenant Cullum continued searching throughout the day with little in the way of rest. It was exhausting, but by early evening they had marked thirty-seven locations the dogs had alerted to.

"We've done about half the grid so far," Cullum spoke up. "It's getting close to sundown, so we better start making our way back. This swamp is no place to be after dark."

Coffy spoke up. "Lieutenant, what about animal predation on the bodies during the night? Is there going to be a search crew out here tonight?"

"No, ma'am. It's too dangerous. Have you ever seen someone catch a gator with a chicken on a hook?"

"No," she answered.

"I have," Flint said. "They suspend a dead chicken on a hook several feet above the water. When the gator jumps out of the water to get the chicken, it gets hooked, and their own weight keeps them suspended on the line."

Lieutenant Cullum added, "A gator can jump four or five feet out of the water to get to that chicken. If I'm a gator, and the heavens had just opened up and rained food down upon me, I'd want to make the most of my day. I don't think I want to be here tonight when they get that all figured out."

"Good point," Coffy said.

The Zodiac turned and headed south through the middle of the channel. Looking out in front of them, the number of red stakes surrounding them was staggering. It was going to be awful for the divers tomorrow.

In front of them, slightly to the right, a big piece of the plane's tail section was sitting in shallow water. This particular piece of debris was outside their search grid, but Lieutenant Cullum steered the boat so they would pass close by it. There was a white stake visible, so someone had at least marked it.

As they approached, Cullum slowed the boat down so they could get a good look at the hulking wreckage. It was surreal. The tail's rudder rose eight or nine feet out of the water and leaned at a forty-five-degree angle. The right side aileron jutted out of the water ninety degrees to the rudder, forming a sort of giant 'V' reaching toward the sky. Flint took his eyes off the sight for just a moment to grab a water bottle out of the ice chest when he noticed Argo's posture tighten up. His nose hit the air, and his ears went up.

"Coffy!" Flint shouted.

Coffy turned to see Flint pointing at Argo, who was now on full alert. "Lieutenant, stop!"

Cullum put the boat in neutral as Coffy led Argo to the bow. They both laid down over the front of the boat and got as close to the water as they could. As they approached the tail section, Argo became more animated. When he finally bit at the water, Coffy shouted, "Stop right here!" She looked back at Cullum. "I see a white stake for the wreckage, but not a red one, and there's definitely someone down here. Let's mark it."

Cullum reached back, grabbed a red stake, and handed it forward to Flint, who passed it on to Coffy. Still lying over the bow, she reached out to push the stake into the muddy bottom below. Something hard prevented the stake from penetrating the mud. She tried moving it to another spot nearby, but to no avail. Using the end of the pole, she tried prying aside whatever piece of wreckage was blocking its insertion until, finally, she found a soft spot and plunged the stake into the ground. As she did, the body of a young child broke the surface of the murky water, just inches from her face, dead eyes open, staring into the very depths of Coffy's soul.

Coffy stood, looked down at her husband's body and screamed, "You evil, fucking bastard! What have you done?" The blood on her hands mixed with her tears as she tried to wipe away her blurred vision. It was no use. She was no longer in control of herself. She knelt down, putting her knees on his chest and began to slam her fists into his face once again. With every blow, she felt the heat of rage rising in her soul, making every blow stronger than the last until finally spent; she could go no further.

Stephen's face was unrecognizable now. If she had had a knife with her, she would have cut his heart out and stuffed it into his mouth. He had taken the one thing in this life she cherished more than life itself, her son.

Coffy struggled to her feet and stumbled to her son's body which still lay submerged in the shallow, clear water of the Animas River. Each step required exhausting effort as her mind fought against her every movement. She knelt next to him and caressed his face one last time. His lifeless, brown eyes were open, staring up at her. She collapsed prostrate into the river next to him and cried out, "Oh, Justin. What did he do to you? What did he do?"

She lay next to him crying, sobbing, and holding him for what seemed like an eternity. She prayed to God to let the cold water wash over her and take her life away. It was her fault Stephen had killed Justin, and she couldn't live with that.

Her body eventually grew numb, but she never lost consciousness. Kissing her son one last time, she let him go and dragged herself through the shallows to find swifter water near the middle of the river. Using everything her body had left to give, she rolled into the fast, deep current and let go as she whispered, "I'm sorry, Justin. Please forgive me."

CHAPTER TEN

Flint parked his rental car, walked through the hospital's front doors, and rode the elevator to the second floor. He'd been here the night before, but the nurses wouldn't let him in to see her. They had told him she was still too unstable, and unless he was family, he wouldn't be allowed to see her anyway. This time, though, he wasn't taking no for an answer.

Walking through another hospital had given him a strong feeling of déjà vu. The last time he visited Coffy in a hospital hadn't ended well. He hoped this time it might end differently.

Entering the psychiatric wing required him to push a buzzer at a locked door and wait for someone to answer. He identified himself as Coffy's brother and, to his surprise, was allowed in. The nurse informed him that Coffy was doing better, but she needed intensive follow-up care. She was scheduled to be transferred to a psychiatric facility in Baton Rouge the next day. There they would help her with determining a diagnoses and the medicines she would need.

Flint had little to no experience with mental illness and based on the information he had just been given, he half expected to see Coffy sitting in the corner of her room, nearly comatose. He was happy to find her resting comfortably in her bed watching the Showcase Showdown on *The Price Is Right.*

"Don't you know daytime television isn't good for your mind?" he said as he walked through the door and stood next to her bedside.

She looked up at him and smiled. "Doesn't matter anyway. Didn't you hear? I'm bat shit crazy already."

Flint leaned over and hugged her. "You're not crazy. Believe me, in my career as a cop, I've seen crazy, and crazy you're not." He pulled the only chair in the room closer to the bed and sat down.

"Well, that's as close as I ever want to come," she said.

"You seem a lot better. How are you feeling?"

"I'm all right. "Tell me what happened."

"Are you sure you want to hear that right now? The doctors might not--"

"Tell me Flint!"

"All right, do you remember anything that happened the day before yesterday? Do you remember the search in the swamp?"

"Yeah, most of it. I remember looking for plane crash victims. I remember you, the boat, the lieutenant. I remember doing something near the tail section of the plane, but everything just kind of dissolves at that point." She reached for the TV control and switched it off.

"Do you remember a child's body coming to the surface as you were placing a marker in the water?"

"No."

"Well, it happened. The marker must have dislodged a young boy's body that was hung up in the wreckage. It came to the surface right in front of you. When you saw it, you screamed and jumped into the water to grab him. You insisted we put him into the boat, then started yelling at us to help him."

"Oh." Coffy relaxed her head and let it sink back into her pillow.

Flint hesitated, not sure it would be good for her to hear any more.

"What else happened?" she prodded.

"Coffy, I'm not sure that this is--"

"What else happened, Flint?" she demanded.

"We tried to assure you there was nothing we could do for the boy, but you didn't want to hear it. You insisted we give him CPR. We didn't do it, of course. We thought maybe you had seen something we didn't, but Coffy, the boy had been dead for hours, and there was nothing we could do, but you kept insisting."

Flint stopped again, not sure what to do. Coffy was staring at the ceiling, which made him nervous.

"What else?" she said with little emotion.

"Well, I reached out to try to help you back into the boat. You uttered some not so kind words, took off your life jacket, and started swimming toward the middle of the swamp. Argo jumped in and followed you. I didn't know what to do, so I jumped in, too. By the time I caught up to you, you had given up and gone under. You just went totally limp. Like nothing was there. I found you right away, and we loaded you back into the boat and took you back to the staging area. We couldn't get you to respond to us, so one of the ambulance crews brought you here."

"So everyone at the base knew I had gone mental?"

"No, actually, Lieutenant Cullum and I are the only ones. Well, besides the ambulance crew. They were local, so no one else should know. I figured you wouldn't want too many people finding out, especially since you have a contract with FEMA."

She lifted her head and stared at him with a huge grin. "Flint, you really did that for me? You covered this up?"

"Well, as much as I could. I asked Cullum to keep it private. He said he had no reason to say anything. He hates the feds. Said he lived in New Orleans when Katrina hit."

"Oh my God. You really are one of the good guys, aren't you?"

He was relieved to hear her say that. "Heck yeah," he said with a smile. She seemed perfectly fine.

"I think I owe you an explanation," she said as she adjusted her bed so she could sit up straight.

"You don't owe me anything. I just want you to feel better."

"I already do," she said. "You being here for me now is the best medicine. I should have never told you to leave when you were in Colorado." Flint was surprised to hear that. "I need to tell you something that few people know about me." Flint suddenly got a nervous feeling in his gut.

There was a knock on the door and a nurse walked in. "Hello, Miss Coffy. My name is Janice, and I'm going to be your nurse for the evening shift. How are you feeling?"

"I'm good, thank you."

"Great," the nurse replied and began taking her vitals. The nurse was in no rush, which was driving Flint crazy. He began agonizing over what Coffy was about to tell him, hoping it wasn't a reason she couldn't be with him. He had great hopes for this relationship, mental breaks and all.

The nurse finally finished. "Is there anything I can get for you?"

"No, thank you." The nurse left the room.

"What were you going to tell me?" Flint suddenly felt bad for rushing her.

"Do you remember when we first met, I told you I had a husband and a son?"

"Yes."

"And do you remember I told you that they both disappeared, and I've never seen them since?"

"Yeah," Flint replied hesitantly.

"Well, I didn't tell you the truth."

Flint took a moment to steel himself for the bad news. He was positive she was about to tell him she had remarried and had a family in Silverton somewhere.

"My husband was an alcoholic. It wasn't too bad in the beginning, but over the years it got worse, a lot worse. He straightened up some when Justin was born, but only for a little while. One afternoon at the cabin, I'd finally had enough. Stephen had been drinking a lot when he yelled at Justin over something stupid. I told him I wanted a divorce. I didn't want my son growing up in that kind of an environment. Stephen didn't take it very well. He threatened to kill Justin and me and burn the cabin down to make it look like an accident."

"Oh, that's awful," Flint said, completely taken off guard.

"It was bad," she replied. "I was afraid he might really do something stupid like that, so I got some camping gear out of the closet, grabbed Justin, and left. The train had already run for the day, so I couldn't get to town for help. I thought about going over to Frisco's to stay the night, but I didn't want to take the chance that Stephen might come looking for us there, so I decided Justin and I would hide in the woods that night and catch the train in the morning."

"What the hell, Coffy!" Flint didn't know what else to say.

"Justin and I camped out by the river a mile or so from the cabin, pretty close to Frisco's place. My son thought it was a great adventure, and we actually had a pretty good time. We were both happy. For me, it was going to be the start of something new and exciting, away from the sadness that Stephen had been bringing into our lives. But Stephen couldn't let it be. He had to take that last hope of happiness away from us." Giant tears began rolling down her cheek crossing over a very sad smile.

Flint lowered his head.

"The next morning when I woke up, Stephen was sitting on a rock watching me sleep. He had this big, evil smile and a gun in his hand. He actually had the nerve to say good morning to me. I could tell he was still drunk, bad drunk. I sat up, told him he could do what he wanted with me, but please don't hurt Justin." Her voice broke. It took a minute or so for her to catch her breath. Flint rose from the chair and sat beside her on the bed. He stroked her silky black hair as he had done in Colorado.

"Stephen said, 'Guess you should have thought of that before you left,' and he aimed the gun toward the river. I looked to see what he was pointing at and it was Justin, face-down in the water. The man had drowned him in the middle of the night. Can you believe that? Stephen drowned his own son so he could punish me. What kind of a sick person does that?" She was sobbing heavily now. Flint reached out and hugged her tight.

"I don't know," was all he could say as she buried her face in his chest. He held her tightly as her body shook with each sob, warm tears soaking through his shirt. He could only imagine the emotional pain she must be living with knowing her husband killed her child.

After a long while, the sobbing began to slow, and she lay motionless in his arms. Eventually, she looked up at him, wiped her tears, smiled weakly, and continued. "I ran into the river to help Justin. He was face-down, and when I turned him over, I saw he was dead. His face was lifeless. I remember being so angry that everything began to turn black. I had tunnel vision. All I wanted to do was destroy the man who killed my son. I grabbed a rock and walked toward Stephen, who was standing on the bank. He aimed the gun at me, but I didn't care. Dying wasn't a problem. At that point, the only reason I had for living was to kill the man. I had enough anger that he could have shot me ten times, but I wasn't going down until I caved in his skull." Flint had little doubt that she could have done it.

"I kept walking toward him expecting him to shoot me any second, but he never did. The son-of-a-bitch never fired a shot at me. Instead, the big coward put the gun to his head and shot himself."

"Damn, Coffy!"

"It was his plan all along. He was going to kill himself and punish me by leaving me nothing but the memory of my son. On top of that, I was sleeping, dreaming about how good things were going to be without Stephen in our lives. Now, I have to live the rest of my life knowing my son was being murdered less than fifty feet away from me while I slept."

"Coffy, that's not your fault. Surely you don't--"

"Oh, it's my fault, every bit of it. If I hadn't argued with Stephen that day, my son would still be alive. If that's not good enough for you, then if I had stayed awake like I should have, Justin would still be here. Or if I had left Stephen sooner, or if I--"

"Coffy!" he interrupted. "You're not responsible for the actions of a sick man. The man was evil. I'm a cop and I've been around many bad people in my life. There's never any reason for what they do. When people do something terrible like that, they always blame their actions on others. They always leave someone behind who's left searching for answers. But in the end, it's just evil people doing evil things."

"Yes, he was evil, but I should have been there for my son. I'll always regret my weakness."

Flint smiled at her. There was no point arguing right now. This was an issue that was going to take lots of time to resolve, if it could be resolved. "I'm honored you chose to share that with me."

"I did it because I trust you. I felt like I was holding back from you and I didn't want anything like that to be between us. It's the reason I lost it out there. I guess when I saw the body of that young boy, it reminded me of Justin. In all my search and rescues, that's never happened before. My mind couldn't take a repeat of what happened to Justin, so it just shut down."

"I can see that. I knew you weren't crazy. Your mind just went into self-preservation mode for a while," Flint said.

"Yep. That's what I think, too."

"I have something delicate to ask you, and I don't want my question to make you angry. Think you can keep an open mind?"

"I hope so. What is it?"

"When we were in the hospital in Colorado, you got angry with me for asking if you had a reason to cause harm to yourself. Do you remember that?"

"I do, and I'm sorry for how I reacted. I've regretted asking you to leave every day since. Please understand, I was in a lot of pain, and I was afraid of you. I was getting close to you, and it was scaring me."

"Why was it scaring you?" he asked, suddenly sidetracked.

"I don't know," she said. "I guess I don't trust men. I haven't had good experiences with them. It seemed like Stephen and every man I've ever met was trying to take something from me that I just wasn't willing to give. You're the first man who has never asked me for anything, and I didn't trust that about you."

Flint just stared at her.

She smiled and said, "When you asked if I had a death wish, it pissed me off. Why can't a woman be strong and take chances without being labeled as suicidal or crazy? I didn't have a death wish. I just wanted to save that young boy on that mountain. Maybe I value life above all else, and if it takes my life to save another life, I'm okay with that. That's not a death wish. That's just a woman with courage and a healthy respect for life in general."

Flint was completely dumbfounded. She was absolutely right. How many times had he, as a cop, put his life on the line and been labeled courageous? Why was it when a woman did the same thing, it was a mother's instinct or hormonal? Why couldn't it just be courage?

"You're right, Coffy. I was wrong to ask that."

Coffy's eyes widened. "What did you say? Did I hear you say you were wrong?"

"Yep. I was wrong to assume that what you did was anything less than courageous. I can be a real jerk sometimes."

"Oh my God, Flint! Take me now!" They both laughed. He had never seen her so joyous as at this moment.

"We got sidetracked. What did you want to ask me?" Coffy asked.

Flint wanted to ask why she tried to drown herself in the middle of the swamp. Given the sudden uptick in her mood, he decided that could wait for another day. "I can't remember. It must not have been important."

The conversation soon turned to dogs and what Flint had been doing over the last couple of days. He told her he'd been taking care of Argo and had continued with the search operations in the swamp. He said he was proud of how he and Apache had performed the last couple of days and now he had the confidence they could conduct search and rescues on water with little difficulty. He told her he was tired and ready to go home now as the search and rescue had turned into a recovery effort, which it had really been all along.

He updated her on the search progress. Crews found the plane's black box yesterday, and all the search grids had been gone over twice. Divers were in the water gathering as much as they could. DNA evidence was going to be crucial in identifying the passengers and crew aboard the ill-fated trip and he and Coffy had done their part to make sure it was possible. Most of the K9 teams were going home tonight, but he wasn't quite sure what he was going to do. He wanted to make sure Coffy was going to be all right first.

"What are you going to do when you get out of the hospital?" he asked, not sure he wanted to hear the answer.

"I guess I'll go back to Colorado. I'm sure Frisco is probably tired of taking care of my dogs by now."

"The nurse said you were going to be transferred to Baton Rouge tomorrow for evaluation and follow-up."

"I heard that rumor, too. Tell me, do you think I'm crazy? Do you think I need to go?"

"Hell no, you're fine. It would be a waste of your time."

"I agree. That's why you're going to help me get out of here."

The escape from the hospital sounded a lot more audacious in their minds than it actually was. They spent at least an hour planning the details of their getaway, but that was half the adventure.

In the end, Flint casually walked to the electronic door, waited for the nurse to hit the button at her station, and held the door open for Coffy, who ran from her room, down the hallway, and through the door. They ran to the parking lot and jumped into the rental car. Flint caught a glimpse of the security guard exiting the building, but they were already on the street and headed to the highway.

The escapade had lifted Coffy's spirits as they traveled east on I-10 back toward the Command Center. Flint asked if she was hungry. "I am, but do you think we should? I wouldn't want to give anyone a chance to catch up to us."

Flint laughed out loud. "We're not exactly Bonnie and Clyde here. I'm pretty sure what we did wasn't illegal. At least I hope so," he said with a grin.

Coffy laughed, too. Flint was glad to see her smile. "Let's stop at this Cajun diner up the road. I saw it last night coming into town, and it looked kind of interesting."

"Fine by me. I've never had Cajun food, but I don't mind experimenting," Coffy replied. "Wait a minute, you came to see me last night?"

"Yeah, but they wouldn't let me in. I wasn't family."

"How did you get in today?" Coffy asked.

"Told 'em I was your brother."

Coffy laughed out loud again. "Guess you're lucky it wasn't the same nurse this time."

They pulled off the highway and found the restaurant Flint had seen the day before. He helped Coffy pick out something from the menu. They decided her first foray into Cajun food should be jambalaya. He chose the Boudin sausage. The conversation while waiting for their order to arrive was familiar and comfortable. It reminded Flint of their front porch conversations while he was in Colorado.

"How is Frisco doing?" Flint asked.

Coffy snorted. "That old man has been mad at the world lately. The tax assessor paid him a visit a couple of months ago. It seems the county never knew there was a flying saucer on his property, and now they're trying to collect on ten years of back taxes."

Flint cocked his head and squinted at Coffy. "Oh man, I bet he's livid."

"Yes, he is. He's threatened to have a helicopter pick up his house and drop it on the Tax Assessor's office. I told him to try and settle first. He has more money than he knows what to do with."

"Really. Frisco's rich?" Flint asked.

"I wouldn't say he's rich, but he is well off, though he would say otherwise. He was an investment banker in Albuquerque when his son was killed. He and his wife split, and he moved to Colorado."

"I would have never guessed."

Their food arrived, and Flint helped Coffy doctor the jambalaya with some Tabasco. Not enough to make it uncomfortable, but just the right amount to let her know it was there. To his surprise, she loved it.

"So you like spicy food?" he asked.

"I do. You know I've traveled around some in my line of work. I enjoy a little kick to my food."

"Oh yeah? What states have you been to?"

"Well, this is my first time in Louisiana, but I've been all over the northwest. Oregon, California, Utah, Wyoming. I've been down to Arizona, New Mexico, and Texas."

"Wow, you really have been--"

"Then there's Guatemala, Mexico, Portugal, Turkey, Japan." She smiled at the look on Flint's face.

"You've done search and rescue in all those places?" he asked, genuinely impressed.

"Yes, and probably half-a-dozen or so other countries."

"That's hardcore, Coffy."

"Did you think I was just a one-state operation?"

"Well, I mean, I figured you must be good if you got called to Louisiana, but--"

"My dogs and I go all over the world. Argo and I may get called out for a lost Boy Scout in Ft. Collins tomorrow or maybe my entire team could be called for a building collapse in Argentina next week. It just depends on who needs us when."

"That's amazing. I had no idea."

Flint took another couple of bites and thought about what she had just shared with him. This woman was incredible. He'd been thinking about her all day, all week. Hell, who was he kidding? He had been thinking about her since the day he met her in Colorado. He'd never *stopped* thinking about her. He dared himself to ask her, "Have you ever been to Florida?"

"No."

"Would you like to go tonight?"

Coffy woke up and caught Flint watching her sleep. It took her a moment to remember she wasn't in Colorado, smiling as she remembered last night's five-hour trip to his home in Florida. She agreed to go to Florida with him as a gift to herself. She was physically and mentally exhausted, and she knew she needed time to recuperate. What better way to recover than in the arms of the first man she'd trusted since the death of her husband? Not that she had ever trusted her husband that much.

"What are you doing?" she asked as her eyes finally focused on Flint's face.

"I'm observing what beauty looks like when it has stood firm against the ugliness the world has to offer."

She took a moment to think about what he just said to her. "I believe that's the kindest thing anyone has ever said to me," she said, smiling at him. "But that was before the fire on the mountain. I'm afraid my backside isn't as palatable as it once was."

"I would disagree! From what I saw last night, it looks pretty spectacular."

"Now you're just being polite. I know the scars are pretty bad."

"Coffy, to me, those scars are a just a reminder of how you were willing to give your life so another human being could live. There's nothing on this planet more beautiful than that."

Coffy rolled over into Flint's embrace and said not a word the entire time they made love.

Flint drove to Troy's house taking the long way so Coffy could enjoy the beach scenery. They were a little late picking up Sam, so he didn't want to go too far out of the way, just enough to give Coffy a taste of what a Florida beach was like.

"Why are some of the homes on stilts and others are not?" she asked.

"Well, the idea is that when a hurricane comes through, the tidal surge that comes with it will flow under the house and not through it."

"What about the wind?"

"The wind can do a lot of damage, but if the house is built sturdy enough, it can survive it. What a home can't survive is the scouring effect of the tidal surge. When that wall of water comes in, it takes the sand out from under a foundation and destroys the house. If the house is on stilts, it doesn't affect it as much."

"So these houses that are on the ground, what keeps them from washing away?"

"Pure luck," Flint replied.

Flint passed the turn to Troy and Liz's house and kept driving east on Via De Luna Drive out of town. He pulled into the East Beach parking lot and turned off the truck. This would be the perfect place to show Coffy the famous sugar white sands of Pensacola Beach.

They climbed the weatherbeaten, wooden stairs to the elevated boardwalk, crossed over the dunes, and stepped onto the beach. Coffy at last saw what Flint had talked about many times before. Pure white sand stretched from the dunes behind them to the clear, turquoise water of the Gulf of Mexico ahead. The dunes were six to ten feet tall and punctuated with brown sea oats that fluttered in the slightest breeze, not unlike the golden leaves of the aspen trees in Colorado. Flint smiled as he experienced Coffy's joy of seeing something wonderful for the first time. For him, just another day in paradise, except for the thrill of being able to share it with someone he cared about. Flint took her hand in his as they walked to the water's edge.

"What do you think?" he asked her.

"I don't know what to say. It's just, so different. So expansive. It's beautiful. It smells good, too! I can almost taste the salt in the air," she said, laughing and sticking her tongue into the air.

"Come on, let's find some shells," he said, leading her by the hand along the water's edge. "Most of the time, you'll only find small ones, but now and then you might come across a big one."

They had fun running back and forth in the sun, seeing what each other had discovered in the sand. Flint knew it was just what Coffy needed. She had been alone for so long. He wanted her to know the happiness that can be found in the company of another. Hopefully, a little laughter, and a lot of conversation, might show her a different path. One that allowed for living a life of love and hope for the future, rather than the path of self-destruction from living each day in the past. Ultimately, it would be her decision, but he was going to do his best to help her make it the right one.

Coffy admitted to Flint she was a little nervous as they pulled into Troy's driveway. She explained it had been a long time since she had interacted with a child she wasn't searching for and she didn't want to appear awkward. She took a couple of deep breaths to try and calm herself.

"Relax," Flint said. "Sam never met anyone she couldn't be friends with, but so you know up front, she likes to kid around. That's how you know she likes you." He placed his hand on her knee. "I'll be right back."

Liz opened the door, greeted Flint with her usual hug, and invited him in. Flint loved this woman with his heart and soul and was glad to see her. Anyone who could remain this kind after spending a lifetime with Troy had to be a saint.

"I'm so glad to see you, Flint. How was your trip?" she asked him.

"Interesting, to say the least. I learned a lot, but I'm glad it's over. The last couple of days were hard."

"We've been watching it on the news. It looks bad. It sounds like someone blew up the plane."

"It certainly seems to fit the profile. The debris was all over that swamp. I hope they figure out who did it."

"Me, too. Let me get the old man. He's out in the garage trying to show Sam how to use the radial arm saw. You know, I believe he thinks of Sam as the son he never had." Flint laughed and followed her through the kitchen and out to the garage.

"What the heck are you two doing?" she said, placing her hands on her hips. Flint looked up to see Samantha standing on a chair peering through the garage door windows out to the driveway. Troy was standing beside her doing the same.

"Nothing!" he replied, quickly grabbing Sam under her arms and lifting her down from the chair.

"What are you looking at?" she asked again.

Troy, looking as if he'd just been caught by surprise, confessed. "We were looking at the woman in Flint's truck."

"What?" Liz rushed to the windows to look for herself. "I'll be. There really is a woman out there." She turned to look at Flint. "Flint Westbrook, that's not Christine!"

Flint showed a huge grin. "No, it's not Christine. Her name is Coffy."

"Coffy?" Troy shouted. "Like in Coffy from Colorado?"

"Really, Troy? How many other people named Coffy have you ever heard of?" Flint said. Liz put her hands to her mouth and giggled. Sam just stood there wide-eyed.

"I don't believe it! What did you do, drive up to Colorado and snatch her?" Everyone laughed.

"Nope. We ran into one another while I was in Louisiana working the plane crash. She was called in by FEMA. She's the one who got them to fly me out there, though I didn't know it at the time."

Troy turned back to look through the garage windows again. He waved at Coffy. "She's beautiful, Flint! Bring her inside. We need to make sure she's real." Liz nodded in agreement.

"Not so fast, guys. I want to introduce you to her, but how about we have dinner later in the week. It's been a while since she's been around a group of people so I'd like to take it slow."

"Okay," Troy relented. "I understand. Liz is hard for people to like at first."

"Troy!" Flint and Liz shouted in unity.

"Truth be told, Troy, I like Liz a whole lot more than I like you." Liz smiled at Flint and walked toward him to give him another hug. Sam joined in.

"We would love to come over sometime," Liz said. "What can we bring?"

"Just yourself, Liz. Leave Troy here."

Flint helped Sam into the back of the truck, then hopped into the driver's seat. Sam couldn't help staring at Coffy until Flint got settled. "Coffy, I'd like you to meet my little champion of terror, Samantha. Sam, this is Coffy, the lady who gave us Apache."

"It's nice to meet you, Miss Coffy. Thank you for Apache. She's a great dog," Sam said from the back seat.

"It's nice to meet you, too, Samantha. I'm glad you like her. She's a special dog."

"It's okay to call me Sam. Everyone else does."

"All right, Sam it is." Coffy smiled at her.

"You're beautiful," Sam blurted out without a second thought.

"Oh, thank you!" Coffy said, suddenly surprised at Sam's comment. "That's so sweet of you to say! But I have to tell you, you're much prettier than I am. I just love your cute blonde hair and your gorgeous blue eyes!"

Samantha smiled. "We're just a bunch of good looking people, aren't we, Dad?" Everyone in the truck laughed.

"Yes, we are, sweetheart," Flint replied. "How do you guys feel about going out for lunch, then doing a little souvenir shopping at Quietwater Beach?" The vote was unanimous.

CHAPTER ELEVEN

It was a beautiful afternoon on the beach, and Coffy was in a great mood. It had been a long time since she'd enjoyed the company of several people at once, and her time with Flint and Sam had been a pure joy. Lunch at Flounders had been fun. At Flint's suggestion, she tried the blackened redfish, which she declared delicious. She'd not eaten much seafood in her lifetime, and everyone made sure to make fun of her because of it.

Samantha kept Coffy laughing the entire time. The things effortlessly coming out of that kid's mouth were hysterical and poignant at the same time. It was easy for Coffy to see she was quite the character.

After lunch, they went shopping at Pirate's Cove, a local tourist shop where Flint encouraged Coffy to buy a swimsuit she could use at the beach later that day. She toyed around with the idea of getting a bikini, but found herself embarrassed about the scars on her back. She decided on a more modest one-piece.

It was a short hike from Flint's house to the beach, so they decided to allow Apache and Argo to tag along. Coffy and Flint sat in folding chairs near the water's edge watching Sam play with the dogs in the surf. Coffy hadn't felt this relaxed in a long time.

"It's a little different than what you're used to, isn't it?" Flint asked.

"Yes!" she answered. "It's warm! Right now it would be almost cold back home, and everything is so wide open here. You can see forever without the trees or mountains blocking your view. There's a *horizon* here. I'm not used to seeing it except when I'm traveling."

The dogs were having a great time running through the surf retrieving sticks of driftwood that Sam was throwing into the water. It was obvious Argo had never been in warm saltwater before and was having the time of his life. It was good to see he and Apache playing together again.

"Sam seems to like you," Flint said while handing Coffy a beer from the ice chest.

"I really like her. She's a funny little girl, and I mean that in the best way. She says things that make me laugh, spontaneous things, but sometimes she says things that someone a lot older would say, almost like she's thirty years old. She's amazing."

"Really? Like what?"

"When we were shopping today, she asked if I had ever been married."

"Really?" Flint looked at Coffy with a quizzical look. "Why did she ask you that?"

"I don't know, but after I told her that I had, she said, 'Good. My dad needs someone who has *experience*.'" They both laughed. "I mean, how innocent and at the same time adult is that?"

"Wow!" Flint went silent for a moment. "I'm not sure why she feels the need to look after me so much. I mean, I do a pretty good job being her father. I make sure she has what she needs, that she's safe, that she's happy. But sometimes, I feel like she spends too much energy trying to take care of me."

"That's so sweet."

"It is, but I don't know how to get her to stop doing it and just be a kid. I think after Rachael died, Sam felt it was her job to take over for her mother. I'm not even sure she's aware she's doing it."

"I didn't mean to start a--"

"Oh no, it's okay, Coffy! I haven't had a chance to speak to anyone about this other than Liz, so I'm glad you brought it up."

"What does Liz think?"

"She says that it's natural, and that she only does it because she loves me so much. But I just want her to be a kid and not a mom right now. I can take care of myself, and I don't think it's something that Sam needs to be concerned about at her age."

"Well, please don't ever hurt her feelings over it. She's just doing what she feels in her heart."

"Oh God, no. I would never do anything to hurt her feelings. I'm still her proud Papa! She's the love of my life."

"Does she remind you of Rachael sometimes?" Coffy asked softly.

"Yes," Flint answered. "More often than not."

"How so?" Coffy wanted to know more about his love for Rachael, and this seemed like an innocent way to approach it.

"Well, in the first place, Samantha looks a lot like Rachael. They have the same blonde hair and blue eyes. They get more similar with each passing year. Unfortunately for both of us, though, she acts more like me. Rachael was kind and gentle at home. She was a cop, so she had to be assertive on the street. But she had this amazing ability to switch it off when she walked in the front door. Even when we would occasionally fight, she never raised her voice."

"Now that little one over there," he said, pointing to Sam still playing with the dogs in the surf, "She has a mouth on her. She can get mad at the funniest things. But she got that from me. It's not her fault."

"You can be a hothead?" Coffy asked, looking at him. She didn't see how it could be possible from what she had seen thus far. She had spent too much time around people like Stephen who couldn't control their tempers. She would have none of that again.

"No, not in that sense. I've never lost control or been mean to someone who didn't deserve it. I used to be the type who held on to my anger and not share it with anyone. Let me tell you, that can make you toxic. I would get depressed, start hating the world and everyone in it. It made me not want to be around people, which is hard to do when you're a police officer."

"Do you still feel that way?"

"No. I've learned to deal with it. Well, Rachael taught me how to deal with it. I channel most of that anger into other projects. She taught me how to redirect that anger and depression and put it into something useful, like K9 search and rescue. I'm passionate about it because it was Rachael who taught me to use all energy, good, and bad, for the purpose of helping people. She helped me start liking people again." He paused for a moment. "Well, almost everyone. Maybe not so much for the occasional drunk asshole who disturbs everyone else in the campground at two in the morning. Those are tough to warm up to." Coffy laughed.

After a few moments of reflection accented by the squawk of a few nearby seagulls, Coffy asked, "Do you think you could teach me to start liking people?" Flint thought about the question for a moment.

"I can try, but it doesn't happen overnight."

"I want you to teach me everything you know by the end of the week."

Flint chuckled. "End of the week. I'm afraid it'll take a little longer than--"

"End of the week," Coffy interrupted.

Flint smiled. "I'll do what I can, but for now, start with another beer."

The tide was coming in, occasionally bringing a gentle wave onto the beach. The warm water lapping at their feet and the soft breeze had relaxed them both to a state of tranquil bliss. The alcohol helped a little too.

Sam was soaking wet and grinning ear-to-ear when she trotted up to Coffy, trailed by two equally wet and equally happy German Shepherds.

"Look, Coffy." She handed Coffy something from her hand. "It's a sand dollar."

"A sand dollar? Really? Like those at the store today? But those were white."

"Yep. But this is what they look like when they're alive. They're brown and fuzzy. There's a whole bunch of them out there," she said, pointing to a spot farther out in the water. "Come on, I'll show you." She grabbed Coffy's hand and helped her out of the beach chair.

"Dad, did you bring the masks?"

"Yes, sweetheart. They're in the bag behind Coffy's chair." Sam reached into the red and white striped bag and pulled out two scuba masks and a pair of snorkels.

Coffy was a little apprehensive at the prospect of going into the water.

"Are you coming?" she asked Flint.

"No. I probably should watch the dogs while you two are out to sea! Don't worry, Coffy. Sam is the best snorkeler in Pensacola. She knows how to snorkel like no one's business, and she's pretty good at keeping the sharks at bay when necessary." Coffy shot him a wide-eyed look. "I'm just teasing. The sharks here like to nibble first before dining." Sam pulled Coffy out into the water.

Flint watched as Sam taught Coffy how to snorkel in the shallow water. Coffy seemed to pick up on it quickly. He made a note to ask if she played sports in school. Her movements and coordination in the water showed athleticism.

It was bittersweet seeing Sam having so much fun with someone he cared for. It brought back memories of Rachael and Samantha playing together when they would go on family outings. Often he would just sit there watching and thinking about how lucky he was to have such a beautiful family. The two of them would always gang up on him over everything, and he didn't want it any other way.

After losing Rachael, he had come to the stark realization that Samantha had also lost her mother. It was almost like grieving for the loss of two people in his life. His wife, his soul mate and lover for eleven years, and his child's mother, the woman who had given birth to his daughter and helped raise her to be strong and independent. He missed both visions of Rachael immensely.

There was a pang of guilt in his heart as he sat there, watching another woman playing with his child. It should have been Rachael, but then that argument was settled several years ago on a chilly autumn night when a drug dealer pulled the trigger and removed her from his and Sam's lives forever.

Yes, there was sadness, but there was also happiness. In a way, it had been Rachael who put the wheels in motion for Flint to meet Coffy by pushing him into the K9 service. Each turn of the wheel led them here, to this beach, to this moment. He looked out at Coffy, who was inspecting something Sam had brought to the surface for her, and he silently thanked Rachael. He knew he would have her blessing.

Dinner that night was Sam and Flint's specialty, spaghetti. The father-daughter team proudly worked together to provide Coffy with the finest in bachelor cuisine. With just the right amount of heat provided by the crushed red pepper packets left over from a recent pizza delivery and the addition of frozen, straight from the bag, spicy meatballs, it was delicious, though Coffy wasn't sure which she enjoyed more, the food or the show put on by the cook staff.

It was evident that Flint and Sam had made spaghetti many times before. Each person had their own task in contributing to the dinner and would loudly proclaim an injustice if one interfered with the other's duties. Coffy, no stranger to eating alone, was getting dinner *and* a show.

Afterwards, Coffy and Flint made their way to the wooden back porch of the house so they could watch the sun set over Pensacola Bay. Sam had excused herself to her bedroom; she had something she wanted to show to Coffy, but needed to retrieve it first.

Flint took the white wooden rocking chair on the left and invited Coffy to sit in the multi-colored but predominantly bright aqua chair on the right. The chair had paintings of pelicans, clouds, and starfish all over it. Coffy stood there admiring it for a moment before sitting.

"That's my daughter's chair. She painted it," Flint said proudly.

"It's beautiful," she said, still looking at it.

"Yeah, she's the creative one for sure. The chairs on your porch may be hand-crafted, but these excellent examples of mass production came from the Cracker Barrel store up on I-10." He laughed a little. "We bought them unpainted, but Sam insisted they were ugly so I agreed we could paint them. I painted mine white, but you can see she never does anything halfway."

"I love it! I may have to hire her to make one for me."

"You don't think it would look a little out of place on your porch in the mountains?" he asked.

"It would be the perfect reminder of my visit here. Every time I sat in it, I would think of the ocean and the little girl who taught me all about sand dollars." She looked at Flint, smiled, and took a seat.

Coffy took in the view. Pensacola Bay was about thirty yards away and the Ft. Pickens Fishing Pier was straight ahead. Across the bay, she could see several large buildings and, to her right, the skyline of downtown Pensacola.

"What are those buildings straight across?" she asked.

"That's the Pensacola Naval Air Station. Have you ever heard of the Blue Angels?"

"Yeah. I saw them out in California once. They were practicing in the distance when I was looking for a missing hiker."

"Well, this is their home base. They stay out here most of the year, but go to California to train during the offseason. Did you find the kid?"

"Yeah. We found him. He committed suicide in the desert." Feeling happy and not wishing to discuss the death of others, she quickly changed the subject back to the original topic. "That's interesting about the Blue Angels. I thought they were based in California."

They rocked in silence for a while. Coffy was not yet at ease with talking much, and Flint seemed happy enough not to worry about the long pauses in their conversation. Finally, as the sun began to lower toward the water's horizon, Flint spoke, "Have you ever seen the sunset over water?"

"No. I've seen the sunrise over water, but never set."

"Sometimes, if you're lucky, just as the sun slips behind the horizon, there will be a flash of green light. It only happens when the sun sets behind open water, though, and even then, it doesn't always happen."

"Do you think it will happen tonight?" Coffy asked.

"Don't know. But we'll find out in a few minutes. The old sailors used to say that if you're fortunate enough to see it, it means you're on the right path to your destination. There will be smooth sailing on your journey."

"Well, I know we could all use some smooth sailing right about now," Coffy said.

The sun grew larger and deepened in color as it met the horizon. After a minute or so, the sun was almost gone except for a tiny bit of the top.

"If it's going to happen, it'll happen any second now." They stared intently as the last remnants of the sun slipped behind the horizon without the mythical green flash.

"I didn't see it, did you?" Flint asked Coffy.

"Nope, not a thing. I think you're yanking my chain."

"No, I swear it! I'm not! Sam and I have seen it!"

"Uh huh. I bet you have," Coffy replied sarcastically. "Hey, speaking of Sam, where is she? She had something she wanted to show me."

"Good question. Let me find her." Flint got up and stopped at the door. "Would you like another beer?"

"Sure. Thanks."

Flint returned with two beers, twisted the top off one, and handed it to Coffy before returning to his chair. "Sam is sound asleep on her bed.

155

She must be exhausted."

"You don't think she's feeling sick, do you?" Coffy asked.

"No. I think Troy kept her up all last night. He likes to play video games, and his wife hates it, so when Sam comes over, he uses her as an excuse to play. Of course, she loves it. She beats him most of the time." They both laughed. "The Burnsides have been good to Sam and me. I've known Troy since my early days of being a cop in Dallas. He was a cop, too. We hung out a lot after our shift was over. He married Liz about the same time I married Rachael, and we were all best friends." Flint took a sip from his beer.

"One day, Troy decided he'd had enough of police work in the big city, and he took a job out here as a police officer with the National Park Service. After Rachael died, he and Liz talked me into coming out here and taking the park superintendent's job. I'm still a cop, but I don't have to deal with a rough crowd anymore, and since Troy and Liz never had a child, they get Sam as a surrogate. Worked out for everyone!"

"Sounds like it," she replied. "Do you really like it out here?"

"Oh, heck yeah. I love it. It's given us a safe place for Sam to grow up and a peaceful place for me to work. I mean, after working at the office all day, no matter how tough it is, I can come out here and sit, enjoy the beautiful view, and relax. There's an old adage that park rangers have. They say, 'I get paid in sunsets.' I may not make a ton of money, but by God, I make a fortune in sunsets."

"I believe that you do," she replied. "You are fortunate. I don't often get to see the sunset. Up in the mountains, there's no horizon. Everything is three-dimensional, up-and-down."

"Well, you may not get to see the sunset often, but there's a beauty in the mountains that can't be matched. When I was up there last summer, I saw some beautiful colors you typically don't see down here near the water. I'll never forget standing on the cliff that evening with you; I'd never seen anything that beautiful."

"That was a gorgeous evening, I have to admit. But you have colors here that are just as beautiful. The white sand, the blue water, the red setting sun, they're all just as colorful as what you see in the mountains. It's just that it's something different, and something different is always more attractive."

"True," Flint said. "I guess we're both lucky then."

"Yes, we are," she replied.

"So, I guess that means that you probably wouldn't consider moving your operation down here?"

Coffy wasn't sure she heard him correctly. "What?"

"Think about it, Coffy. During the winter, it's cold up there in the mountains. Maybe you should move your operations down here where you could train all winter long. I mean, it gets a little cool here, but it hardly ever gets below freezing, and it never snows."

Coffy thought about what he was saying. It made sense, but it was what he wasn't saying that struck her. He wanted her to spend more time with him. With Sam. He wanted her, here. She didn't know how to respond to that.

"Did I scare you?" Flint asked.

"No. You didn't scare me. It just caught me off guard."

"I'm sorry. I didn't mean to spring that on you. It just seems like you could make it work here. We could make it work here."

Coffy looked at him and smiled. "We?"

"Yes, 'we.' It's no secret. I told you that I felt like I could love you in Colorado, and our recent time together just made me more certain of it. I love spending time with you. You could bring the dogs down after you shut down the cabin for the winter. We could set you up a training facility in the old store behind the house. It would be perfect. You could continue training the dogs, and we would get to spend more time together." Flint was all in now. No holding back as he had surprised himself by blurting out the things he had been thinking for a while now. "I want you to think about it. If it doesn't work out, you haven't lost anything. You could go back to Colorado in the spring. But at least then, you would have had an opportunity to spend more time training your dogs."

"And more time with you?"

"Yes. More time with me."

Coffy reached out and held his hand. It felt good to be wanted again. It had been too long, but moving her operations now wouldn't be possible. She still had a price to pay. To feel love again, to know companionship wasn't in the cards for her. She'd had that chance once before and blew it, but for now, she didn't have the heart to tell this man that, though he cared for her, she couldn't, wouldn't, let herself feel wanted again.

"I'll think about it," she said.

Argo laid on the floor next to the couch as Coffy adjusted her blanket. She was warm and comfortable, but if there were ever a time to be wrapped in the arms of another, it would have been now. She ached for the man in the other room, but they had agreed that spending time together in the bedroom was something that neither felt was a good idea with Samantha in the house. It seemed improper. It was probably a good thing anyway. Coffy was still feeling emotional after Flint had expressed his hope that she would consider moving to Florida. Spending time in bed together right now would only get his hopes up.

As she lay there in the dark, she wondered how it would all end when she had to tell him no. Would he be angry with her? Would he be broken for a while? Or would he be fine with it? There were so many questions racing through her mind that it caught her by surprise to find herself wondering if it might actually be possible to spend a winter here? She quickly disposed of that thought and shut her eyes.

Coffy was just to the point of falling asleep when Argo began to growl. Coffy opened her eyes. "What is it, Argo?" Coffy soon saw the source of his concern. Sam slowly opened her bedroom door and walked out with a flashlight in hand. "Quiet, Argo," Coffy whispered after he let out another growl.

"Hi, Coffy," Sam said, softly walking toward the couch. "Did I wake you?"

"No, sweetheart. I was just lying here thinking about what a great day I had with you and your dad."

"I had fun, too. Can I show you something?" she asked.

"Sure. Come on over, and sit next to me. What do you have?" Coffy leaned up on her elbow as Sam put down the flashlight and sat on the floor next to the couch. Coffy could see she had an old cigar box in her hands.

"This is what I wanted to show you, but when I went to get it, I guess I fell asleep. I'm sorry."

"That's all right. I know you were tired. We had a long day."

Samantha opened the box and raked her fingers through the contents. Coffy could see some of the treasures inside, but one object in particular made her heart catch. It was a police badge. Coffy almost asked about it, but decided to wait to see if Sam wanted to talk about it first.

Sam pulled a small brown bottle out of the box and poured the contents into her hand. She picked up her flashlight and shined it on her open palm. Coffy saw what looked like broken bits of seashells.

"These are shark's teeth," Sam said, barely veiling her pride.

"Oh, my gosh, Sam! Where did you get those?"

"I found them on the beach. Aren't they pretty?" She held her hand out for Coffy to touch them.

"That's so cool! You just picked them up off the beach?" Coffy asked.

"Yep. You have to have a good eye, though. Not just anybody can find them."

"Oh Sam, I'm so impressed," Coffy said truthfully. "Can you help me find some while I'm here?"

"Sure!"

Coffy shifted her finger through the teeth. She was surprised at how pretty they were. Some were tiny, but there were a few bigger ones scattered throughout. She picked up one that caught her eye.

"That's from a bull shark. It's my favorite."

"Yes, it's a pretty one. Why is it your favorite?" Coffy asked.

"I found that one when my Dad and I first moved here. I was pretty scared of the beach, and I wasn't sure I wanted to live here. When I found that one, I started learning more about sharks, and pretty soon I was an expert, and now I love the beach."

"I can't imagine you being scared of anything."

"I was then. It was right after my mother died and I wasn't very happy then."

"Oh, I see. I can't imagine. It must have been pretty rough for you?"

"Yeah, but my Dad and I are pretty tough." She smiled at Coffy, who tried not to return a sad smile but couldn't help it.

"Why is this tooth your favorite?" Coffy asked.

"See the nick on the side?"

"I do now. I didn't notice it before."

"It means the shark bit something with it before it fell out. I keep imagining that whatever the shark tried to bite was so tough that it got away." Sam looked up at Coffy with another smile. "My dad says it reminds him of me. He says I'm pretty tough and that even a shark couldn't hurt me." She and Coffy laughed together. "He also told me that the most interesting things in the world are not perfect and that it's those little flaws that make something special."

Tears welled in Coffy's eyes as she handed the treasure back to Sam. This child had been through a lot and still saw life as something precious, something mysterious. Why was it so hard for herself then, to still find wonder in the world? Maybe this girl, as young as she was, could help her reclaim the part of herself that had disappeared so long ago.

"Sam, I noticed a police badge in your box. Did that belong to your mother?"

Sam stared blankly at Coffy for a second or two before she answered. "Are you crying?"

"No, sweetheart. My eyes are just tired."

"Okay. Yeah, that was my mom's." She looked down at the box for a moment before opening it. Coffy was immediately afraid that she shouldn't have asked. "Do you want to see it?"

"Yes, if you don't mind?"

"I don't mind," she said, handing it over to Coffy.

Coffy held it up to the light that Sam was shining on it. It was beautiful, with a big Texas star on the front and Dallas Texas Police Department engraved on the shield behind it. Imprinted on a silver banner near the bottom of the star was the number twenty thirty-three.

"This was her badge number?" Coffy asked.

"Yes. Twenty thirty-three," Sam replied without looking at the badge.

"Judging from what I know about you, I bet your mom was a great police officer."

"Dad says she was the best."

"I'm sure she was," Coffy said with a touch of sadness. "But I know one thing she was good at for sure."

Sam looked away from Coffy's hand and looked her in the eyes with a questioning look.

"She was great at raising a little girl into a wonderful young lady," Coffy said while smiling and returning the badge to Sam. She received a warm smile in return. "Thank you for sharing your treasure with me, Sam. That makes me feel special."

"You're welcome." Sam closed the lid to her box and stood. She leaned over to pet Argo. "Coffy?"

"Yes, sweetheart?"

"How long can you stay with us?"

Coffy didn't know how to answer.

"I don't know, Sam. For a few more days probably. I've got to go home and take care of my other dogs, and I don't want Argo to get too comfortable with the beach life. He's a working dog, and I'm afraid he might get lazy."

Sam laughed. "Well, I hope you can come back to see us. I think my dad likes you, and I think you're pretty nice, too."

"Thank you, Samantha. That's sweet of you to say. I think you two are special also."

"Oh, we are!" Sam said with a grin as she turned and trotted off to her bedroom.

CHAPTER TWELVE

Coffy woke the next morning before anyone else and decided she would take both of the dogs for a walk. Quietly making their way out the back door, she decided to make the fishing pier their first stop. She entertained herself by watching the dogs stare into the water which was clear enough for them to see fish schooling under the old wooden structure. She actually had a difficult time getting them to break their attention so they could move on.

It was another beautiful morning, clear skies and just enough of a light breeze to keep the dogs' noses working overtime. She walked the dogs to the beach where she unleashed them and let them play in the water for a while. It reminded her of watching them play in the meadow next to her cabin in Colorado. She hadn't realized until now how much she and Argo had missed Apache.

On the way back to Flint's house, she decided to check out the abandoned store Flint was talking about in his bid to convince her to move to Florida for the winter. The building, located just behind his home, was rustic and visually appealing, made from rough hewn cedar planks which had darkened with age. It reminded Coffy of an old stagecoach way station from the 1800s.

She climbed the wooden steps and tried the door. Finding it locked, she walked around to the side where she found a large sliding door similar to those she had seen on old barns. She opened it just enough for her and the dogs to squeeze through.

It was dark inside, but there was enough light streaming through the door that she could make out a large room with open beams in the ceiling and a wooden floor which was in pretty good shape. The room was large; she estimated forty feet long by thirty feet wide. She unleashed the dogs to let them investigate on their own.

At the far end of the large room was a small set of steps leading to a door that she thought might give her access to the front of the building. She climbed the steps, opened the door, and walked into what looked like an old museum. There were lots of old glass display cases full of weird and wonderful things. In one of them stood two old stuffed raccoons posed to look like they were fighting over some kind of fish. The dust on them suggested they had been fighting over the same fish for at least a decade or more. Another glass case held a diorama of the actual Civil War era fort the park had been named after, complete with cannons and tiny soldiers. Seeing the layout, she was certain this must have been the place Flint was talking about. It must have been the park visitor's center from years ago where they sold books, snacks, camping supplies, and such. The big room she had first come through was probably storage for the store and maybe even for old park equipment. Whatever it was used for and despite the dust, it was most definitely well taken care of.

She dared herself to think about how she could use it for training her dogs. The store would make an excellent apartment, and the storage room would be perfect for sheltering her dogs inside. By putting a chain link fence just outside the big room with a small door in the wall, the dogs could come and go outside anytime they wanted. It seemed like a perfect setup, if only...

The front door to the store shook as someone inserted a key to unlock it. She knew it was probably against the rules to be in here, and she didn't know how to explain her presence to whatever staff person was trying to enter. As the door swung open, she saw Flint standing there with a big smile.

"You couldn't stand it, could you?" he said as he walked through the doorway.

"Am I in trouble?" she asked.

"Oh, heck no. I'm glad you found a way in. What do you think about it?"

"Well, to be honest, I love it. It's quaint."

"Yes, it is, but what I'm asking is what do you think about this place for training your dogs?"

"Flint I--"

Flint didn't let her finish. "Now we can't change the layout because this is considered a historical building, but imagine this being your office and work space, and that big room over there would be perfect for sheltering the dogs. There are plenty of old World War One redoubts around here for training areas, and you can train anywhere in the park since you would be my guest for the winter."

"Flint, it sounds great, but--"

"But what? It sounds great but what?"

Coffy sensed the agitation in his voice. This was the very thing that she was trying to avoid. She didn't have it in her to tell him no right now. She just wanted to enjoy the time they still had together.

"But nothing. It's a great building with a lot of potential. I'll think about it."

Coffy could see the sadness in his smile. She was stalling and he probably knew it. Her heart told her he was a good man. Most men get vicious when they are heartbroken, but this man wasn't capable of that. It made her love him even more. Telling him that she loved him, though, would be the same as torturing him.

"I tell you what," Coffy said as she walked up and put her arms around him. "How about we talk about this later. Right now, I'm hoping *you* will teach *me* how to fish."

Flint's happy smile returned as he hugged her. "You don't know how to fish, and you live next to a river?"

"Nope. No one has ever taught me."

"Well, I know just the person to help you with that. Let's go wake her up."

It was early afternoon on Coffy's last day on the island when Flint announced that he wanted to show her something. It wasn't far from the house, but Flint wanted to take the truck. They still needed to pick Sam up from school, then the three of them were going out to celebrate Coffy's last night on the island. He drove the truck a short distance along the park road and pulled off next to a grove of Naval Live Oaks. From there they hiked a short trail through the trees and after climbing a short, sandy incline, made their way to the top of a concrete redoubt.

There were several redoubts in the park, a leftover curiosity from World War I when they were deemed necessary to protect Pensacola Bay from marauding German vessels occasionally seen in the Gulf of Mexico. The fortified bunkers, built to protect the big guns that were once installed within them, made the perfect retreat during summer thunderstorms that frequented the island. This particular one was Flint's favorite spot in the park.

It was built about seventy-five yards behind the sand dunes and high enough to provide an unobstructed view of the beach for several miles in either direction. Flint loved coming up here during work with his binoculars to look for illegal fishing activity. It was also a peaceful place to visit when he wanted to get away from people.

The week had gone by too fast for both of them. Flint spent as little time in the office as he could, but there were still things that needed to be done. He spent most mornings until noon handling work affairs while Coffy spent her mornings walking the beach or exploring different trails in the park. Afternoons seemed to be the perfect time for lovemaking and pillow talk while Sam was at school. Evenings were reserved for family time usually spent in town or on the front porch, watching the sunset with the dogs.

One evening, Troy and Liz took everyone out on their fishing boat for a sunset cruise. Coffy had never laughed so hard in her life as when Sam reeled in a cartoon version of a fish that was all bone from the neck down. Triggerfish had eaten the flesh off it as Sam reeled it to the surface, and the shock on everyone's face as it popped out of the water was too much for Coffy to take. She couldn't stop laughing. For the remainder of the week, every time Coffy thought about it, she would laugh.

The sunset that night and every night after was spent in anticipation of seeing the elusive green flash that Flint had told her about. She wasn't sure if he was making the whole thing up or not, but she kept hoping to see it regardless.

Flint led Coffy to the edge of the redoubt and sat with his legs dangling over the drop-off. She joined him and, together, they silently took in the view. The view of the clear blue water contrasting with the sugar

165

white sand of the beach was breathtaking. There was no one on the beach. It was as if they had the whole park to themselves.

"I wanted to bring you up here to show you my world," he said, placing her hand in his.

"It's beautiful up here, isn't it?" she said, still taking in the colors.

"Yes, it is, and it could be your world, too, you know. Or, if you prefer, part of your world."

She looked into his eyes and sensed the hope welling inside him. It was a hope that she dared not crush, but it was a hope that she couldn't be allowed to share. Her life was set in stone. It was not to be one filled with love and happiness; it was one that had to be spent in the service of others. She must spend the remainder of her life paying for a sin so grievous that it could never be atoned for. She would be kidding herself if she thought she could ever make a life for this man and herself. No, it couldn't be, and this was the moment she had dreaded from the day she arrived in Pensacola. Now was the time to tell him.

She placed her hand on top of his. "Flint, I thought hard about it. I really did. You know I care for you deeply. Please know that. But I can't. I'm sorry, I just can't." Like a child at Christmas opening a gift sweater, she watched as his face turned from joyful excitement to one of disappointment in an instant. God, she hated this.

"You know I'm not asking you to marry me, right?" he said, grasping for the right thing to say as if the correct incantation of magic words would change her mind. "All I'm asking is to spend more time with you, even if it's just during the winter. When it gets too cold in Colorado, you could bring the dogs down and train them right here in the park. It makes perfect sense."

"It may make perfect sense to you, Flint, but it doesn't work for me. My organization is based in Colorado, and I can't risk the disruption it would cause being out of state for months at a time. It's all I have."

"I don't understand why you can't start another organization here. There's no organized search and rescue group down here. It's just me and a few people doing what they can with no leadership. You could start a new organization and keep doing what you do now."

"It won't work Flint. It just won't work. There are people up there who depend on me and my organization to help them find their loved ones when they're missing. What about them? If I'm not there, who will help *them?*"

"Well, what about the people here who need the same kind of help? Whether a person is missing in Colorado or Florida, they still need help."

"But you're here for them."

"I'm beginning to think you're just making excuses. Is there something about me you don't like? If there is, just say so." Coffy knew she needed to tread lightly. The man in front of her was a good and decent man, and for her to allow him to think anything less than that would be wrong.

"Flint, there's nothing about you that I don't like. That I don't love."

"Is it because I have a child?"

Flint's words stung her. She had been clear to him that Sam had been a joy to be with. "God, no. Sam is an angel, and believe me, I would love nothing more than to spend more time with her."

"Then what is it, Coffy? Why don't you want to be with us?"

The pain in Flint's eyes was too great for her to bear. She let go of his hand and looked out to the ocean, taking a moment to calm herself. "Flint, when I look at you, I see everything I desire. You live your life without malice, and you love and protect those close to you. I truly want to be one of those people. But I can't.

Things haven't been easy for me in my life, and there are things about me that you don't know. Things that I can't bring myself to even think about, much less share with someone else. Please, try to understand. I am twisted and broken in ways you can't fathom. How can I take care of someone else if I can't even take care of myself? It wouldn't be fair to you or Sam. I can't be the person you need me to be."

Flint looked hopeless, and Coffy was starting to unravel. Tears welled in her eyes as she struggled to keep her emotions inside.

"We don't need someone to take care of us, Coffy. We just need someone to care about. We want to care about you."

An uncontrollable sob came out from somewhere deep within her as she leaned against him and buried her face in his shoulder. Flint must have known that he had pushed too hard as he put his arm around her and held her tight. He ran his fingers through her hair until the sobs began to soften. She sat back up and wiped tears from her face. They sat in silence for a while, not knowing what to say to one another. Embarrassed that she had collapsed emotionally in front of him, Coffy struggled to regain her composure.

"Coffy?" Flint asked.

"Yeah," she said, wiping the last tear from her face.

"I'm sorry. I didn't mean to hurt you."

"You didn't hurt me, Flint. I'm afraid it's been a long time coming. It's been a while since I've been around people, and this is one reason why. When you avoid being around people as I have, you don't get emotionally attached."

Flint reached for her hand once again. They sat in silence until Coffy, for the first time since they had been above the redoubt, spotted something on the beach that took her breath away. She had been so focused on Flint and his words that she hadn't noticed the words written in large letters in the sand down below, *WE CAN WALK TOGETHER TO ILLUMINATE THE PATH FOR OTHERS*. At first, she thought it was a fluke. Someone else must have written it. Someone who had no idea about the words she had written high up on the cliff in Colorado, but it couldn't be. It was too coincidental. Tears started to flow again as she realized that the man sitting next to her must have written them in the sand. This must be what he had wanted her to see.

"Flint," she said, choking on her words. "Did you write that?"

"Yes. I remembered what you carved into the canyon wall the day you took me up to your favorite spot. You wrote that you must walk alone in darkness to light the path for others. I wanted you to know that you don't have to walk alone. You and I can walk together and be happy as we help others find their way."

"Oh my God. Oh my God. No! You don't understand, do you?" Coffy began to cry again. "I can't be with you. It isn't possible for me!"

Flint looked at her with utter bewilderment as his own tears began to appear.

"I have to go. I'm sorry, but I can't be here anymore. It's too hard." She stood and backed away from him.

"Coffy, I didn't mean to--"

"I know, Flint. Dear God, I know it. I can't expect you to understand, but I love you, and because I do, I can't stay here. I know it hurts, but please, if you know what's good for you, and for me, forget about me." She turned to walk down the trail.

"Where are you going?" Flint asked.

"I'm going to get my things, then I'm going back to Colorado where I belong. I'll call a cab to pick me up at your house. I should be out of your house by the time you get back with Sam. And Flint, please tell her I'm sorry and that I said goodbye." With that, she was gone.

Coffy walked to Flint's home as quickly as she could. She knew Flint needed to pick Sam up from school, and she wanted to be gone before they arrived home. She called for a taxi, packed her bag, and did her best to hide her red and swollen eyes with a splash of water and a bit of makeup. She said goodbye to Apache and waited on the front porch with Argo until the taxi arrived. The driver was hesitant to let Argo into the car, so it took a bit of convincing for her to get across that he was a working service dog. It also cost her an extra twenty dollars, but she was in no mood to argue with anyone.

The drive along two-lane Pensacola Beach Highway from the park into town was usually a beautiful one filled with images of sea oats growing atop white sand dunes with blue water as a backdrop. Coffy had never tired of the drive which they all had taken many times together this last week. This time though, as she sat in the back seat staring out the window, her eyes took in the scenery, but her mind wouldn't let her see the beauty in it. All she could think about was what she was leaving behind. She had never known anyone like Flint. She loved him yes, but she knew she couldn't have him. He was meant for someone other than her, someone better than her. He was kind and considerate. He was the kind of man any woman would desire, and he would have no problem finding another. What right did she have to claim him for her own when she couldn't even take care of her own child? He had no idea of her past indiscretions. She is capable of doing evil things when necessary, and no one who is good and kind should have to live with someone capable of that. No, she didn't deserve him, and he most certainly did not deserve her.

"Ma'am, do you know the guy in the truck behind us?" the driver asked, bringing Coffy out of her thoughts.

"What?" She turned to look out the back of the taxi. She was heartbroken to see Flint in his truck behind them flashing his headlights. She was especially saddened to see Sam sitting beside him in the passenger seat.

"He was headed the other direction, and when he passed us, he turned around and got up close. Is that someone you know?" the driver asked looking in the rear view mirror.

"Yes, I know him. Please don't stop," she said.

"Is he dangerous? I mean, should I call the cops?"

"No, he's not dangerous, and he is a cop. I just don't want to see him right now."

"I'm afraid you might not have a choice. The light is red up here, and I'm going to have to stop."

"Let's just see what he does. He's not out to hurt anyone."

As the taxi came to a stop, Coffy couldn't bear to look behind her.

"Looks like he's getting out. Do you want me to run the light?"

"No. Let me see what he wants." Reluctantly, she rolled down the window. "Flint, I don't want to talk right now."

"I know!" he said as he handed her a padded envelope. "I'm sorry. I hope I didn't scare you. When I picked Sam up from school and told her you were leaving, she got upset. When we saw the taxi, she asked me to see if I could get you to take this. She made it for you. She said not to open it until you got home." Coffy reached up for the envelope. She placed it over her heart and began to cry. "I'm sorry, Coffy. I didn't mean to upset you again. Samantha says goodbye." As he turned to leave, Coffy tried to call out his name but couldn't make a sound. Her heart was broken for the second time today, and it was all she could do to just breathe. How easy would it be to open the taxi door and walk back to a family she could be with for the rest of her life? Paralyzed with indecision, she sat motionless until finally the light turned green, and the taxi moved forward. She turned to look back one last time and saw Sam, her eyes reddened and her face streaked with tears waving goodbye to her out the passenger window as the truck made a U-turn and headed for home.

It was dusk as the plane backed away from the service ramp and began the long taxi out to the runway. Apache was lying on the floor in front of the two empty seats next to Coffy. Service dogs were usually allowed to travel with their handlers if there was enough room in the passenger cabin and, fortunately tonight, the plane was only half-full. Fewer people meant less time spent explaining why the dog was on the plane in the first place, and tonight, Coffy was grateful for that. She needed to be alone.

The jet engines roared to life as her plane took off and headed south over the Gulf of Mexico. Coffy looked out the window as they passed over the white sands of Pensacola Beach. Soon the plane began its long, slow turn back to the northwest as it headed for Denver. The sun was about to set over the western horizon, but the sight of it through the plane's plastic window was less than perfect compared to watching it from Flint's front porch.

Coffy sighed as she reached for the carry-on bag under her seat and retrieved the white envelope Flint had given her. There was little doubt that whatever was in it was going to fill her with regret for leaving. She wanted to get it over with. She carefully ripped one end open and pulled out the contents. She was surprised to find she still had tears to shed as she looked at the black leather necklace from which dangled a shark's tooth with a nick in it. The gift from a little girl of her prized possession.

Instinctively she held it to her breast as she wiped her tears and looked out the window so that others on the plane wouldn't see her crying. It was then, while wiping the tears from her eyes as she watched the sun disappear behind the horizon, a small green flash of light suddenly took her breath away.

CHAPTER THIRTEEN

Coffy turned the truck into a small parking lot just off the Fort Pickens main road. Koda knew the routine and showed her excitement by crowding Sam against the passenger door and pawing at the window. Sam tried to push her back to the middle of the front seat, but didn't stand a chance against the young forty-five pound German Shepherd. Coffy laughed at Sam's exaggerated efforts and reached over to pull the dog back by the collar as she tried to park the truck at the same time. It was a comedy show, one that brought her great joy.

Coffy managed to bring the truck to a stop, though it straddled the parking space line. No matter, hardly anyone used the lot this time of year anyway. It was early April, and the auxiliary lots in the park wouldn't be used for another month. She would be back in Colorado by then, missing the big summer season. Flint had told her about some of the crazy things that happen during the summer months, and she was looking forward to experiencing them for herself, but it would have to wait until next year. She needed to spend this summer back in Colorado preparing to move her operations permanently to Pensacola.

As it turned out, the decision to move to Florida hadn't been so difficult after all. Sam's act of kindness, giving Coffy one of her most treasured items, the shark's tooth, caused her to think about how her actions affected others. Flint and Sam had made her feel as if her life was important and that maybe she did possess the basic human desire to share it with others.

Then there was the flash. Used to making decisions on her own without outside influence, when she saw the green flash in the sunset on the plane ride back home, even she had to consider the possibility of divine intervention. To Coffy's dismay, Flint and Sam had taught her to like people again. Hell, maybe even love a select few. She had spent a long time in the mountains, avoiding people when she could. She had forgotten that there was joy to be had in the company of others. It just had to be *certain* others.

Coffy called Flint from the airport in Denver and let him know that she would be bringing the dogs down over the winter so she could continue her training activities. Of course, he was ecstatic and so was Sam, which was important to Coffy.

The time since her arrival in late October had been spent training new dogs in search and rescue and enjoying time with Flint and Sam. She decided to live in the old storefront building instead of living in Flint's home as a courtesy to Samantha. She didn't want to come on too strong, too soon. Like her, Sam was independent and used to helping her father. Coffy didn't want to interfere with that dynamic and decided instead to let Sam ease into the idea by being neighbors first.

Coffy still had plenty of alone time with Flint. There were lots of midnight visits, Friday night dates, and her personal favorite, night sex on the beach, but her absolute favorite thing to do was spending time together as a group. She liked to think of it as 'family time,' although she was hesitant to use that term in front of anyone. Things were working out well. So much that in the back of her mind, she had decided to make the arrangement more permanent after the upcoming summer season.

Cellphones and Internet service, which wasn't available to her in the mountains, had suddenly expanded her horizons as far as maintaining her business. These new tools had made communications much easier for her and her organization. She realized there was no need to stay where she had always been. She could move her business anywhere, and right here in Florida seemed a whole lot more desirable than spending winters in the cold mountains of Colorado.

Koda tried to follow Coffy out the driver's side door, but Coffy intentionally pushed her back toward Sam. She wanted Sam to learn to control the dog who was half her size. Koda had come into Coffy's stable of dogs last October as a three-month-old from a German Shepherd breeder in England. She had great potential, but as soon as Koda arrived in Pensacola, Sam laid claim to her. She was a beautiful all-white dog with all the markers that search and rescue dogs need to be successful. She was smart, curious, and loved to play.

Not long after Coffy returned to Florida, Sam began showing an interest in doing what her father was doing as a K9 handler, and Coffy had taken it upon herself to teach her. By teaching Sam how to train a dog, then letting her do the training herself, she was learning about the entire operation. Coffy knew Sam would make a great partner in the business someday.

With Sam and Koda in the lead, they followed the trail from the parking lot to one of the old concrete bunkers once used to store ammunition when Ft. Pickens was an army training facility. They spent the afternoon running different scenarios of what a handler might encounter during a search and rescue mission.

During one exercise, they were working on getting Koda to stay focused on the task at hand even during circumstances which would distract the average K9. Coffy beamed with pride as Sam kept control of Koda after a swamp rabbit ran across the trail in front of them. The kid had a natural instinct for working with dogs.

The rest of the afternoon went by quickly, and Coffy was thankful for it. The boundless energy of the young German Shepherd and her enthusiastic trainer had worn her out. She was ready to head back to the house. She had plans to enjoy the sunset on the storefront porch with Flint.

When they arrived back home, they found Flint on the porch in his rocking chair with a margarita he'd made for Coffy. He had already changed out of his uniform and was in full weekend attire, Hawaiian shirt, khaki shorts, and flip-flops. As they approached the building, Coffy asked Sam to feed Koda and put her in the kennel they'd built behind the old store. Sam gladly accepted, as she did anytime she got the chance to play with all of the other dogs.

"How did it go?" Flint asked as Coffy reached for her drink and took the rocking chair next to him. When Flint got the call from Coffy saying that she would be coming down for the winter, he and Sam had traveled to the Cracker Barrel and bought Coffy a rocking chair to match theirs. Sam had taken it a step further by painting it like hers, complete with sea shells, a dolphin, and even a German Shepherd lying beneath a palm tree. The sight of it made Coffy cry the first time she saw it.

"It went well! Your daughter has a gift for training dogs."

"She's had many years of experience training her father." Coffy laughed and took a sip from her glass. It was the special moments like this that she had missed in her life. Not so much the moments with her ex-husband, as those were few and far between, but those times when she could sit down and relax with someone totally and completely. No one putting a guilt trip on her or berating her for some imagined slight, just sharing a moment of joy. Like watching the sun go down. She dreaded the thought of leaving, even for a little while.

"Time is getting short, Flint. I need to start thinking about getting home for the summer. The train will start making the full run to Silverton in a few weeks, and I need to start planning on how I'm going to get everything down here."

"I know it. I hate it, but at least I know this time you'll be coming back." He looked at her with a furrowed brow. "You are coming back, right?"

She laughed. "Of course, and once I get back, you won't be able to get me to leave."

"I'm counting on that. Sam's counting on it, too."

After several minutes, Sam came around the corner, claimed her chair, and all three of them talked about dogs until the sun finally slid behind Pensacola Bay with a small but distinct green flash. She was on the right path.

"Flint? Honey?" Flint woke when he felt Coffy's hand on his arm. She'd laid next to him on the bed and was trying to wake him.

"Hey. What's up?" he said sleepily as he rolled over to face her.

"I just got a phone call from a FEMA Coordinator. "There's been an earthquake in Mexico, and he's asking if my organization can respond."

"Are you going to?"

"Yes. I need to. I still have a contract with them, and it sounds bad. They need a lot of help down there."

"I didn't hear anything about it on TV," he said before he realized he didn't watch TV last night. In fact, there had been little TV watching in the house since Coffy had arrived. She didn't have a television in Colorado, and she didn't enjoy wasting a lot of time watching it now that she had access to one. That was one of many good habits that had rubbed off on the Westbrook family.

"It happened overnight, but it's bad enough that they already know they'll need search and rescue teams. There are a lot of people trapped in their houses and a lot of the public infrastructure is gone."

"Oh, that's awful. What do you need from me, a ride to the airport?"

"No, Honey. I need you. How do you feel about going to Mexico with me? You can take Apache, and I'll take Argo."

"Really? Mexico? I don't know, Coffy. I don't have a lot of urban disaster training."

"You might not, but Apache does, and I'll be there with you. It'll be good experience for both of you and, God knows, those people need everyone they can get. From what the FEMA guy told me, it was a 7.2 quake near Taxco in the mountains outside Mexico City. One of the worst ever recorded there."

"Well, all right. Sure, I'll go. I need to get Sam over to the Burnsides and notify someone at work. Oh, but I don't have a passport."

"That's fine. We'll be taking a government charter flight down, and there are ways around it."

"When do we leave?" he asked.

"It's two in the morning now. The flight will land at the Naval Air Station at seven. That gives us five hours from now."

Flint threw the covers aside and jumped up. "Then we better get a move on!"

CHAPTER FOURTEEN

The Air Force C130 landed in Mexico City at the Benito Juarez International Airport. Most of the regional airports around Taxco were too small for the large military aircraft or had been too badly damaged by the earthquake to use. The plan was to make it to Mexico City, then travel by helicopter the seventy miles or so to the city that sat 5,800 feet up in Sierra Madre del Sur mountains. The mountainous terrain would feel like home for Coffy, though living the last several months at sea level was sure to take a physical toll. Flint would have to suffer through it.

During the flight to Mexico, Coffy and Flint had been introduced to John Owen, the Incident Commander for the American team. Coffy had never worked with John before, but had heard of him from encounters with other rescue groups, and by all accounts, he knew what he was doing. There were others on board whom Coffy recognized, and she took time to introduce Flint to most of them. In addition to her and Flint, there were two dog teams from Maryland, one from Vermont, and two military teams from Dover Air Force Base in Delaware. She had supplied several dogs to the program at Dover and was happy to see one of them, Booker, on the plane. There were also a large number of doctors, nurses, structural engineers, and federal administrative types on board, a typical contingent of the various professionals needed for a large scale natural disaster response.

The team transferred their dogs and equipment to three Mexican military helicopters waiting for their arrival on the far edge of the airport property. The flight to Taxco took only twenty minutes, but it seemed like a lifetime as they surveyed the damage from the air. The helicopter convoy flew over the edge of town where they could see cars and trucks traveling at a slow crawl, weaving back and forth through the debris that lay in the cobblestone streets. The buildings were made predominantly from stone and masonry, which now lay in large piles where they fell. A few homes were still upright, but judging from the cracks in the walls and their collapsed roofs, they were beyond repair, assuming there was anyone inside left to repair them.

The helicopters landed on the damaged concrete tarmac of the town's small airport where several Mexican Army cargo trucks transferred the Americans to the Command Center for incoming aid and rescue groups. After a short welcome and briefing from someone high up in the Mexican military, the American team departed to set up tents and an administrative command center. Owen stayed behind to consult with the Mexican officials as to what they needed the Americans to do first.

It was four forty-five in the evening local time when the tents finally got set up, satellite communications were operational, and military rations were passed out. The American briefing was scheduled for 5:00 so many of the group showed up still eating out of their MRE food packets. Coffy, who had grown weary of spaghetti in the last several months spent with the Westbrooks, changed her spaghetti packet with Flint's, who had opened a pack of turkey tetrazzini. She didn't allow him to protest.

John Owen briefed the search and rescue personnel first so they could load up and get on with the mission. Medical personnel would set up operations afterwards at another location inside the airport. The greatest need, according to the Mexican officials, was to search various damaged and collapsed apartment buildings close to the center of town. The mission would be a night operation, which was always the most difficult, but all were in agreement that waiting until morning would only cause further loss of life. It had been nearly nineteen hours since the main quake and there had been a dozen or more tremors since, each causing further damage to the buildings already weakened by the primary quake.

Team assignments were handed out. Coffy and Flint were paired with Conner Tate, a young structural engineer from Washington D.C., who would lead the team, and an Emergency Medical Technician named Sal

Romero, who would assess the injured, handle radio operations, and translate for the team. Crews were instructed to reassemble in thirty minutes, and local transportation would take them to their assigned areas.

Bravo Team, as Flint, Coffy, the dogs, and the two new members would be known by, disembarked from the van, gathered their safety gear, and made the walk to their first assignment, a collapsed three-story apartment building on the edge of downtown Taxco. The van could only get within a quarter-mile because the roadways were jammed with debris from the taller buildings. It didn't help that there were no sidewalks in Taxco, and the buildings were built right up next to the roads. The closer they had gotten to the taller buildings of downtown, the more difficult it was to get a vehicle through.

Conner and Sal had the two radios assigned to the team, and Sal used one to notify the command staff that they were now on scene. He was immediately rebuffed by Conner.

"Romero, I didn't give you permission to talk to command."

"I didn't know I needed your permission," he replied smartly.

"I'm in charge of this team. Any communication with command needs to go through me first."

Sal looked over at Flint and Coffy. "Yes, Sir!" he said as he rolled his eyes. He was easily twice the young man's age and didn't appreciate being admonished in front of the others.

Conner took a position on top of a broken piece of concrete and turned to face the others. "All right, our first assignment is this apartment building behind me. Since the quake took place last night while people were sleeping, there are most likely people still in here. I don't want anyone entering the building. Either stay on the ground or on top of the debris, but under no circumstances do I want to see anyone inside or under the debris. Is that clear?"

Coffy was first to speak. "You're kidding, right? How are we going to find anyone still alive without looking under the debris?"

"You can send your dogs in. They can alert you!" Conner said somewhat nervously.

"That's crap, Conner," Coffy said sharply. "I won't let my dog in that building without me. He could get hung up or injured. If I don't go in, he doesn't either."

"That's your choice. Stay on the outside then," he said sharply.

Flint couldn't hold back. Even though he'd never conducted an urban search and rescue, he knew enough to know this guy was out of his element.

"I've got to ask, Conner, have you ever worked with a K9 search and rescue team before?"

Conner looked hurt for just a moment, but quickly recovered. "I've been on three deployments for FEMA. I know what I'm doing."

"That's not what I asked you. Have you ever worked with a K9 search and rescue team before?"

"I have training in urban search and rescue. I know what I'm doing."

It was obvious to everyone from his refusal to answer Flint's question that the kid didn't know squat about K9 search and rescue.

"Get back with me when you figure out the answer. Till then, stay the hell out of the way." Team Bravo, minus the young engineer still standing on the rock, took off and entered the apartment grounds to begin their search.

"Flint, there's not a lot of difference between a disaster search and a wilderness search except the bodies don't move around like a living person does when they're lost. Apache will alert on anyone in there dead or alive, but she can't indicate to you the difference. That will be up to you to determine. If she alerts, yell into the area she alerts to and listen for a reply. If you hear something, let Sal know so he can use the radio to get help. If you don't hear anything, mark the spot with the orange tape in your pack, just make an X with it and move on." She reached down to make sure her lead was firmly attached to Argo.

"Doesn't sound too complicated," Flint said, unconsciously following Coffy's movements by checking his connection with Apache.

"A couple of things." She stood back up and grabbed his hand. "Despite what that dumb ass said, he is right about this stuff being unstable. Try not to get underneath the debris if you can avoid it. Earthquakes always come with aftershocks, and that's when a lot of people get killed. You never know when or how strong they'll be, and this debris will try to settle."

"Understood," he said.

"Last, it's all right if the dog wants to investigate something in the debris while following a scent. But don't let them disappear anywhere while on a leash. If it gets tangled onto something and you can't reach them, it's possible you won't get your dog back."

Flint shook his head and squeezed her hand. "Got it."

"Do you want to follow me for a few minutes to see how I do it?" she asked him.

"Nope, I'm good. I don't think it's too far above my pay grade."

Coffy smiled at him. He was damned near as independent and stubborn as she was.

"Flint?" She pulled him back to her.

"Yep?" he said, looking into her eyes with a grin.

"Don't get hurt. I don't want to lose my summer home."

They both laughed and shared a kiss before they separated and began climbing the remains of the apartment building.

It didn't take long for Apache to alert. Barely a minute after Flint's command to 'find,' she stuck her nose into the debris and sat, staring up at Flint for further instruction. Flint got down on his hands and knees and yelled, "*Hola!* Anyone there?" There was no answer. Flint shined his light into the hole and could see nothing. He yelled once more and again received no response. He marked the location by making an 'X' on a nearby piece of debris with his orange tape, stood, and commanded Apache to continue her search.

Ten feet farther up the debris pile, Apache alerted again. Flint yelled into the broken concrete with the same result as last time, no response. He looked in Coffy's direction and saw her move a large chunk of debris to the side before she leaned headfirst into the hole and yelled. He was amazed at her strength. Sal, who was just behind her marked the position with an orange 'X.' He began to worry that they might not find any survivors in the apartment building. If the heavy cement floors pancaked on top of sleeping occupants without warning, and it certainly looked like that was what happened from the way the debris lay, most victims never had a chance to protect themselves.

The sun slipped behind the tall mountains just on the edge of town and daylight was quickly fading as they continued their search of the apartment building. After almost an hour, no one had been found alive. Coffy sent Sal over to tell Flint that he should start wrapping up his search area and prepare to move on to the next building. Flint had already finished his area, but was going back over a few spots he wanted to double check when Sal arrived.

"Sal, how many of these earthquake search and rescues have you been called out for?" Flint asked as Sal followed behind.

"This is my third event. I went to Nepal once, and Haiti. The one in Haiti, man, that was a bad one."

"Worse than this one?"

"Yeah. Those poor people, they had nothing to begin with, then to see all that hurt and misery come down on them at once. It was sad."

"Do you ever get used to it? I mean the suffering?"

"Nope. Never. You just have to keep your mind focused on helping those you can. Not on those you can't."

"I guess so. Are you ready to move on?" Flint asked.

"Yep, nothing here."

As Flint turned to head downslope, Apache alerted. "Got any tape? I'm running low," he asked Sal.

"I do."

Flint almost decided not to yell, but thought twice about it. He got to his knees and shouted. "*Hola! Alguien ahí?* Anyone in there?"

Flint was stunned when he heard a weak reply, "*Por favor, ayúdame.*"

"Sal! Someone is alive in there!"

Sal moved closer to the opening and shouted, "*Estás herido?*"

The voice sounded female. "*Sí, me lesiono! Por favor, ayúdame!*" Sal translated, "She said she's hurt."

"*Señora ayuda está en camino,*" Sal shouted back. "I told her help was coming," he told Flint.

As Sal began to radio for help, Flint stood and looked at Apache, who was patiently waiting for her reward. Flint took off his pack and reached in for Apache's favorite towel, the one they used for tug of war. He happily engaged her in her favorite sport.

It was well past midnight as Bravo Team made the long walk through the rough cobblestone streets to the hospital. They had been dispatched there by the American Command Center after searching two office buildings and a school just south of the main square where not a single person was found alive. Fortunately, the bodies they did find were few as most everyone had headed home for the evening before the quake hit.

The street leading to the main hospital building was on a steep uphill incline, and it was no small effort to negotiate the debris that covered it. There were no sidewalks, and it reminded Flint of the uphill, rock-strewn trails he had experienced during his training in Colorado.

As usual, Flint struggled silently trying to keep up with Coffy. She most definitely had the home field advantage here in the mountainous terrain of western Mexico.

"Come on, old man. You need to keep up!" she shouted at Flint while she walked backward up the hill with Argo leading the way.

"Freaking showoff! Wait till we have a search in Florida in the middle of summer and it's a hundred percent humidity! You won't be so perky then!"

Sal chimed in from even farther behind Flint, "That's nothing. Try hauling a three-hundred-pound man down the stairway of a thirty story tower in New York! That's when you know you're a bad ass." They all laughed at that one.

Coffy slowed down a little to let them catch up. The engineer was somewhere ahead, trying hard to prove himself again.

"So how do you feel?" Coffy teased as Flint got a little closer.

"I'm fine. You just worry about yourself."

"No, I mean finding your first urban disaster survivor."

"It's all right I guess. You know I've found people before, right?" Flint said with a grin.

"Yes, but not in the middle of an earthquake zone and under several tons of concrete."

"I think I'm digging it!" he admitted.

"Digging it?" Sal protested as he caught up with the other two. "You know 'digging it' isn't cool anymore right?" Sal patted him on the shoulder as he passed by and continued up the hill.

Coffy turned and walked beside Flint and Apache. "I'm proud of you. You and Apache did well."

"Shoot, Apache did all the work. All I did was follow her."

She reached up to whisper into his ear, "Yes, but she did it for you and you listened to her tell you what was going on. You two are a real team, and I love you both." She sneaked a quick kiss on his cheek. His huge grin made her smile.

The team reached the apex of the hill where they, at last, saw what remained of the hospital in front of them. The large, white masonry building which had once been a symbol of help and comfort for the community now lay mostly in a crumbled heap. The jagged and broken walls still standing looked dangerously close to toppling backward down the hill. Mexican Police had set up barricades across the street from it to keep people from wandering into the danger area. At least a hundred people stood behind the barriers, each turning to look at the Americans as the team pushed through the crowd until reaching the white, wooden barricade. There was a great cheer from the crowd, mixed with enthusiastic applause when they saw the police let the team through to enter the vacant street in front of the hospital.

Sal walked forward to listen in as Tate, who had evidently arrived a few minutes ahead of them talked to one of the police officers while Flint and Coffy hung back and stared at what remained of the hospital walls. It looked to have been a three-story, possibly four-story building with an ancillary wing to the right that lay in a pile of smoking rubble. Parts of the front wall to the main building were still standing, reminding Coffy of the shell still standing after the Trade Tower collapse. A fire was burning somewhere deep inside, its presence given away by the occasional flicker of orange light against the white painted rubble seen through the few surviving windows in the facade.

"Man, that's one scary looking building," Flint said to Coffy.

"Yes, it is. I'm surprised the aftershocks haven't sent it down the hill yet."

"*Señor! Señorita! Por favor*, please, come." They both turned to see a young man in the crowd behind the barricade, beckoning for their attention. Flint tugged on Apache's leash and began walking toward the man with Coffy and Argo behind him.

"Thank you, *Señor!* Thank you!" The man reached out and shook Flint's hand. "*Señor*, are you here to help find the lost ones?"

"Yes, we're here to help." Flint kept his words short and to the point.

"Thank you!" The young man looked at the middle-aged woman standing next to him and spoke to her in Spanish. Speaking back to him, the young man translated for her.

"*Señor*, my English is not good. Please try to understand me. *Esta es mi madre*," he said, pointing at the woman he had just spoken to.

Coffy stepped forward so she could hear his broken English better.

184

She knew little Spanish, but she knew the lady he was pointing to was the young man's mother.

"*Mi Madre*, she got ah, phone message from my sister. She is *atrapado*, ah, lost in hospital."

Coffy looked into the red and swollen eyes of the mother, who was obviously desperate to find her daughter. The pain was evident for all to see. Coffy reached over the barricade to hug the woman.

Flint asked the young man, "Is your sister still alive? How long ago was the phone call?"

"It was soon after the *terremoto,* the earthquake. *Mi Madre* has not talked to her since."

"Is she a patient?" Coffy asked him.

"No, she is a nurse. She helps babies, and *Señorita*, before the phone die, my sister, she says there are four babies still alive."

Coffy's eyes went wide. "Tell me again, how long has it been since your mother talked with your sister?"

"It was just once, soon after the hospital fell. She told *mi Madre* she is hurt; she cannot move."

"Do you know what part of the building she's in?"

The man turned to his mother, "*Qué parte del edificio fue ella en?*"

The woman spoke quietly, "*Ella estaba en la sala de maternidad.*"

The woman's son translated. "She was in the baby room."

"Where is that?" Coffy said abruptly.

"In the back of the hospital. In the bottom. Under the number one floor"

"The basement?" Coffy asked.

"*Si,* the basement," the man said, nodding his head.

Coffy looked at Flint. "Let's go." They started toward the building.

"Where in the hell do you think you're going?" Tate shouted their direction when he saw them move toward the building.

"There are people still alive in there!" Flint shouted back at the young engineer. He didn't like catching attitude from people half his age. "We're going to do what we came here for!"

"Hold up! You're not going anywhere." Tate started walking over to them, puffing himself up as he approached. "The building is too dangerous."

Flint looked at the young engineer and grinned. "Son, you need to grow a pair before you start ordering people around like that."

Coffy stepped out behind Flint and gave Tate the finger, to which the crowd responded with a loud roar of approval. There was no translation needed.

Romero had obviously had enough of Tate's incompetence as well. Walking up next to him, he locked eyes, muttered, "Chicken shit!" and fell in next to Flint and Coffy. The three members of Bravo Team began making their way over to what was once the main entrance to the hospital.

"Summerfield! I've already been in touch with Central Command. If you disobey my orders one more time, they will pull your contract. Do you understand me? I'll see to it that you and your organization are never called out on a FEMA job again!"

Coffy stopped suddenly. "Here, Flint, take Argo's leash?" She turned to face Tate, who had stopped about twenty feet away and was suddenly looking concerned.

Flint had seen that look on her face once before, just before she jumped out of the helicopter. "What are you about to do?"

"Nothing," she said as she began walking calmly toward the skinny engineer. "I'm just going to politely inform this prick that he has hurt my feelings."

"Don't do it, Coffy!" Flint said, but it was too late. She closed the distance between Tate and herself before Flint could hand the dog's leashes off to Sal. Tate began to back up, but at the last second decided to hold his ground.

"Summerfield, I don't--"

"You sorry son-of-a-bitch! Don't you ever threaten me again!" With that, she threw a right-handed haymaker that connected squarely with the engineer's chin, knocking him to the ground. She stood over him, commanding him to get up so she could knock him down again.

Flint ran toward her, grabbed her, and tried to pull her away from Tate, but it was too late. The Mexican police officer whom Tate had been talking to earlier was already walking toward them with his handcuffs out.

Flint woke up not recognizing where he was at first. Rolling over in his cot, the soreness in his body reminded him of the activities from the day before. The bright, late morning sunlight streaming into the open tent stabbed at his eyes as he struggled to open them. Apache, lying on the ground next to him, stood and licked him in the face. She was ready to go again. Flint most certainly was not.

As some semblance of alertness began to filter into his sluggish brain, he looked around and realized Coffy wasn't in her cot and Argo was nowhere to be seen. *Probably trying to cool off by taking the dog for a walk*, he reasoned. That was a good thing. When the group returned to their tent early this morning, she was still furious with Tate and wanted to finish the fight she started with him the night before.

As a cop and a park ranger, Flint was used to negotiating when necessary to get things done, but he had never haggled with anyone as hard as he had last night trying to get the police officer to let Coffy go without a charge. He finally convinced the officer that no harm was done as the fight was between two Americans who were trying to help his country through a time of crises. The three-hundred dollars he paid the officer to take the handcuffs off of Coffy didn't hurt either. In any case, it was an awkward van ride home with Tate in the front and Coffy in the back.

Flint changed clothes, took Apache for a short walk, and returned to his cot to open two military ration meals. One for himself, and one for Apache, which she ate in three gulps. She wasn't dainty when it came to eating human food.

Twenty minutes went by without any sign of Coffy, so he decided to start looking for her. Not finding her in camp, he began asking others if they had seen her that morning. Only one person, a nurse, had reported seeing her briefly. She said she had seen a woman matching Coffy's description walking her dog near the transportation depot at about seven o'clock this morning.

Flint thought at first she was sent on an assignment in the middle of the night without his knowledge, but Command was pretty displeased with her right now. It wasn't likely she would have been sent out so soon after her battle with Tate, and surely she would have told him first. Suddenly, an alarming thought coming from somewhere in the back of his mind caused a surge of adrenaline to flood his body. She went back to the hospital.

Last night, she had been hell-bent on rescuing the babies. She must have gone without him, probably to avoid getting him into any more trouble than she had already caused him. He should be with her, and he was determined to make sure she heard about it when he found her. They were a team whether she liked it or not.

He quickly made his way back to the tent and assembled his gear. He looked over at Coffy's bunk and saw her rescue pack was missing. He cursed himself for not noticing it before; it might have saved valuable time. The only thing on top of her bunk were the clothes she had worn the day before. He grabbed her shirt and threw it into his pack. He might need it later.

It took almost an hour for Flint to get his gear together, find transportation, and get himself and Apache to the ruins of the hospital building. He'd thought about asking Sal to go with him, but it would have been unfair to ask him to risk his career on a hunch.

There was still a crowd in front of the hospital. Flint studied several of their faces until he recognized the man he had talked with the night before. The man was pleading with a police officer who had his back turned toward him, apparently trying to ignore him.

"Sir, I need to speak with you," Flint said as he approached. The police officer walked away, leaving Flint alone with the young man.

"Yes! Are you here to help?" The man gave Flint his full attention.

"I am, but I need some help from you first. The woman and the dog I was with last night, have you seen them this morning?"

"Yes. She is inside the hospital looking for my sister and the babies."

"How long has she been in there?"

The man looked at his watch. "Sir, about three-and-a-half hours and we are worried for her."

"Why are you worried?"

"Because, *Señor*, two hours ago, something exploded. There was lots of fire and smoke."

Flint's shoulders fell as he absorbed the blow to his gut. Remembering that she had survived a fire once before, he hoped she could do it again.

"Where did she enter the building?"

"Through that window," the man said, pointing to one of the few remaining openings in the partially standing facade.

"Thank you," Flint said as he turned to run to the spot where Coffy was last seen.

"Please, sir, find my sister," the man shouted.

Flint pulled Coffy's shirt out of his pack and let Apache get a good scent lock on it. He didn't imagine she would have much trouble recognizing the scent, but the shirt would tell her to concentrate on Coffy's scent only. Flint knew there would be plenty of distractions coming from the bodies of those buried beneath the rubble. He hoped Apache could ignore them and concentrate on Coffy alone. Flint disconnected Apache's lead and she wasted little time figuring out which direction Coffy had gone.

Carefully climbing the debris pile, Apache found several openings large enough that she and Flint could negotiate. Several of the tunnels had smoke rising from them, an indication that there were still fires burning deep within. She stopped at each opening, carefully smelling the scent molecules floating upwards from them until, finally, she disappeared downward into one. Flint followed closely, though the hole was only big enough for him to crawl through.

Flint turned on his helmet light to help see through the smoke and darkness that filled the empty spaces. Twenty feet in, he encountered the first body. It appeared to be a woman, though he couldn't be sure because of all the white dust that coated her face. She wore medical scrubs and stared lifelessly at him from below one of the thick concrete columns. He crawled past her and focused on his dog several yards in front of him. Apache had ignored the body, which was a good sign she was doing her job correctly.

Every twenty feet or so, he stopped to mark his location with orange tape and yell Coffy's name. There was no reply. The deeper into the debris he went, the denser the smoke became. At one point, the fire must have been directly below him because the heat was almost too much to take. Apache, however, never gave it a second thought.

Several times Apache would enter a hole only to back out and start through another. Flint always removed the orange tape when this happened so that when it came time to find their way out, the tape wouldn't lead him to a dead end.

After almost an hour of crawling through the debris pile, Flint entered a crawlspace where the smell of burning bodies began to overwhelm him. It was as if he were crawling through the bottom of one of those big funeral pyres in India he had seen pictures of. The bodies he'd seen thus far weren't burned, but somewhere nearby, plenty were. He saw flickers of orange now and then in the darkness, shooting up through the debris in the distance. There were multiple fires all around, and he began to worry about his endgame strategy here. At what point should he give up and climb back out to safety, but then he would find himself thinking about Coffy and how she never backed down from that raging fire in Colorado. He wasn't about to quit either.

Flint and Apache struggled on until they entered an area full of twisted, lifeless bodies, ghostly in appearance due to the plaster dust that covered them. Flint could see at least ten bodies from where he lay. He was surprised that thus far, he hadn't seen a live person anywhere. If there had been anyone alive down here, then they were probably finished off by the shifting debris during the aftershocks. Flint called Apache back to him. They both needed to rest a few minutes.

Apache carefully negotiated the debris back to Flint and sat next to him. Flint was lying uncomfortably on one of the concrete beams as he studied her face in the light from his helmet. Her eyes weren't as bright and happy as they normally were. It wasn't a game for her this time. Flint reached out to rub her ears. "You know, don't you, girl," he said. "You know who we're looking for. She'll be all right. We all will be." He petted her in silence for a long while. With every stroke of her fur, a cloud of white dust would fly through the beam of his light. There was no telling what toxins they were ingesting with every breath. Suddenly, Apache's ears stood straight up as she cocked her head and focused somewhere behind Flint. Flint heard nothing.

"Coffy!" Flint yelled. There was no reply. "Coffy!"

After several more tries, he heard someone calling his name. It wasn't Coffy.

"Flint! Flint!"

"I'm down here!" Flint shouted back. The voice was too far away and too distorted from all the strange angles of the debris surrounding them for him to tell who it was. After several minutes, the voice was much louder.

"Flint, can you hear me?"

"Yes!" Flint yelled. "You're getting closer!" It was Sal Romero. He couldn't believe Sal had found him.

Flint watched as the light from Sal's helmet suddenly appeared near his feet as he crawled around and over some debris until, finally, they were close enough to see each other. Apache negotiated her way around Flint to inspect this new development. Sal reached out to scratch her between the ears.

"Sal! Damn glad to see you, sir!"

"Likewise!" Sal grinned as he petted Apache.

"How did you find me?"

"Easy, I followed the orange tape."

"No, I mean, how did you know I was going to be here, at the hospital?"

"When pecker head Tate got our assignments and couldn't find you or Coffy, he went ballistic. Started asking me where you two were. I told him I had no idea. Then I caught the next ride I could get to the hospital. It wasn't hard to figure out."

"Well, hell, Sal, I appreciate it."

"You should have told me you guys were headed here. I would have come with you. Where is Coffy? She up top?"

"No, that's why I came here without telling you. She took off on her own this morning. She didn't tell me what she was planning; I guess because she didn't want to put anyone else at risk."

"So she's down here somewhere?"

"Yeah, I'm trying to find her."

"Damn! That woman has some brass cajones. Are you sure she's down here?"

"I'm positive. Apache is on her scent, so she's come through here. Besides, I know her pretty well, Sal. She doesn't put up with anyone telling her she can't do something. I think she decided to do it the second Tate said she couldn't. She probably had it all planned before we got back to the tent last night."

Sal chuckled. "Good on her."

Any good feeling from Sal's sudden appearance was soon replaced by terror as what was left of the building began to shake.

"Aftershock!" Sal yelled.

Dust began to fill the air in their tiny space. They could feel the vibration build to a crescendo of full movement back and forth throughout the building as pilings shifted and debris settled downward through the empty spaces. Somewhere below and to the right, an explosion, most likely from an oxygen bottle or some other compressed gas cylinder typically used in hospitals, lifted the heavy beams and laid them down again. Apache whined. There had been nothing in her training that had prepared her for this scenario. It was over in twenty seconds.

Flint looked down toward his feet. The dust was thick, but he could see Sal's light was gone. Fearing the worst, he yelled, "Sal! Sal! You okay?"

Sal's light reappeared. "Yeah, I'm all right!" he yelled after lifting his face from under his arms, then he mumbled to himself, "Think I might have just shit my pants, though."

"What?" Flint asked.

"Nothing! False alarm," he said, wiping the dust from his eyes. "Flint, this isn't good, man. I mean, this is some dangerous stuff."

"I know it, Sal. I can't leave her down here, though. Why don't you head back up?"

"Hell no. I'm here for the duration. Besides, I'm thinking our path out of here may have just changed."

"Roger that!" Flint leaned out to comfort Apache, who was still looking at him with fear in her eyes. "It's okay, girl. Are you ready?" Apache turned her head and stood. "That a girl! Seek!" With that, she was off again. There was work to be done.

Another twenty-five minutes of crawling among the bodies and smoke and wallowing through the dirt and debris had resulted in little, except for cuts and bruises among the two men. Apache's behavior of following Coffy's scent one direction only to turn and come back told Flint that wherever she was, she must be exhausted. She was searching for survivors, not one particular person. She must have crawled down each false hole only to back out and try another. Flint and Sal had the ability to let Apache do the hard work. If Apache went one direction, they would wait for her to come back and try another. It was a lot easier for them than it had been for Coffy.

It was when Apache returned from the darkness of one of those holes that Flint got the shock of his life. The light from his helmet would always cause the bright reflection of Apache's eyes when she was returning from the darkness of one of her tunnel explorations. This time was no exception. Except this time as she emerged from the hole, there was another pair of glowing eyes staring directly at them from the darkness.

CHAPTER FIFTEEN

"Argo!" Flint shouted with disbelief. "Where did you come from, boy?" Flint was joyful, calling out for Coffy and hoping to see her show up behind her dog. There was no answer. His heart sank as he realized seeing Argo alone without Coffy wasn't a good sign. "Sal, we may have an issue."

"I see that." Both men shouted Coffy's name, but again there was no response.

Flint reached out and pulled Argo closer. He stroked the dog's fur and checked him for injury. It was then he noticed the piece of paper wrapped around Argo's collar. After carefully removing it, he read the words loud enough for Sal to hear them.

I'm trapped in the nursery. Need help. Three babies alive. Coffy Summerfield. Flint suddenly felt more optimistic about their chances of finding her until he noticed that congealed into the white dust that coated the paper were droplets of blood.

"We need to hurry, Sal. She's injured." Flint put the paper into his pants pocket and looked at Argo. "Take me to her, girl. Show me!" Both dogs took off in the direction they'd come from with the rescuers crawling on their bellies right behind them.

It took less than ten minutes to get as far as the men could go. One of the concrete beams holding back tons of concrete debris was blocking their path. Coffy had to have been here as both Argo and Apache stood at the end of the debris tunnel with their noses to the ground.

193

"Coffy!" Flint called out. Nothing. "Coffy!" Again, nothing. Half out of desperation and half out of anger toward her for going off and dying alone, Flint yelled one more time. "Coffy! God damn it!"

Both dogs and humans cocked their heads at the same time as they heard the faint voice.

"Hello?"

"Coffy? Coffy, is that you?" Flint shouted.

The voice suddenly got stronger. "Yes, it is! My God, is that you Flint?"

Flint laughed, though he didn't know why. "Yes! It's Flint. Where are you?"

"I'm in the nursery." Coffy sounded loud and clear now like she was just on the other side of the beam. Flint crawled closer and found a small hole under the concrete beam, maybe a foot and a half in diameter. It sounded like Coffy's voice was coming from the hole. Out of the corner of his eye, he saw something that shocked him, a dust-covered human hand reaching up from under the beam. He recognized a ring on the hand as one he'd seen many times as it had caressed his face during endless nights of lovemaking. It was Coffy's hand under the beam.

"Oh shit, Coffy, are you trapped under this beam?"

"I was. Not anymore. I'm about twenty feet beyond it in what's left of the nursery. Flint, there are four babies in here; three of them are still alive. We've got to get them out of here. They're dehydrated and in bad shape."

Flint was stunned. All he could picture in his head was Coffy trapped in a room just out of reach, probably bleeding to death with what must be a horrible injury. Despite all that, she was more concerned about the babies than herself. He looked back at Sal with disbelief.

"Like I said, brass cajones," Sal quipped while shaking his head.

Flint shouted back into the hole. "Coffy, first you have to take care of yourself so you can help those babies. Are you still bleeding?"

"Yes, but it's slowed down. I have a tourniquet on it."

"How bad is it, Coffy?"

"Not good. I was climbing out to get help when a tremor hit. A beam shifted and caught my arm. It pinched it off at the elbow. I crawled back into the nursery, wrapped it up, and I guess I passed out for a while. I woke up when another tremor started, and now the hole in the wall is closed up. I can't get out of the room."

"The nurse who called her mother, is she down there with you? Can she help you?"

"No, she's dead!"

Flint thought about the situation for a moment. "How did Argo get out, sweetheart?"

"There's a small opening in the wall just big enough for him to get through. I wrote a note and sent him through hoping he would find a way out. I guess he did."

"Yeah, we found him. He got out through a hole underneath the beam that got you. It's not big enough for us to get to you. We're going to have to find another way in."

"Who's with you?"

"Sal is here. We're going to find another way in."

"There's no time for that. There's a fire down here, and we don't have long to get these babies out. Listen to me; I have an idea. Do you think the dogs can get through to me?"

Coffy tried to ignore the pain, but it was impossible. Her arm had been pinched off by the massive concrete column just below the elbow. A clean cut by a sharp implement would've been far preferable. Losing a limb by having it smashed off ensured that every possible nerve ending was affected and screaming at her in agony. She was in shock, which helped some, but with every passing minute, the pain grew. It clouded her judgment.

She found the babies after several hours of searching in the debris, with Argo as her guide. When he alerted her that he had found something, she thought it was just another body. She crawled with him through the dark and cramped voids until she happened into the nursery. The narrow hole through the wall gave way to a dark and dusty space barely bigger than her kitchen back home.

The first thing she saw through the light from her helmet were baby cribs. Six of them. She squirmed her way through the opening and, upon standing, saw two of the cribs were empty, but the other four had infants in them. All four were covered in plaster and dust and lying motionless. She was heartbroken at first as she thought they must all be dead. When she checked on them, however, she was shocked to find three of them still alive. They were no doubt close to death and needed to get out of here immediately. They most likely had not had liquids or formula in at least thirty-six hours and their still delicate respiratory systems had been taking in a significant amount of dust. Still, they were alive. It was an incredible find.

She decided the best course of action would be to grab one of the infants and climb back out the way she had come in. She would alert rescue workers above and lead them back in to get the other two.

Coffy reached for the closest baby, who opened her eyes as soon as it was touched. They were beautiful brown eyes which stood out behind the stark white dust caked on the baby's face.

"Hello, little one," Coffy said sweetly. The baby began to cry, which made Coffy smile. "Don't you worry one bit. I'm going to get you and your friends here out into some fresh air and get you something to fill your tummy. You're going to be just fine."

Argo startled her with a bark. Coffy had forgotten about him for a moment.

"What is it, boy?" She swung her head around to illuminate what had gained Argo's attention. What she saw made her cringe. Lying on the floor, crushed from the pelvis down by a large chunk of concrete that must have fallen through the ceiling, was a nurse judging from the medical scrubs she was wearing. She was dead. Lying next to her was a cellphone. It had to be the daughter who was able to connect with her mother to tell her about the babies. Coffy stared at her for a moment.

"You saved a lot of lives with your phone call. I hope you somehow know that now." Coffy looked at the cellphone. If the nurse had been able to use it, maybe she could do the same. She reached down to pick it up and tried to make it work realizing after a moment that either the battery was dead or, the phone was broken.

Returning her attention to the babies, Coffy wrapped the infant girl in a bed sheet, instructed Argo to lead the way, and crawled back into the narrow passageway. It had taken nearly three hours to get here, but it should take a quarter of that to get back out. She barely made it twenty feet.

The aftershock hit just as she told Argo to slow down. She was reaching outward with her right hand to pull herself and the baby forward when the concrete beam slammed down, catching her forearm between it and the concrete slab underneath it. The beam slid forward, grinding her arm off at the elbow. At first, she wasn't sure what happened as she lay there waiting for the tremors to stop. Her fear of further collapse on top of her and the baby had somehow masked the pain. It wasn't until the building grew quiet again and she looked up in front of her that she saw the terrible damage.

She lifted her arm to see blood spurting from the elbow. The shock of seeing it made her chuckle for some odd reason. The humor of the situation quickly disappeared as the pain set in, and the seriousness of what had just happened quickly became apparent. She and the baby were now trapped, she was missing an arm, and they were both separated from Argo if he was still alive. She screamed, half out of desperation, half because of the pain.

Crawling back to the nursery nearly killed her. She was losing blood at an alarming rate, trying to push backward with one arm and carry the baby at the same time. It was an impossible task, one that took every ounce of energy she could muster.

Barely conscious when she reached the room, she lay the baby on the floor and crawled over to one of the empty cribs. Not having the energy to stand, she reached up and pulled one of the sheets out of the crib. Using her teeth to tear a strip, she did her best to make a tourniquet. In the debris on the ground, she found a piece of lathe board once used to reinforce plaster, inserted it into the cloth, and twisted it, tightening the tourniquet as much as she could bear. She crawled back to the baby lying on the floor and did her best to cradle it in the crook of her good arm. Despite the baby's weak attempts at crying, Coffy finally passed out.

Argo wouldn't even let her die in peace. She woke to his giant tongue giving her long, wet licks on the side of her face. She opened her eyes to see that big, cold black nose coming in and out of her vision with every lick. "Argo!" Through her confusion, she reached out to him until she was forced to remember once again that she had no right arm with which to embrace him. The pain from the movement was sharp and heavy. She grimaced. "How did you get back in here, boy?"

She lay there in the dust trying to focus on what her next move should be. The baby next to her had quit crying. Coffy leaned over and gently pinched the child's arm. The child's eyes opened, but there was no crying. *Good. I've got to find another way out of here.*

Trying to ignore the throbbing pain, Coffy sat up, which increased the flow of blood from her arm. It was worrisome. She looked around to find something suitable to wrap around the lower part of her arm. She saw several folded towels on the floor that had fallen from one of the cabinets above. Crawling over, she grabbed one and looked for something with which to tie it on. She found a small supply of surgical tubing inside one of the bottom cabinets. Using her teeth to gnaw off a short piece, she quickly wrapped the tubing just above what remained of her elbow and tied it off. It did a much better job at staunching the blood flow than her first attempt with the tourniquet. She wrapped the towel around the bottom of the stump and used another piece of surgical tubing to tie it in place. It would at least keep the dust out of the wound. It was the best she could do.

She was weak, but as her adrenaline began to flow once again, she was finally able to stand. She checked the other two babies still in their cribs. They were still breathing though she didn't know how. She shined her light toward the other side of the small room and saw a chair at a small desk against the wall. She struggled to make it over and sit. She tried to think of what to do. There must be something. She looked at the desk and saw a couple of pieces of paper with the hospital logo on it. A pen lay nearby. She had an idea.

After struggling to write a message as well as she could with her left hand, she called Argo over. He sat next to her.

"Argo, I need you to do something." She folded the paper around his collar several times. "I want you to take this note and give it to someone. Understand?" She looked into his eyes. "Of course, you don't. Listen, I don't know how you got back in here, but I'm hoping you can find your way back out." She guided him to the hole in the wall. "Home, boy!" she shouted. "Go home!" Argo looked back at her, and she waved her good arm to point the direction. "Home!" He disappeared into the hole in the wall.

Using her last bit of strength, Coffy made her way back to the baby lying on the floor. Fighting through the pain, she knelt, scooped the baby with her good arm, and struggled back to her feet. She walked to the chair, collapsed into it, and gently began rocking the precious child in her arm. Memories of how she rocked her son to sleep filled her head and kept her mind off the pain. She closed her eyes and began to hum a nursery rhyme from years ago.

The aftershock that woke her didn't feel as strong as the one that had taken her arm, but the structural damage was far greater. A fire started from an explosion somewhere nearby, and she could already feel the heat through the rubble. Looking at the baby, she could see its eyes were shut, but not having the energy to check to see if the baby was still alive, she passed out once again.

The sound of Flint's voice woke her. He was yelling her name, though she didn't know at first if it was merely a dream or if he was really out there.

"Coffy! God damn it!" she heard him yell. It was Flint. He always cursed when he got frustrated.

"Hello?" Coffy tried to answer.

It was a simple plan, a brilliant plan really, the kind of plan that could go spectacularly wrong in an instant. Coffy got the idea from summers spent helping her father build the cabin in Colorado. She didn't like crawling under the cabin's floor. There were too many spiders under there for her liking, so she developed a method of using dogs to help get things like pipe, wire, and insulation to her father when he needed them. She would tie a rope to the dog's collar and send it to her father under the house. Coffy would tie whatever he needed to the other end of the rope which he would then pull toward him. Her father would laugh every time she did it, but it worked.

She quickly explained her plan to Flint, who expressed his doubts that it would work, but agreed that he could think of nothing better. They would send the dogs through, each with one of the infants swaddled in bed sheets and foam from the crib mattresses tied to the dog's harness. Argo had been able to make it through the narrow passageway so it could work. The biggest worry was if the child became lodged in the debris somewhere along the way. If that happened, both child and dog would be lost. There was no way for a human to get to them if it happened. With fire now visible in the back of the room and getting bigger by the minute, there would be no time for a second rescue attempt.

Coffy struggled to move. Blood loss was making her weary and confused. She fought against the pain, wishing she could just lie down for a few moments, but she knew if she did, she would never get up again. She yelled to Flint to send a knife through with the dogs.

Both dogs arrived at the opening in the nursery wall, and Coffy did what she could to help them get through. Each dog was forced to lie on its side and wallow through as if it were trying to dig under a fence. Coffy used her good arm for support to keep them from falling to the floor.

Using the knife Flint had tied to Argo's collar, she retrieved one of the mattresses from an empty crib and began to cut at the foam padding which was made much more problematic by having only one arm with which to work. Once the foam was out of its cover, she laid it next to one of the babies to get a sense of how much she needed. She cut off the excess and found that by placing the baby perpendicular to the original length of the mattress, she had enough foam from this one mattress for two of the three babies.

It took an eternity in her mind as she watched the flames in the back of the room begin to eat away at the cabinetry that was still standing. She put aside any thoughts of not being successful. There was no other option but to get these babies out of here right now.

She laid the foam on top of a bed sheet in one of the empty cribs, then struggled to get the baby girl on the floor up onto the foam. The only way she could manage it was to pick the baby up by the diaper and flop it onto what remained of her other arm. She couldn't stifle her scream from the pain.

"Coffy! What's going on? Are you all right?" Flint yelled into the hole.

"Yeah. Just give me another minute," she said, feeling sick to her stomach and on the verge of passing out again.

She carefully laid the baby onto the foam and, using the bed sheet underneath, wrapped the baby to form a crude papoose. The baby opened its eyes, but it never made a sound. Coffy thought it might be too late for this one, but she had to try. Using the surgical tubing she found earlier, she tied the sheet around the baby, leaving two long pieces to tie to Argo's harness. She lifted the baby by the padding and laid it on the floor. With Argo sitting on the floor next to her, she tied one piece of tubing to the left side of Argo's harness and another to the right side, creating a crude sled.

She scanned the room for something to use as a ramp to aid her in getting the dogs off the ground and into the hole in the wall. Finding nothing suitable, she improvised by rolling the chair up to the hole. It wasn't tall enough, but it was all she had. "Come on, boy. You've got a job to do." She patted the chair. Argo hesitated once he felt the weight of the baby behind him, but following Coffy's command, he dragged the baby across the floor. It was working, at least on the smooth floor. The real test would be in the tunnel.

Coffy picked the baby up by the swaddling and held it as Argo jumped onto the chair. "Okay boy, in the hole." He reached his front paws up to the hole and tried using his rear legs to climb, but the plaster wall gave him no traction. Coffy used her shoulder to boost him into the hole while still holding onto the baby. He finally wallowed through as Coffy slid the baby into the hole right behind him. Shining her helmet light into the hole, she watched as Argo struggled to pull the baby along. It was working!

"The baby, it's on its way to you!" she yelled. Unable to stand any longer, she collapsed back into the chair and passed out once again.

"Coffy! Coffy, we got the baby!" Flint's shouting brought her to.

"Great," she said weakly, struggling to her feet to get to the next baby. Smoke from the fire was filling the room, causing her to choke. She was running out of time.

She struggled to repeat the process with the second baby. Like the first, it was lethargic and needed help immediately. She secured the baby in its foam and cloth cocoon, but there wasn't enough surgical tubing to make the connection to Apache's harness. Improvising, she tore several strips of cloth from a bed sheet to make the connection. Using every ounce of strength she could muster, she to lifted the dog to the hole and guided the baby through.

She didn't wait to hear from Flint before wrapping the third baby. Coughing and gagging from the smoke, she laid the baby in her lap as she sat in the chair to catch her breath and wait on another dog. She wasn't sure how long she was unconscious. Had it not been for Argo yelping from the pain of falling to the concrete floor when he returned to the nursery, she might not have woken up. She was almost done. Soon she could rest. She struggled to attach the baby's protective bundle to Argo's harness. Knowing this was the last time she would ever see her gentle giant of a dog, she spoke gently, "Argo, this is it, baby. You're one hell of a dog. We've saved a lot of lives together, you and me." Argo leaned down to lick her face. "I love you, boy." She reached out with her one good arm and drew him close. She whispered into his ear, "You take care of Apache."

She struggled to her feet and held the baby as Argo jumped onto the chair. She gave Argo one last command. "Home, boy! Go home!" She painfully supported him as he struggled to get through the hole and pull the baby along with him. When it was done, Coffy turned, placed her back against the wall, slowly slid to the floor, and closed her eyes.

Flint watched as Argo's head appeared out of the hole. He couldn't believe the plan actually worked. Argo struggled to get through the hole dragging the extra weight behind him, but the foam swaddling that Coffy made for the baby was too bulky to make it through. With the baby still on the other side of the beam, Flint cut Argo loose from the tubing connecting them together.

Working blindly by reaching through the hole with one arm, he loosened the straps holding the foam bundle together, and separated the baby from the cocoon that kept it safe during the trip through the tunnel. Carefully, he pulled the baby through, and reached back into the hole to retrieve the bundle. He handed the baby and the swaddling to Sal, who using Flint's orange tape, did his best to reassemble the package, making sure the baby had plenty of space to breathe.

"I'm worried Flint. This baby isn't crying. It's dehydrated and weak," Sal said with great concern in his voice. "It needs help right now."

Flint shouted back into the hole, "Coffy! Coffy, we got the baby! Coffy!" There was no answer. He yelled out for her several more times before finally hearing her weak reply that she was still alive.

Apache soon brought the second baby through and, like the first, Flint had to disassemble the foam bundle before he could gently pull the baby through. He handed the baby to Sal and reached back in to get the bundle of foam. Sal worked quickly to get the baby wrapped back into its protective covering.

"Flint, these babies are in critical shape. We have to get them back up top now," Sal said as he tore a piece of orange tape with his mouth and wrapped it around the foam.

Flint looked at Argo. "Sorry, boy, you've got to give it one more shot." He turned Argo back toward the hole. "Go!" Argo knew just what to do. Flint turned his attention back to Sal. "There's one more left. Can you handle those two?"

"Yeah, I got 'em. But when that third one comes out, you need to get it street level as fast as you can. It probably won't be in any better shape than these two."

"Roger that. Leave me the tape and go ahead," Flint said, having no intention of leaving Coffy down here alone. "When you get up top, radio the Command Center that we have a trapped rescuer, and we need all the help we can get."

"I will, but you're coming out as soon as that baby gets here, right?"

"Yes."

"All right, I'm out of here. Don't be too far behind me." Sal tossed the tape in Flint's direction, gathered the babies as best he could with one arm, and used the other to begin his climb out of the debris.

"Sal!" Flint yelled.

Sal turned back to look at him. "Yeah?"

"Thank you."

Sal smiled at him. "See you up top." With that, he turned and crawled off into the darkness.

"Coffy! Can you hear me? Coffy!" Coffy opened her eyes and took a moment to remember where she was. The blood loss was starving her brain for oxygen, and the flames which were getting closer didn't look real to her. The heat from them told her they were.

"Coffy, talk to me!" The desperation in Flint's voice sharpened her focus, but only briefly.

She could muster only enough energy to barely speak. "I'm here."

"Thank God! I have the last baby! You got them all out!"

"And the dogs?"

"They're out, too. They're right here beside me."

"Good. Now get that baby out of here!"

"Not yet. We need to get you out of there."

Coffy looked at the flames that were now just a few feet away. Her skin was beginning to redden and the smoke burned her eyes. If she told Flint how dire her situation was becoming, it would be impossible to make him leave. "The baby doesn't have time for that right now. What needs to happen is that you get that child some help." She took a deep breath and struggled to her feet. Leaning against the wall, she spoke directly into the hole. "Flint, that baby isn't going to make it unless you get it help right now. If you love me, you will take care of that baby!"

"Coffy, you know I love you and I'd do anything for you, but I'm not--"

"Flint!" she screamed, using too much of the little energy she had left. All bets were off. She needed to make him understand that it was hopeless to believe in a miracle this time. "Listen to me, dammit! In about five minutes, I will no longer exist. There's a fire in here, and it's not stopping for you or me. This is it, baby! I have no way out. But you do, if you leave now. More important, that baby will have a chance. If you don't care about yourself, then care about that baby. If that's not enough for you, think about Sam! Either you live on without me, or Sam lives on without either of us and the baby dies, too!"

There was a long silence. Coffy wasn't sure that Flint heard her. "Flint, did you hear what I said?" Coffy shouted.

"I heard you!"

"Then go! Please, Flint. Get that baby out of here!"

"All right, I'm taking the baby, but I'll be back to get you out of there. Do everything you can to stay alive till I get back. Do you hear me?"

"Yes, I hear you," she said with a sense of relief even though she knew time had run out. She was too weak to cry.

"I love you, Coffy. I'll be back."

"I love you, too. See you when you get back. And Flint?"

"Yeah?"

"Tell Sam that Koda belongs to her now. It's my gift to her for making me laugh so much this summer."

"That, my dear, you'll have to tell her when you get back."

Smiling at his optimism, she turned her back to the wall and slid slowly down to the floor. Her weary mind turned back to the horrible day in Colorado when she woke up to find her son face-down among the rocks in the river. The guilt she carried for not helping him when he needed her had defined every moment of every day of her life since. It guided every decision, every option, even every emotion she had in her life. She chose a solitary life of hardship and self-discipline to atone for her failure that morning. Years of saving the lives of others to absolve the sins of a mother.

It was Flint who showed her the way back from the darkness she endured for so long. He'd taught her that love and respect were still a possibility in a world of hurt and mistrust, and Sam, she had shown Coffy how to bring joy and wonder back into her life. Though it was only for a moment, she had been part of a family again.

Thinking of Flint and Sam in the kitchen making yet another awful pot of spaghetti and laughing together caused her to smile. She hoped Flint would forgive himself for having to leave her in this room. She hoped he would find his smile again. She needed to tell him not to allow the guilt that would come later to invade his life as it had hers. She needed to tell him now.

With her good arm, she reached out to the chair beside her and slid it closer. Struggling to her knees, she stood briefly before collapsing into it. "Flint!" she yelled. "Flint!" There was no answer. It was too late, he was gone. The man wanted to get the child out as fast as possible so he could return in time to save her. It was then she realized, he had already saved her. "I love you, Flint! Thank you for loving me!"

She looked back at the flames. The forward movement of the fire had slowed, but it hadn't decreased in size. She began to believe she might die from the heat before the flames ever got to her. She tried to focus on the empty cribs and smiled at the thought that, hopefully, three brand new lives had been saved here. She knew that she had done well and could now, finally, release the burden she had imposed upon herself of doing everything she could to save another. Soon, she would be with her son again and could tell him how sorry she was for what happened, but that some good had come out of it.

She looked at the crib closest to her, which still held the body of the baby she couldn't save. With everything she had left, she struggled to her feet and stumbled over to it. With pain still sharp and nauseating, she picked the child up by sliding her good arm underneath and steadying the tiny body with the bloody end of her other arm. She staggered back to the chair and collapsed into it, cradling the baby with her good arm. She stared at the child, who still looked as if it were peacefully sleeping.

"Hello, sweetheart," she said softly. "You didn't have long in this world, did you? I'm so sorry." She looked up at the flames and knew that it was time. She slid her arm out from under the baby and removed the towel from the end of her damaged arm. Soaked with her blood, it was easy to pull off. Reaching higher, she slowly removed the two tourniquets that had helped to staunch the flow of blood from her terrible wound. The pain was profound and intense as the blood flowed into the oxygen-deprived nerve cells at the end of her arm. The artery opened up and blood poured freely to the floor.

Coffy sighed as she slid her good arm back under the baby's body and rocked back and forth like a mother holding her newborn for the first time. She ignored the tormenting pain and concentrated on the baby's face.

"You know, little one, I have someone I want you to meet. He was brave like you, and handsome. He never met a bug he didn't like, and he was so smart. I know you would like him. Just in case you've already met him, if you see him, tell him his mom is coming to see him soon, okay?"

The room grew darker, and her head began to swim. She tilted her head back and closed her eyes as the rocking stopped. "Justin, please don't be angry with me. There was so much I had to do. I can't wait to tell you some of the stories that--" As she slumped back and fell silent for the last time, a slight smile formed as the joy of going home replaced the burden of a life spent with too much sadness.

CHAPTER SIXTEEN

Flint leaned back in his chair and watched Sam and Frisco going through their training exercises with Koda down near the barn. As usual in the evenings, Apache and Argo were having a great time chasing each other through the meadow next to the cabin. His daughter's natural ability to understand what motivated a search and rescue dog reminded him so much of Coffy's talents. Nearly fifteen now, Sam already had two successful searches under her belt. Her tenacity had brought her a long way in a short amount of time. She was determined to be as good as Coffy, and she was well on her way.

There was a fresh, crisp feel to the air as fall was quickly approaching. It was almost time for Flint and Sam to start packing for their winter training facility in Durango. There wasn't much to it, really, just a small rented farmhouse near the edge of town, but it afforded them the luxury of roads that were cleared of snow more often than not and a way for Sam to get back and forth from school. Flint dreaded the thought she would be driving on her own next year, but it would free up a little more time for him to work with the dogs.

The cabin changed little in the year-and-a-half since Coffy died. Flint went to great pains to keep it as he had known it when he first met her almost three years ago. The only exception was the addition of two objects to the fireplace mantle that Flint added himself, a silver urn and a picture of Coffy, Sam, and the dogs that he'd taken while they were together in

Florida. He cherished that picture and the memories it held for him. He'd had it enlarged and framed along with the shark necklace that Sam had given Coffy.

Flint found the necklace tied around Argo's collar during the bus ride back to the Command Center after their attempt to rescue Coffy. She knew she wasn't coming out of the building alive, so she must have tied it to Argo's collar while she was rescuing the babies. It was her last gift to Sam, besides Koda.

Flint often thought about the babies they'd rescued and what they might be doing now. He learned from the American Consulate in Mexico not too long after the disaster that all three of them survived. He imagined them at a year-and-a-half old now, running around their home, bumping into things, terrorizing their parents.

Around the one-year anniversary of the quake, a Mexican television station called asking to interview him and Sal together. He declined politely, explaining that he wasn't the one who rescued the children, it was all Coffy. He knew Sal would say the same. In the time since the rescue, they both avoided all accolades regarding the rescue out of respect for Coffy. She gave her life for those three children. He and Sal had given little. In fact, the way Flint saw it, he abandoned Coffy and would spend the rest of his life trying to make it up to her. She had atoned for whatever perceived sins she had. He must now do the same.

His imagined anguish of her dying alone haunted his dreams every night since the failed rescue attempt to save her. By the time he reached street level and handed the baby off to Mexican Police, a specialized rescue crew out of California, alerted by Sal's radio call when he got to the surface, was already assembling in the parking lot. Flint and Sal spent a few minutes briefing the team on what happened, then prepared to lead them back down to the nursery.

Before they could finish giving their information, a white minivan pulled up next to them and two men got out. Flint recognized them both, John Owen, the Incident Commander for the American team, and the man with a black eye, Conner Tate, Coffy's punching bag.

"Flint, tell me," Owen asked. "Is she still alive?"

"Yes, sir. At least she was when I left her forty-five minutes ago. But she's severely injured, and there's a fire in the room she's trapped in. We've got to get down there as quickly as possible."

THE SCENT OF REDEMPTION

"We? There is no we!" Tate protested. "I told your team not to go into that building because something like this would happen! You're not going back in there. You countermanded my orders, and now these guys have to risk their lives to fix your mistake," he said, pointing to the California team.

Flint surveyed the faces of the rescue group, several of whom were shaking their heads in dismay at what the man just said. He looked back at Tate and dropped Apache's leash to the ground. "Fuck you, you arrogant prick! The woman who beat your ass last night just saved three lives by not doing what you ordered. I suggest you back your cowardly ass away from me before I make you the next casualty!" Apache, picking up on Flint's anger, began to growl at the engineer. Several stifled laughs came from the California team.

One of the team members spoke up, "Hey kid, why don't you head back to the food tent and make me a ham sandwich." Even John Owen smiled.

"Tate, these folks think you need to go back to the staging area," Owen said as he pointed to the minivan. "I would tend to agree." Tate sighed, turned, and sloughed away. Owen turned to face Flint. "Get down there and take care of Coffy. You tell me what you need, and I'll make it happen."

The team, led by Flint and Sal, tried for several agonizing hours to get back down to the nursery. Twice, smoke caused them to turn back. Air packs and specialized pneumatic chisels were sent down along with airbags to support the massive concrete beam blocking their way to the nursery. When they finally got to the point Flint and Sal had reached earlier, Flint frantically yelled Coffy's name. There was no answer. The jackhammers went to work, and whenever there was a momentary break in the noise, Flint would again yell. There was never a reply. Finally, four hours after Flint had last heard from Coffy, they broke through.

The team was stunned by what they saw as they entered the nursery. They found Coffy, peacefully slumped back in a chair, holding the body of a baby girl. The fire had moved on after consuming most of the room, leaving Coffy and the child untouched. The concrete wall behind her and the lack of combustibles in proximity to her had stopped the fire short of her body. It was obvious to everyone, she had simply ended things on her own terms, choosing to bleed to death rather than succumb to the

209

terrible heat from the fire.

It was the image of Coffy holding the baby that haunted Flint most. If he had stayed with her, perhaps he could've talked her through surviving the injury. Or maybe he could've found another entrance into the room? Those were questions he would never be able to answer. The doubt of his decision crushed him.

Others, in an effort to comfort him, told him there was no way she could have survived the fire. If she hadn't bled to death, she would have died from smoke inhalation, or worse, the heat alone would have killed her. They told him it was far better that she had died from blood loss than from any of the other ways that could have killed her. She simply faded out of existence, but he heard none of it. He hadn't been with her when he should have and, because of it, she wasn't with him now. He would have to live with that for the rest of his life.

The funeral was held a week to the day after her body arrived from Mexico. As per her wishes, she had been cremated. The memorial service was held at her cabin and was attended by many who knew her and many more who didn't. The Durango and Silverton Narrow Gauge Train Company had put a special train in service to accommodate everyone wishing to attend the funeral. There must have been thirty different search and rescue dogs on board with their handlers.

The ceremony was simple. Members of her beloved Colorado Search and Rescue Association were there to share stories about some of the people Coffy had rescued. Flint's emotional recap of what happened in Mexico brought tears to many in the crowd, and even Frisco got over his hatred of other people to stand and deliver a toast to Coffy. There were no family in attendance. Frisco told Flint there wasn't a chance of finding any of them, but if there were any to be found, she hadn't had contact with them since before he had known her.

After the funeral, many members of Coffy's organization stayed behind to camp out overnight near the cabin and shared more stories of her life. They asked Flint to join them. He was hesitant at first, but decided that Coffy would have liked for him to know her friends. He asked Frisco to join him, but Frisco told him he'd had enough of others and was going home. It wasn't long before the alcohol came out and the laughter began as they traded stories with each other around the campfire.

In the early morning hours, several of the members asked Flint to take over the organization and run it as Coffy had. He was honored, but politely declined, explaining he lived too far away. Not taking no for an answer, they told him that Coffy had sold the cabin to the organization for a dollar years ago, and now that she was gone, they would have to sell it if they couldn't find someone to take over where she had left it. They all agreed it would be best if it remained the central training facility for the organization's search and rescue dogs.

When Flint asked why they wanted him and not someone from within the group to carry on the work, he was informed that Coffy had been bragging about Flint's expertise with search and rescue and that she felt she had finally found someone to share her passion with. Flint was dumbfounded. He had no idea she talked about him to others. He wondered if they'd known about her plans to pack everything up and move to Florida permanently.

He expressed his appreciation again, but there was just no way for him to do it. He had responsibilities in Florida and a daughter still in school. He apologized sincerely, shook everyone's hand, and retired to the cabin. As Flint walked past the fireplace on his way to the bedroom where he and Coffy had shared their love passionately several years before, he stopped and looked at the silver urn that now sat atop the mantle. "Coffy, I'm sorry. I hope you can forgive me. I know I can't forgive myself," he whispered out loud.

Back home in Florida, he'd had plenty of opportunities to talk about what happened because Troy and Liz wouldn't leave him alone. They did their best to convince him there was no reason to carry any of the guilt. He'd done what Coffy begged him to do in those last moments by getting the baby to safety. To appease them, he would tell them they were right and change the subject, but the pain never faded. For months, he struggled to bury it, but it would always come roaring back in the form of anger and resentment. There were times that Sam would stay with Troy and Liz for days at a time. Sleep became a fading memory, and others began to worry about him. He even sought counseling, but nothing he tried would give him any peace. He could never rest if he couldn't atone for what he had done.

Finally, after nearly coming to the end of his sanity, he decided to consider the possibility of being part of Coffy's organization. He needed to find a way to carry on with her work. If search and rescue work had helped her cope with guilt and sadness, then maybe it could do the same for him.

Flint asked Sam if she would be willing to move to Colorado and was surprised to hear that she was in favor of it. She knew she would miss her friends, but was excited about the chance to work with search and rescue dogs and to continue with what Coffy had begun teaching her. Besides, beating Troy at video games had become tiresome. That night, after his talk with Sam, he thanked Rachael out loud for helping him raise such a wonderful young lady. It took another month of phone calls and making preparations before the trailer was loaded, and the Westbrooks, Apache, Argo, and Koda were on their way to Colorado.

Flint looked up to see Frisco walking up to the cabin. "How's it going, Frisco? Sam got it figured out?"

"She's teaching me at this point." He climbed the cabin steps and took a seat in the chair next to Flint. "She seems to know what a dog is thinking before the dog knows what it's thinking."

Flint handed him a beer from the cooler next to him. "Yeah, she's good. Coffy would be pleased." Flint took a sip of his beer. "I guess we'll be headed down to Durango in another week or so. Sam starts school in two weeks, and we have to get the kennels set up."

"I figured it was getting close. Coffy used to stay out here until October, but then she didn't have a school age kid."

"Sam graduates in another three years, then we can start staying longer. I can't believe I'm saying that. She graduates in three years."

Frisco chuckled. "Welcome to the old man's club."

"Sam coming up?" Flint asked.

"She said she'd be up after she fed the dogs." Frisco took a sip of his beer and turned to Flint. "So how are you doing? Sam said you had a rough day today."

"Oh you know, it varies. Some days are good, some bad. Today wasn't great. I just keep thinking about how unfair it was that she was taken so soon. She was doing so many good things for people. I can't get over knowing that it's my fault she's gone."

"You know what your problem is? You're just like Coffy. You have to have a reason for every bad thing that happens. I've got news for you; sometimes shit just happens for no reason at all." Flint realized he had hit a nerve with Frisco. "My son was killed because someone planted a bomb on a dirt road in Afghanistan. It wasn't because he deserved it or because the Army didn't do their job; it was just the way the cards were played. The guy who planted that roadside bomb couldn't have cared less who it killed. Sometimes, there's no rhyme or reason. It just happens. Coffy always blamed Justin's death on herself, and she had nothing to do with it. You blame yourself for Coffy's death, and you had no part in it. The two of you would have been perfect for each other."

"Frisco, you weren't there. I might have found a way to help her."

"From what I heard, if you'd stayed, the baby would have surely died, and most likely you would have, too. Now that would have been a much bigger tragedy. I know it's hard to hear it, but Coffy would have died either way. And what about your daughter there?" Frisco said, pointing in the direction of the barn. "She would have been left without a mother *and* a father. How could you justify that?"

Flint looked at Frisco. "I hear what you're saying. It's just that I can't get over the feeling that I let her down."

"You've got to find a way to let it go. It'll eventually kill you just like it killed her. Guilt led her down a path that could only end one way. It'll end that way for you, too, if you don't find a way to get rid of it."

Flint stared across the canyon. "If she could live with it, I can, too."

Frisco sighed, set his beer on the porch, and leaned forward in his chair. "Flint, Coffy had more going on in that head of hers than you could ever imagine. She carried guilt for a lot of things, not just her son." Flint looked at Frisco waiting for an explanation. "It's time you knew about it. I was hoping it would die with her, but I see now it won't."

"What are you talking about?"

"I'm talking about Coffy and the night her son died. You don't know the whole story. No one does except for me, now."

"I don't understand."

"Of course, you don't. But it's important for you to know why Coffy was the way she was. I'm afraid you'll follow the same path she did and never find your way out."

Flint thought back to the afternoon Coffy left him alone on top of the redoubt. She had told him she was broken and twisted beyond his understanding. He never understood what she meant by that statement and was never willing to ask her about it when she came back to Florida. He sat silent for a moment and waited for Frisco to gather his thoughts

"Coffy took responsibility for her son's death, but she had nothing to do with it. Stephen killed her son. What added to her guilt and made her life so difficult with was the fact that she killed her husband. There, I said it."

"What the hell? Why would you say something like that?"

"Because I know. I was there." Flint sat in stunned silence. "Listen, that morning, I was drinking coffee on my porch when I heard people arguing down by the river. I thought it was someone hunting on my property, so I decided to go down and see what the hell was going on. When I got down to the river, I thought I saw a body floating by, so I waded out to grab it. It was Coffy. She was almost dead from the cold water."

"She told me the story," Flint said. "She found her son dead in the river and her husband sitting on a rock next to where they had been camping. She said he committed suicide by shooting himself."

"That's not what happened. I mean, the part about her son being murdered is true, but her husband didn't commit suicide, and there was never any gun. Stephen was just sitting there, on a rock, watching the look on Coffy's face as she discovered what he had done. She told me he was smiling at her. Can you believe that? He was actually enjoying the pain he was inflicting on her. When she saw him sitting there with that grin, she grabbed a rock from the river, walked over to him, and beat the ever loving shit out of him with it."

"My God, Frisco!"

"Yep, the man never tried to defend himself. He just sat there and smiled when she raised the rock and smashed his skull with it. She told me she kept hitting him with the rock until there was so much blood it slipped out of her hands, so she proceeded to beat his face in with her fists. Afterward, she walked out into the river, kissed her son goodbye, and tried to drown herself. She would have succeeded, too, if I hadn't found her first."

Flint went silent. He was having a hard time believing Frisco's story. How could she have kept something like this from him all that time? If it was true, though, how painful it must have been for her to hold it inside for so long. How alone she must have felt.

"The bastard deserved it, Flint! He killed the boy!"

Flint held up his hand to calm Frisco down. "Hang on, Frisco; I agree with you! There's not a jury in the world that would disagree." Frisco leaned back in his chair and let out a heavy sigh. Flint was stunned. The information wasn't processing fast enough in his head, and he needed a break. They sat together for several minutes not speaking a word.

Finally, Flint spoke, "Who investigated it?"

"No one. I think that's what Coffy regretted the most."

"So no one knows about this. As far as anyone is concerned, it's still a missing person case?"

"Yes. Coffy was scared she would be accused of killing them both. I suppose that might have been one of the reasons she tried to kill herself." Frisco took another sip from his beer and stared at the canyon wall across the river.

"So, I have to ask, what happened to the bodies?" Flint avoided looking at Frisco.

"Justin is buried on the trail to my house. There's a big rock and a little memorial garden that Coffy made."

Flint finally looked at Frisco. "I've seen it. Is that where Stephen's buried, too?"

Frisco returned Flint's gaze. "No, Coffy couldn't bear the thought of that piece-of-shit being buried near her son. I told her I would take care of it and I did." There was another moment of silence as the two stared at each other.

"I don't suppose you're going to tell me what you did with him?"

"Nope. That was between Coffy and me." Frisco turned away and focused across the canyon again. "So, you're an officer of the law. What are you going to do now that I've told you all this?"

Flint turned and stared in the same direction as Frisco. "Well, Frisco, the way I see it, Coffy saved the citizens of San Juan County a ton of paperwork."

The next morning, Flint walked to the fireplace and stared at the picture of Coffy, Sam, and the dogs. The story Frisco told him the day before had freshened some old wounds. He'd been up all night, unable to sleep as thoughts of what might have been raced through his head. What would he have done as a parent facing the same situation as Coffy? Would he have killed his child's murderer? Damn straight he would, as would almost any parent he'd ever known.

If only she'd told him what really happened that dreadful morning on the river, he might have found a way to ease the pain she had endured for so long, and maybe, just maybe, she wouldn't have taken the chances she did that day in Mexico, but then three children would have lost their lives after they had barely begun to live. There was Jason, the boy she nearly gave her life for on the mountainside in Colorado. He would be gone, too, his parents lost in a sea of sadness. There were countless others who owed their lives to this remarkable woman, as damaged as she was. His eyes gazed at the simple silver urn under the photograph. It was time.

"I'll be back in a bit Honey," Flint said to Sam as he walked out the back door of the cabin. The climb up the side of the canyon wall was one he had made many times since Coffy's death. It was a way of being close to her. Reaching the top, he stood there looking out over the river flowing south through the canyon. They shared this same view not too many years ago, and it gave him great joy to be here with her again. He turned and looked at the rock wall where Coffy had inscribed the words, I MUST WALK ALONE, IN DARKNESS, TO LIGHT THE PATH FOR OTHERS. She was right all along. As hard as it was for him to say it, she was right. Her inability to forgive herself, the flaw she suffered from the most, was the very same thing that made her so perfect, so willing to sacrifice herself so that others could live.

He turned back to the edge of the canyon wall. "Coffy, I'm sorry we didn't have more time. I was hoping to get to love you for the rest of my life. Guess I'll just have to do that without you here. You should know that the little time we had together changed me forever. In giving your life to save others, you also saved mine. I will always love you." He removed the top of the urn, raised it to the blue Colorado sky, and ever so slowly, let the canyon winds set her free.

Made in the USA
Columbia, SC
04 August 2024

39409283R00133